TEMPORARY

SARINA BOWEN
SARAH MAYBERRY

ONE

New York, New York

Grace

"HAVE YOU SEEN MY METROCARD?"

Later, when I looked back on the whole disaster, I'd settle on this innocent-sounding question as the moment it all began.

"No..." I told my fifteen-year-old sister. "Shouldn't it be in your wallet?"

"You'd think," she mumbled.

We spent the next fifteen minutes tearing up our tiny living space. It was astonishing that anything could go missing in four hundred square feet. "Olivia, how much money was on that card?"

"Not sure," she dodged. "But I'll find it."

She didn't, though. And as the clock ticked forward, I panicked, letting my opinions on her housekeeping and life choices fly as I sorted through the papers on our dining table and searched the pockets of Olivia's two jackets.

She'd suffered in silence, but I knew I'd pay for it later, in the form of sullen dinner-table conversation.

Finally, I dug my own MetroCard out of my wallet and thrust it at her. "Take this and go."

"But..."

"Just do it. I can't be this late. You *know* I need this job." I was only a temp, but I was hoping against all odds that my current assignment would turn into a permanent role.

Sparing more arguments, Olivia took my card, and we hustled out the door and down the creaky stairs of our apartment building. It wasn't even eight a.m., but my blood pressure was already sky high, and I hadn't had a sip of coffee.

"Have a good day at school," I told my sister as we parted ways.

Olivia's only reply was to shoot me the kind of glare that comic-book villains used to kill people. Then she stomped away, up Essex Street toward the subway stop at Delancey, while I headed west toward the Grand Street station.

"Deep breaths," I coached myself as I hurried along the sidewalk, hugging my trench coat to my body. The stiff November breeze off the Hudson River sliced right through the thin fabric.

I'd become a New Yorker at eighteen, when I'd started design school. And I'd thought of the city as the brightest, shiniest, most exciting place in the world. Mornings had brought the scent of dark coffee and lemon lavender scones wafting from pristine cafes. Boutique windows were decked with beautiful things that I might someday own—or design.

I'd looked at all the luxury and thought, *Why not me?* When New York had smiled at me, I'd seen opportunity everywhere.

But these days New York was really good at giving me the stiff arm. I could never stop inside one of the cute little cafes on the way to the subway. Coffee and a scone would cost six dollars, maybe seven. That was money I didn't have. And my dreams of designing beautiful things were derailed long ago. My college degree took years longer than I'd expected. Even though I'd switched to a more practical field, a good job was elusive.

On mornings like this one, I no longer asked, *Why not me?* It was more like: *What now?*

Just before I reached the stairs leading down to the subway platform, I spotted a hand waving to me from across the street. It was Mrs. Antonio, the woman who ran the gourmet deli on the corner. Polite to my very core, I paused to wave back at her before dashing down the stairs.

As I tapped carefully downward, mindful of my kitten-heeled ankle boots, I wondered how long it had been since I'd ducked into Mrs. Antonio's store. Months, probably. Before my boyfriend had ditched me for a new job in France, he and I used to stop at the deli for last-minute groceries. Marcus would usually pay, and I'd cook. It was one of the little arrangements that made things work between us.

Then he'd yanked the rug out from under me.

It had taken me a long time to trust Marcus, to believe in him. Yet it had taken him less than a day to decide that a plum promotion in another country was more important to him than I was.

Shaking my head, I jumped the last stair and bolted toward the MetroCard machine. This was no time for a pity party. I had sixteen minutes to get to the office in Midtown. Not enough to be on time, but I could come close.

I was working the touchscreen like a champ when I heard a squeal of breaks in the distance. And then I felt the telltale wind of a train pulling into the station. Still, I didn't panic, swiping my credit card and typing in my ZIP Code so fast my hands were a blur. I could do this.

Why not me?

The train pulled into the station just before I finished my transaction. The doors slid open and commuters began to pour out as I grabbed my new card and ran toward the turnstile. I was so close to victory. But a man in a charcoal suit came storming toward the turnstile from the platform side just as I raised my new card to swipe through.

Now, a good guy would stop. He would clock the panic in my

3

eyes and give me those two seconds that would have made the difference between catching the train and missing it.

But this man looked right at me and levered his briefcase those crucial six inches in front of his body, winning the race and claiming the turnstile first. He pushed through, halting my progress.

And then? He used the briefcase to actually bump me aside as he pushed through the crowd toward the stairs.

"Have a nice day, asshole," I said under my breath, my heart quivering with aggravation.

Ding dong. The train gave its warning song, and then the doors slid closed.

I watched it pull out of the station without me.

———

By the time I finally made it uptown to 60th and Central Park West, I was seventeen and half minutes late for my tenth day of work as an office temp at Walker Holdings. Maybe nobody would notice. There was always a chance that Stephen, my supervisor, came in late on Fridays.

I was hoping to ride this assignment into next week. Walker Holdings was in the throes of acquiring another company and everyone was focused on the deal. I'd been brought in to take care of various day-to-day matters and the workload didn't seem to be lessening, so I figured I had a chance.

Have I mentioned I'm never lucky at all?

The New York offices of Walker Holdings were a small outpost for a big Australian importer of high-end agricultural products. I'd never heard of them before this assignment, but an internet search had taught me that the Walker family were considered business royalty back home, their wealth derived from one of Australia's largest and oldest cattle- and beef-producing operations.

It seemed a bit ridiculous to me that a steak from Australia could taste better than a steak that hadn't been flown or shipped across the ocean. But nobody asked me.

Now, sliding into the chair at the desk I'd been assigned, I found a note waiting for me. It was folded to conceal its contents. *Grace*, the outer flap read. The note gave me an honest-to-god shiver of anticipation. With each temp assignment, I had two hopes: first that the job would become permanent, and second that an employer would ask me do something creative.

But when I read the note, its contents weren't very forthcoming. *Come to Stephen's office the moment you arrive, please. Conference call at 8:15.*

It was now 8:22.

Shit!

I jumped out of the chair and skated toward Stephen's office in the far corner. At least I already knew where to find him. The office door stood open, with Stephen waiting at his desk.

"Sorry!" I gasped. "Should I come in?"

He gestured toward the chair beside him. I sat down and immediately noticed a middle-aged woman's face staring at us from Stephen's computer monitor. She wore the expression of someone who'd just tasted something sour. "Is this the girl?"

"Yes, this is Grace Kerrington," Stephen said with a wide smile that seemed not to fit well on his angular face. "She's been providing admin cover during the acquisition. She's been checking warehouse reports for us this week, with good attention to detail."

"She's late," the woman snapped.

I was.

And yet Stephen only smiled harder, which threw me because until this moment I hadn't seen him smile at anyone. "I needed Grace to make some copies for me this morning. She was waylaid. Grace, say hello to Ms. Victoria Walker, the CEO of Walker Holdings."

My pulse jumped like a frog on a trampoline. Victoria Walker, *the* boss-lady—the woman I'd need to impress if I wanted a full-time position. "How do you do, ma'am. Is there something I can help you with?"

Her nose twitched in high definition on Stephen's seventeen-inch screen. She was sitting at an enormous desk, a plate-glass window behind her. Framed by the window was a picture-perfect view of the Sydney Harbour Bridge, the famous coat-hanger structure gleaming blue-black against the night sky, the water beneath it gold and fuchsia and turquoise from the reflected lights of the city. Impeccably dressed in a black dress with white polka dots, she studied me from half a world away. I felt my face grow warm from her scrutiny.

"My brother died last week," she said finally.

What?

An awkward silence fell as I tried to regroup from her unexpected opener. "I'm *so* sorry," I said a beat too late.

"We weren't close," she said, her tone unmistakably dismissive. "He lived in New York, about twelve blocks from where you are now."

"Oh." I was still playing catch-up. "How can I help?"

"His apartment is at 125 Central Park West. You'll want to write this down."

Stephen thrust a legal pad and a pen at me, and I scratched down the address while I tried to picture Victoria Walker's brother. He'd have shrewd eyes and an Aussie accent like his sister. For his sake, I hoped there was a vast gap in their ages. Victoria Walker—or Queen Vic as some of the less charitable office workers at Walker Holdings termed her—looked to be in her mid-fifties.

Way too young to die.

"I'm the executor and sole heir," she went on. "I've applied for probate, and in the meantime I want to get a head start on winding up my brother's estate. Jack had a large apartment, and his personal effects must be dealt with as efficiently as possible."

Personal effects, I wrote on the paper like a dope.

"Unfortunately, his insurance appraisals are ten years out of date so everything will have to be professionally reassessed. His book collection. His personal wine cellar. His furniture and the artwork on the walls. Stephen will help you find appropriate auctioneers and dealers to provide the valuations. Your job is not to make decisions but to create an extensive inventory, along with appraisals for everything of value, and a short list of dealers and auctioneers."

"Okay," I said, still jotting notes. *Executor. Appraisals. Dealers and auctioneers*. "Yes ma'am."

"Stephen seemed to think you had studied art at some point. Is that correct?"

"Yes!" I said quickly. "For two years. Then I switched to business at New York University."

She nodded slowly. "We're stretched very thinly with the acquisition at the moment. Can I trust you to do a thorough inventory of my brother's art collection, in collaboration with an auction house?"

"Yes ma'am. I did coursework in accounting. I can make a thorough inventory. It would be my pleasure."

"All right then." I saw the faintest glimmer of approval. "You'll use a Walker Holdings laptop, and all your work will be uploaded to our corporate cloud. Your findings will be checked against the old insurance appraisals..."

She gave me the sort of threatening glare that implied she thought everyone was a thief. It wasn't easy to smile reassuringly, but I tried.

"I will review your findings at the end of each day," she continued. "I want to see your notes accumulating—which auctioneers you've spoken with, which rooms you've inventoried."

"Yes ma'am," I said again, because she seemed to like the

formality. Hell, I'd call her *your highness* if it got me a permanent job.

"There's more," she said, and I felt hope rising inside me for the first time in months. *More* meant more paid days and a positive bank balance. And Christmas was coming. I'd been viewing the holidays like a dark cloud on the horizon—fewer meaningful temp jobs, and a little sister who expected against all odds to acquire some of the glittering things her classmates took for granted.

My pen hovered over the notepad.

"My brother ran a small business importing wines from Australia."

I looked up at her face in the monitor. "And what are your plans for his business?"

"Disposal," she said immediately. "I believe he has some stock in a warehouse. We already dismissed his three employees. That leaves you to inventory these bottles as well as his personal collection in the apartment. The wine auctioneer can deal with all of it once probate has been granted. You'll ship all his personal and business files to my offices in Sydney."

"Got it." That would cost a mint. But it wasn't my problem.

"Once the valuables and business are accounted for, you will clean the ordinary things from the apartment, readying it for sale. His clothing and kitchen items can go to charities."

"Yes, ma'am. Are there sentimental items I should keep an eye out for?"

The woman blinked. "He may have had a wristwatch or other trinkets. You can set those aside for family members."

"Of course."

She looked at her watch. "That will be all for now. You can access the apartment on Monday. There has been a fuss over the keys—the co-op president did not wish to hand them over without a death certificate. But Stephen has that sorted now, and you can pick them up from him first thing Monday morning."

The time difference was fifteen hours. It was almost midnight where she was. "Goodnight, ma'am. Thank you for this opportunity. I'll do a careful job with your brother's things."

Her nod was brisk. "I'll look for your first report on Monday evening, your time."

The screen went black, and I relaxed at exactly the same time as Stephen.

"You're late," he said, scrubbing a hand through his thinning hair.

"I'm sorry about that, sir. The trains were so packed I couldn't get on the first two." My neck grew hot at the lie. "It won't happen again."

He didn't say more on the subject, thankfully. "Have you met Taryn in IT? She's waiting to set you up with a laptop."

"Thank you," I said, popping out of my chair. "I'll find her now."

"Before you go..."

I stopped halfway to the door. "Yes?"

"I know you're looking for a permanent role, and there might be something for you here next month if you prove yourself with this project. But Ms. Walker doesn't suffer fools, so you need to bring your A-game, okay?"

"I will. I promise."

He studied my face for a beat before nodding his dismissal. I wondered what he saw there. Hope? Determination? Nervousness?

Probably all three. But I left his office with a fire in my belly—I was going kick ass on this project and earn myself that permanent role, if it killed me.

TWO

A Hell of a Rider

Callan

"YOU ARE SO FUNNY, CALLAN." The blonde's praise was accompanied by a suggestive thigh touch, a maneuver that required her to lean across me at an awkward angle and rest her hand so high on my thigh she was practically cupping my balls.

Just in case I hadn't got the message she was totally up for anything I was offering.

The woman was gorgeous, though, with long, straight hair and real, lush breasts straining at the seams of her tiny dress. Her problem—sad for her, good for me—was that the yacht was heaving with women like her. Beautiful, built, and eager to get into the bed of a genuine playboy.

Over her shoulder, the private marina glowed orange in the last rays of the setting sun. Bali was idyllic this time of year—and every time of year. Soon the whole hillside would be twinkling with lights as the many luxurious villas dotting the landscape came to life for the night.

A warm breeze drifted across my skin as her hand lingered. I swallowed the last of my champagne and tried to decide if I was drunk enough yet to take her up on her invitation.

This was a finely balanced calculation I'd made many times over my thirty-one years. I had to be buzzed enough to forget that the only reason this beautiful woman was throwing herself at me was because I was the son of one of Australia's wealthiest families. But I also had to be able to perform—because God forbid Callan Walker couldn't make her scream.

"What are you doing when you're not drinking champagne in Bali?" my drinking companion asked with a pronounced European accent.

"Drinking champagne somewhere else, of course."

She giggled. They always do.

"It's true," I said, upping the ante. "I'm personally responsible for a three-point bump in the sale of French champagne over the past four years, give or take." That's how long it had been since I walked away from the family business.

"So you don't wrangle cows on a ranch? Hold on—do Australian cowboys wear big hats?"

"Sure," I said with a practiced smile. "We've got the hats, but we don't say 'ranch,' we say cattle station. I learned to ride when I was four, drove cattle when I was thirteen. I'm a hell of a *rider*." I winked at her, and she laughed again.

This was the dance, and I knew all the steps by heart. Since leaving the Walker family business, my new calling was simple—travel the world and seduce beautiful women in exotic locations while giving zero fucks about anything else.

The warm hand on my thigh slid a fraction higher. For a split second, doubt crept in. I wondered what she'd say if I told her anything real about myself. Self-destructive behavior and family infighting weren't very sexy.

I'd gotten very good at pushing those thoughts away and living in the moment, though. "I'm sorry, sweetheart. Tell me your name again?" I asked.

"It's Henna."

"Well, Henna..." I'd decided I could definitely handle getting this woman naked. It was time to put the play into playboy. "You want a tour of the boat?"

The yacht belonged to a mate from my private-school days. My cabin was on the upper deck and featured a spa. Her tanned tits would look stunning covered in bubbles.

Her smile was feline and satisfied. I could practically hear her giving herself a high-five and was almost tempted to issue a warning—because we'd have a good time in bed, but that was all she'd be getting from me.

There'd be no jewelry, no *Pretty Woman*-style shopping spree with my credit card, no joining me on my private jet. There'd definitely be no marriage proposal or an accidentally-on-purpose baby.

The only Walker beef on offer was the kind in my trousers.

I didn't warn Miss Henna, though. She was an adult, and she'd chosen to play the game, just as I had. I stood, and she followed suit, plastering herself to my side. I rested a hand on the small of her back and ushered her forward as a middle-aged man I vaguely recognised stopped in front of me.

"Callan Walker. Should have known I'd find you here at this time of year," he said.

"Justin. Good to see you," I said, dredging his name from some murky place in the back of my skull, where I stored the connections that used to matter to me. This guy was in banking or finance in New York. Something like that.

I offered him my hand.

"I want you to know, I was sorry to hear about your uncle. He was a great guy. The Met Gala won't be the same without him next year."

My hand tightened around his as his words cut through the champagne buzz in my brain.

"My uncle? You can't mean Jack?"

His expression morphed from a polite smile to distress. "God. I assumed you knew? I heard Jack passed a couple of days ago. Heart attack at the health club."

I just stared at Justin, who looked embarrassed now, like he was regretting having pushed his way through a yacht full of partying elites to ask me to invest in whatever it was he did.

Funny the places your mind went when you were in shock. The cacophony of clinking glasses and happy laughter dimmed around me, fading to a background hum as what he'd told me sank in.

Uncle Jack was dead.

No way. Not possible. I couldn't lose the only decent, uncompromised person in my life. The only family member I could ever be myself with, without worrying he'd use the knowledge against me. The only one I'd trusted, no caveats or exceptions.

Gone, just like that?

"I'm really sorry," Justin said, taking a small step backward. Eager to escape the awkwardness.

"Oh, that's *so awful*. Your poor uncle." The blonde tucked her arm into mine and gave me her best sad face.

"Excuse me." I slipped free from her grasp and started walking, pulling my phone from my pocket.

I headed straight for the gangway, because my gut told me I needed privacy for this call. I shouldered my way past drunks and, after disembarking, turned away from the shore, walking up the darkened dock until I'd left the noise and light of the party behind.

I didn't bother calculating the time difference before I dialed. I didn't care what time it was in Australia. Those fuckers had left me out of the loop on my uncle's death.

Claire answered on the fourth ring.

"Callan. We were wondering when you'd surface," she said coolly.

Claire was my mother's right hand, doing her bidding with a

zeal and efficiency worthy of a loyal mob enforcer. She was also my sister. Technically, anyway. Any sibling feeling we'd once shared had withered on the vine long ago.

"When did he die?" I demanded. They *knew* I was close to Jack. That was why they hadn't told me. My mother never missed an opportunity to assert her dominance.

"Sunday. He had a heart attack," Claire said. "They tried to resuscitate him but couldn't get him back."

Today was Friday. Nearly a whole week had passed. "Tell me you haven't had the funeral yet," I said.

But I already knew the answer, because I knew my mother.

"Victoria thought a quick, private ceremony would be for the best, all things considered. He was cremated yesterday, I believe."

The urge to throw my phone at something was so intense I had to consciously remind myself I would need it in order to make things right for Jack.

Victoria Walker had always been embarrassed by her gay older brother. She'd despised his flamboyant friends, his philanthropy, his political activism. Now she'd turned him to ash. No funeral. No eulogy. No honoring of my uncle's life. Just a quick trip to the crematorium.

My mother, consummate control freak, had outdone herself.

Claire was talking again, and I tuned back into her voice once I had a grip on my rage.

"...is sole heir, and she plans to wind up the estate as quickly as possible once probate has been granted. The New York office is handling the disposal of his apartment and effects."

My mother was sole heir to Jack's estate? What new fuckery was this? A couple of years ago Jack had spoken to me about his will, talking of the charities he wanted to endow and asking me to act as executor. I'd never followed up on the conversation, because I'd assumed my uncle would live to a grand old age, swanning about his Upper West Side apartment in one of his many vintage smoking jackets.

I should have listened more carefully, damn it. I should have asked more questions.

I should have fucking been there when he died.

A sudden headache throbbed at my temples. Why was my mother listed as sole heir when Jack had talked about ensuring his favourite causes were supported after his death? Better question —why was Vicky named as executor instead of me?

"I want to see the will," I said, because I knew better than to show my cards this early in the game.

"I can forward you a copy, but it's pretty clear—everything goes to Mum," Claire said.

I could hear the disapproval in her tone—she thought I was disappointed I wasn't going to benefit from Jack's death. That's how fucked up my family was.

"Send me the will," I repeated. Then I ended the call.

I took the kind of deep, slow breath that was always necessary after any contact with my family. I couldn't conceive of a universe in which my uncle had decided to leave everything to his estranged sister instead of the charities so close to his heart. Something was wrong. Very wrong.

I pulled up another phone number. This time I took the time to do some calculations before I hit dial. It would be just three p.m. in New York. My travel agent should still be at her desk.

Sure enough, she answered on the first ring.

"It's Callan. I need you to get me to New York as quickly as possible."

THREE

Talk Artsy to Me

Grace

"HOLY CANNOLI," I said, completely forgetting myself as I opened the double doors to Jack Walker's apartment Monday morning.

"What's wrong?" my friend said in my ear.

Jasmine had called me as I left the offices of Walker Holdings, the keys to Jack Walker's apartment burning a hole in my pocket. We'd spent the last twenty minutes catching up on each other's lives while I walked uptown.

"This apartment I'm supposed to be inventorying. It's unbelievable." I took in the foyer with wide eyes.

I'd been prepared for something lavish, because the Walkers had buckets of money. But this...this was beyond lavish. And I was only in the *foyer*.

The floor beneath my feet was polished stone, but it was the wall in front of me that had blown me away. It was covered in vividly colored giant artificial flowers, so thickly applied the wall beneath was completely hidden. A riot of bright oranges, deep cobalt blues, and the occasional sunburst of yellow, the colorful backdrop was the perfect foil for the snow-white sculpture displayed in front of it—an intricately executed, scaled-down statue of a horse and rider.

"Let me guess—gold stuff everywhere? Velvet? Lots of faux-ye-olde-worlde family portraits?" Jasmine said.

"No. It's *beautiful*. There's an installation in the foyer, a whole wall of flowers. Like Eloise Corr Danch..." It hit me that this *was* an Eloise Corr Danch installation.

Which was when I realized this project I'd landed was going to be Big. Really Big.

"Must be arty rich then, not tacky rich," Jasmine said knowledgeably. The only child of two high-flying lawyers, she was well placed to categorize the many permutations of wealth.

My heels tapped against the floor as I ventured further into the apartment, and even though I was braced for more fabulousness, what I glimpsed through the doorway to my left made me literally gape.

"Oh my God," I breathed as I stepped into what was the most incredible room I'd ever seen.

"What? Tell me what's going on," Jasmine complained. "You're practically having an orgasm. I need details."

I didn't know where to begin. The view? The ceiling? The fireplace?

"You'd have an orgasm, too. Make mine a double. This living room is freaking amazeballs. The ceiling has to be twenty, maybe twenty-four feet high. And it's painted in hazy blues and yellows... like the Chagall at the Opera Garnier in Paris." Jasmine and I had taken art history together our first year of design school, so I knew she'd understand the reference.

"And there are windows—huge, kick-ass windows that go the whole height of the room, and the view... God, Jazzy, I don't even know how to describe the view. The whole of the city laid out in front of you. And there's this fireplace, so big you could probably fit my entire apartment inside it, made out of some sort of old stone with amazing carved pillars... And there's art everywhere. Beautiful, amazing multimedia."

"Oh baby, yes!" Jasmine shouted. "Talk artsy to me."

I tilted my head back as I described the room, taking in the stunning ceiling, the suspended star-shaped sculptures hanging in front of the window, the many prints and paintings on the walls.

When I dropped my gaze I realized there was a big armchair in the corner of the room, angled to face the view—and that a man was sitting right there, in the chair.

A beautiful man. And he was watching me.

"Fuck," I yelped, leaping backward, one hand clutched to my chest like a damsel in distress.

"Let me guess—live panther, chained in the corner?" Jasmine asked.

"I have to go," I said, not taking my eyes off the man in the armchair. He lifted one eyebrow in a silent expression of curiosity. "I'll call you later, okay?"

"At least tell me if there's a panther or not," Jasmine said.

"No panther. I have to go."

It wasn't until I ended the call that I realized I'd made a mistake—because if you're confronted with a strange man in the apartment of a rich dead man, being on the phone to someone who knows where you are is probably a good idea.

"Don't let me interrupt your next orgasm," he said, the last word drawn out and lazy. And holy fuck—that accent. Australian, if my startled brain wasn't too confused to hear him properly. His words had an easy lilt, but the tone of his voice was rich and smoky.

"Who—who are you?" I asked, embarrassed to hear the crack of fear in my voice.

"I think that's my line," he said.

For a long moment we just stared at each other. I took in his dark hair and the angle of his rugged cheekbones. He had two days' worth of scruff on his jaw, his whiskers roughening up an otherwise perfect face. He was a few years older than me, maybe late twenties, early thirties, with blue eyes.

And, me being me, I noticed that he wore an expensive button-down shirt—a finely threaded jacquard pattern with a spread collar. Tom Ford maybe. Or Zegna.

I couldn't tell how tall he was because he was sitting down, but he was clearly in shape, with broad shoulders and long, muscular legs that were stretched in front of him with relaxed abandon.

His eyes weren't relaxed, though. They were watching me with sharp, assessing interest.

"Are you from Walker Holdings?" I asked. Surely they wouldn't have sent someone out from Australia when they'd gone to the trouble of hiring me?

He stood, unfolding himself from the chair with athletic ease. Standing, he was even better-looking for some reason.

Intimidatingly so.

"Are you a realtor?" he asked. The word sounded like *real-tah*.

Say it again, I felt like begging. I crossed my arms and tried to pull my stunned self together. Hopefully he interpreted my silence as a show of force. *I won't answer your questions if you're dodging mine, mister*. Hopefully he didn't see my silence for what it really was—nerves and a very unwelcome bolt of lust.

I took a deep, steadying breath. "Are you a friend of Jack Walker's?" As far as I was concerned, we could keep this up for hours. Butcher, baker, candlestick maker—we could keep throwing professions at each other forever.

"Jack's my uncle. And you still haven't said who you are."

Uncle. *Family?*

I blinked, completely thrown once again. A wave of heat rushed up my neck as I rewound the last few minutes in my head. All the squealing I'd done to Jasmine as I toured the apartment, the things I'd said... Knowing he'd overheard my inappropriate conversation made me pray for my own quick and painless death.

"I'm Grace. Grace Kerrington. I'm really sorry for your loss," I said, steadfastly ignoring the heat in my cheeks as I stepped forward and shoved my hand at him.

He hesitated for a fraction of a second before taking it, his grip warm and firm.

"Callan Walker. You still haven't explained why you're inventorying Jack's apartment," he said.

"I'm working for Walker Holdings," I said, searching for a sensitive way to describe my role. "They hired me to help organize your uncle's estate."

Callan's blue eyes narrowed for a second. "Hired you?"

"Everyone else is focused on a big project, so I'm temping at the moment, helping out—"

His eyebrows shot up. "They asked a *temp* to wind up Jack's estate."

It wasn't a question, but I felt compelled to answer anyway.

"Um. Yes?" I had no idea what was going on here. "Maybe I should call the office." Even though I had zero desire to start pestering Stephen on my first real day on the project, this whole situation felt way beyond my pay grade.

"So..." He paced in front of those incredible windows, his big form prowling like the panther Jasmine had teased me about spotting. "What's the deal, Grace? You draw up a list of my uncle's possessions, then invite the dealers and auctioneers in to sell off my uncle's life piece by piece?"

"I'm going to call the office," I said, because there was some serious shit going down here. "I'll let them know you have questions."

"Who's your direct report?" He whirled to face me. "Allison Miller? Robert Perez?"

"Stephen Campo. But—"

He had his own phone out and was already dialing. "Stephen, it's Callan Walker. I'm at Jack's place with the temp you sent over. You want to tell me what's going on?"

He glanced at me briefly before heading for the arched doorway on the far side of the room, the phone pressed to his ear. I stood there for a full minute after he was gone, floored by his casual arrogance.

I'd been treated dismissively before—snooty waiters had looked down their noses at me, high-end sales assistants had given me pitying looks as I window-shopped on Fifth Ave with my sister—but this guy took the cake.

I reminded myself his uncle had just died, and that this was bound to be an emotional time for him. It didn't help much. He'd made it plain he thought appointing a temp to deal with his uncle's estate was offensive, and I made a bet with myself that he was in the other room right now, telling Stephen he wanted someone else on the project.

Since he was a Walker, there was a high degree of probability he'd get what he wanted, too.

The thought made me feel nauseous. I needed this job so badly. There were bills to pay, school expenses for Olivia. Plus, she'd shot up a whole two inches this year, which meant she'd probably need a new winter coat...

I swallowed past a tightness in my throat and wiped my damp hands down the sides of my second-best suit. Like my first-best suit, it was second-hand but didn't look it, thanks to the skills I'd honed while studying fashion design. When I'd put it on this morning, I'd looked in the mirror and felt confident about the future for the first time in a long time. This morning, I'd imagined a month of work and a bank balance robust enough to offset the expensive winter months.

What a fool I'd been.

Jaw locked, I waited for Mr. GQ Jerk-off to come tell me to hit the road.

———

Callan

"That's my final offer, Callan. Like it or lump it," Claire said. It was the middle of the night on the other side of the world, but she'd answered the moment Stephen patched her into the call, claiming he had no authority to make decisions in regard to Jack's estate.

I'd been wrangling with my sister for the last ten minutes, and getting nowhere. I dropped my head back and stared at the decorative ceiling in the dining room as I considered my decision. A hundred years ago, an artisan had created a masterpiece in plaster on this ceiling. My uncle had spent thousands having it restored when he first moved in.

I needed to keep thinking of Jack, of what he'd want, or it would be too easy to lose it with my sister.

"Fine. I'll work with what's-her-name," I said. I'd offered to handle the inventorying of my uncle's estate personally, but my mother—via Claire—didn't want to play ball. She didn't trust me.

On the flight to New York I'd read the will Claire sent me. It was more than thirty years old. Once I'd had a chance to sort through my uncle's papers, I was confident I'd find a more recent version, one that more accurately reflected Jack's wishes. And then my mother's hired minion could go back to where she'd come from.

That would be a fun moment for me. Not only would Jack's legacy live on, but I planned to drink a very expensive toast to the victory over my mother's callous greed.

"Let's be very clear on this," Claire went on. "Ms Kerrington reports to Victoria, not to you. You have no authority in this situation. If there are any sentimental items you wish to keep, arrangements can be made. But everything has to be accounted for via Ms Kerrington."

"Perhaps you should send me something in writing, in case I

missed any of that," I said, because I knew it would annoy her. Gotta get your kicks where you can find them.

"And Stephen, I trust you'll keep an eye on things," Claire said crisply before exiting the call.

Stephen cleared his throat with a nervous harrumph, his discomfort obvious. "So. You'll be working with Grace. She's a marketing grad, good eye for detail. Let me know if there's anything you need and we'll make it happen."

I wasn't about to apologise to him for rocking the boat or insisting my uncle's legacy be treated with respect and decency. This clusterfuck was my mother's making, not mine.

I ended the call, then walked to the window and looked out across the city, trying to reconcile myself with what I'd just agreed to do: packing up my uncle's home—his life—with a complete stranger who was being paid by the hour.

Jesus, my mother was fucked up.

But that was hardly news. The important thing was that I make sure Jack's final wishes were executed. Everything else was white noise and bullshit.

So. Turning away from the view, I took a moment to pack my anger away someplace safe before addressing the woman I'd be stuck with for the next few weeks. Grace Kerrington appeared to be typical of the sort of ambitious, slick-suited business graduates my mother always hired.

I assumed Grace had dreams of parlaying this temporary gig into a permanent role with Walker Holdings. If my gut instinct was right, that ambition would make her easy to manage.

Holding that thought in mind, I went to find her.

She was standing in front of the Dali nude near the window when I entered the living room, head tilted to one side as she studied it. She was dressed in the modern corporate armour of a black skirt suit, her brown hair pinned in a neat updo. Her body language was defensive as she turned to face me—arms crossed over her chest, shoulders tight.

So much tension. Idly I checked out her figure, noting she filled her suit in all the right places. My gaze got caught on the lush lower lip of her rosebud mouth, and suddenly I found myself wondering what she'd be like in bed. Prissy and uptight? Or was that plump lower lip the key to her true nature?

I shook the thought off. I wasn't here to fantasize about my mother's hired gun.

"Looks like we're stuck with each other for the next few weeks, Grace Kerrington," I said lightly. Offering her a shrug and a rueful smile, I turned on the charm. "But don't worry, you're in charge—hope you can be trusted with that much power."

I widened my smile to make sure she understood I was teasing her.

She didn't say anything for a few seconds, her expression oddly intense.

"You're going to *help* me inventory your uncle's estate?" Her gaze traveled over me. My skin was tan from my trip to Bali and I wore a Zegna shirt, Valentino chinos, and Gucci brogues, I didn't need to be a mind-reader to know she was trying to work out when I'd last put in a full day's work.

"Let's be honest—I'm probably going to get in the way, but I figure someone from the family should be here to pack up Jack's life." I hit her with another smile. The self-deprecating shtick worked most of the time—people love a self-aware, unrepentant playboy—and I watched as her shoulders dropped an inch or two. "How bad could it be? I'll lift the heavy boxes."

"Because I look weak to you?" she countered quickly, chin raised in defiance.

I was used to having women agree with everything I said, no matter what it was. Her response was...unexpected.

"Hey, I'm more than happy to watch you bench press as many boxes as you like. Just trying to be helpful."

"Well...good," she said, putting on her game face.

"So, what's your plan?" I asked.

"I was going to do a detailed tour so I could get my head around the scope of the project. Then I need to start finding dealers to appraise everything."

"Sounds like hungry work. Let's grab something to eat before we dive in. I only landed an hour ago and I'm starving." I patted my pockets, jingling Uncle Jack's keys to make sure I had them on me.

Grace frowned at the sound. "How did you get in here, anyway? Your mother said the co-op board wouldn't hand over the keys without a lot of paperwork."

"I've got my own set." I headed toward the front door. "You ready?"

"But..." I could hear the heels of her shoes tapping as she hurried after me. "Why didn't your mother just ask you for them?"

I stared at her for a moment, then I remembered she was a temp, and therefore not steeped in Walker family gossip like the rest of the office staff.

"Vicky and I aren't really on speaking terms," I said.

"Oh. I'm sorry to hear that," she said awkwardly.

"I'm not." Cutting communication with my mother had made my life infinitely more pleasant. "Let's go." I held the door for Grace, who passed me on the way into the hall. When I turned to close the door behind me, I had an urge to call out, "Back soon!" to Jack, as I'd done every other time I'd stepped out of this apartment without him.

But of course he wasn't there to hear me. And never would be again.

———

I took Grace to a fancy bakery on West 69th Street, where the waiters were always a little cool and dismissive, just in case you forgot you were in New York. These guys never went without a tip, however. Manhattanites knew better than to piss off their waiters. "I'll have the largest cup of coffee you can find me. Also, one of those chocolate croissants in the display case and eggs benedict."

Looking put upon, the skinny boy in charge of delivering this feast made a halfhearted scribble on his order pad.

"Just a cup of coffee for me," Grace said.

"American coffee?" The waiter sneered.

"Yes, please." The tips of her ears went pink. "We *are* in America."

So Grace was a feisty one. I liked that more than I cared to admit. She shrugged out of her suit coat, revealing a pale cream shirt that offered a shadowy impression of the lace of her bra. As I'd noted earlier, she had a great figure.

"So, Grace." Time to get to know the enemy. "Stephen said you're a marketing grad?"

"That's right. My degree is in business from NYU." She said the name of her alma mater as if it should mean something to me. "My concentration was in marketing. I just graduated in May, and I've been doing temp work until something permanent comes along."

So I'd guessed right, then—she had hopes of converting this gig from temporary to permanent.

"What do you like about marketing?" I asked, bored already. I'd met a lot Grace Kerringtons over the years, all of them eager to suckle from the Walker Holdings teat. They didn't care that under my mother's management, the company had an appalling environmental track record. They just wanted a corner office and a triple-figure salary and a good grip on the next rung up.

Grace gave me an unhappy stare. "Do you really want me to talk about brand recognition and relationship management? You look about as interested in marketing as our waiter looks in waitering."

My laugh was a sudden bark. Feisty *and* funny. Not to mention perceptive. "Fine. Spare us both. Tell me something else. What's your secret passion, Grace O'Malley?"

Please let it be sex.

It was the second time my brain had jumped to thoughts of sex with this woman, a realisation I filed away for later examination.

"It's Kerrington," she corrected me. I didn't bother explaining I'd just given her a nickname. She'd work it out soon enough. "I love art," she continued. "Your uncle has some amazing pieces. I promise to make sure they're given the respect they deserve."

"All right. What else?"

"My real interest is design. Especially fashion. But I gave up that coursework when I realized it was impractical."

I considered her suit and carefully conservative blouse. "I would never have picked you for the arty type."

Grace actually rolled her eyes, proving she'd become less afraid of me by the second. "When in Rome."

"I was in Rome last month," I said lightly. Then I realized how much it made me sound like a rich asshole. Although—in fairness —I *was* a rich asshole.

"Not Australia?"

I shook my head. "I travel a bit."

The surly waiter appeared, plunking Grace's coffee cup onto the table, along with my food. It was rude to eat alone. Usually. But Grace was probably on a perpetual diet, like the other women in my life. I glanced at her briefly before tackling my eggs benny. "So, you mentioned doing a detailed tour of the apartment...?"

"Right. Then I need to do some research, find out who the best people are to talk to for appraisals. I can't be sure how quickly they can come around to see the work. And your mother is in a hurry."

I snorted. Of course she was. "The moment you call Christie's and tell them Jack Walker's collection is up for grabs, they'll strap on their jet packs and fly across the park."

Grace's eyes widened. "All right. My preliminary research tells me I'd be better off dealing with a rare-book dealer on the books, though. And another specialist for the wine."

"You'll get the same reaction there, trust me. Jack spent two decades in this town hanging out with people who like nice things. He was well known and well respected."

"I'm also supposed to pack up his personal effects and donate small household items, such as kitchen gear, to charity," Grace continued.

"Okay, let's divide the labor," I suggested. "If you need to visit Sotheby's and Christie's this afternoon, I could get stuck in. Make a start on Jack's private wine collection, maybe."

"Your mother mentioned the collection a few times. I was planning on tackling it personally," she said.

I nodded as though I thought that was a reasonable idea. "Do you have a lot of experience with French and Italian wines? Jack's collection is pretty sophisticated, lots of small estate bordeaux, for example. "

She gave a slow shake of her head. *Bingo*.

"Leave it with me," I said. "I promise I won't fuck it up."

Grace studied me for one long moment, pursing her perfect lips as if trying to decide whether or not I had any kind of ulterior motive. But my expression of innocence had many years of practice.

"All right," she said finally. "Thank you."

"Don't mention it," I said. "Want half?" I asked, pointing at the chocolate croissant.

She shook her head quickly.

Congratulating myself on having disposed of Grace Kerrington so I could enjoy a couple of hours exploring my uncle's file cabinets, I ate the pastry. It was delicious.

FOUR

Spaghetti Again

Grace

THE SPAGHETTI SAUCE was just beginning to simmer when my sister exited her tiny bedroom. Our *only* bedroom. I'd given it to her because I thought it would make her a less moody teenager.

Hadn't worked yet.

"Spaghetti *again?*" she asked.

My blood pressure ticked up another point or two, and it was already approaching the red meter. "We're out of filet mignon and caviar. The maid didn't pick up any at the store."

Olivia didn't even register my irony. "Will it be ready soon? I'm starved."

"What did you eat for lunch?"

She gave the one-shouldered shrug that passed for an answer these days.

"Liv, answer the question."

"I didn't have time for lunch."

I grabbed the wooden spoon from the counter and plunged it into the spaghetti pot. I stirred with a little more fervor than necessary. "You said you'd use those lunch tickets. You *promised.*"

She flung herself into a kitchen chair. "But I couldn't! Jason Matthews walked out with me after geometry. He invited me to sit at his table."

"So...you starved yourself because you didn't want Jason Matthews to see you pay for your lunch with a ticket?"

"Yes, okay? *Yes*. You don't understand how hard it is to use those tickets. It's not even the same *line*, Grace. You have to stand on the other side of the cash register to pay with a ticket. They *literally* separate the poor kids from the rich kids so they can check off the names of whoever pays with a ticket."

I couldn't help but flinch at the visual. "That does sound grue-some." *Damn it.*

"Thank you!"

If I yelled at her for skipping lunch, it would make me a hypocrite. Today I'd eaten my peanut butter sandwich in a brisk forty-degree wind in Central Park so that Mr. Hot Aussie wouldn't notice it and comment. "Except you didn't tell me about the line thing before I filled out all those forms for tickets."

"I thought we'd never be approved."

"Oh." *Ugh.* Teenager logic. But of course she'd been approved for free lunch. I'd filled in *zero* for our mother's income. Mom was still Olivia's legal guardian, and she was off living in an honest-to-God meth lab somewhere in New Jersey. Even if I'd used my own financial status on the application, we'd probably still qualify for benefits. Our rent had been partially covered by my financial aid stipend until June. But it wasn't anymore. And temp work paid very badly.

It was tempting to go back to bartending, which is what I'd done before Olivia came to live with me. But I'd never find a real job while mixing dirty martinis.

"You didn't tell me—how was the job today?" my sister asked, probably because she was smart enough to know we were due for a change of topic.

"Interesting," I grunted, checking the pasta timer. "A nephew of the dead guy turned up, all the way from Australia. So that's a complication."

Stephen had called me when I was on the train on the way home. He'd wanted to make it clear that while Victoria Walker was allowing Callan to help with her brother's estate, I reported to her, not to her son. Stephen hadn't come right out and said it, but I'd gotten the sense he didn't expect Callan to hang around for long.

"Does he have a cute accent?" Olivia asked. "Aussie accents are hot."

Yes, they are. "What do you know from Aussie accents?"

"Duh. Chris Hemsworth. Is he hot?"

"Chris Hemsworth?" I dodged.

"No. The rich guy."

I frowned down at the sauce, because I preferred not to answer the question. Callan Walker was easily as tasty as Chris Hemsworth. Not that he lacked faults. "He was super confident and full of himself." Rich people always were. "But you should see this apartment. It's like an art gallery. All sorts of expensive stuff in there."

"Like what?"

"Wine." After stopping in at Sotheby's and Christie's on the Upper East Side, I'd returned to the apartment to find Callan helping out, just as he'd said he would. The sound of the French vineyard names rolling off his tongue was more enthralling than I'd ever admit. "Some of those bottles cost hundreds of dollars."

"Did you bring any home?" Olivia teased.

"As if. Callan had started taking pictures of each label with his phone. So I did that, too. All the while terrified I'd drop something priceless. One of those bottles was from my birth year."

"When dinosaurs roamed the earth?"

Olivia's dumb joke was punctuated by the sound of my phone ringing from across the room. "Could you check that?" I put the strainer in our compact sink. Our entire kitchen was about five feet wide. We had one of those tiny dormitory refrigerators, and a weird little narrow stove with only two burners instead of four.

"Who's Victoria Walker?" my sister asked, approaching with my phone. "The area code looks weird."

I grabbed it out of her hand and answered. "Hello? This is Grace Kerrington."

"Hello, Grace. This is Victoria Walker checking in."

"Good evening!" No. "Good morning!" The shock of getting her call had me flapping around my tiny kitchen like a chicken. "I made notes this afternoon and uploaded them to the server..."

"I saw them. Thank you. I appreciate the care you're taking. Photos of the wine bottles are a nice touch."

"Th-thank you." Although that was Callan's idea, damn it. "Seemed like the right way to get all the details. I'll try to price them online tomorrow, and then talk to a wine dealer about anything I can't find." For some reason I couldn't stop talking. Queen Vic had an odd effect on my tongue.

"My son is in your way, I expect."

"Um, he's been helping." There was no topic more loaded than this one. So naturally my oven timer went off with a shrill, repetitive beep. I lunged to silence it. Then I waved frantically at Olivia, indicating the sink. *Drain the pasta*, I tried to convey through a series of rapid hand motions.

She looked at the stove like she'd never seen a pot of pasta before.

"—don't hesitate to let me know," Mrs. Walker was saying.

Crap. "I'm sorry? What was that?" I had to ask her to repeat herself. "You cut out for a moment."

Her sigh was heavy, all the way from Australia, and I knew I'd just damaged my chances of long-term employment by at least a percentage point. "I said, I want to know immediately if he causes any trouble. Don't hesitate to contact me directly."

"Okay?" I felt an uncomfortable prickle at the base of my

skull. Exactly what sort of trouble did Queen Vic think Callan could make for me?

"Just let me know if anything comes up."

"I will. Right away," I assured her. After all, I'd be an idiot not to.

"I'll look for more of your progress tomorrow."

"Yes ma'am," I said, feeling the first wave of relief. "You can bet on me. Good night."

I hung up the phone, jammed it into my pocket and then grabbed the pasta pot.

It burned my hands. "*Fuck*!"

"What's with the f-bomb?" Olivia asked from the table.

I grabbed the dish towel and used it as a buffer against my hands, draining the pasta before it turned to porridge. "You could have done this yourself," I grumbled. But my mind was on the call from Victoria Walker, and the complication of her son turning up.

"You didn't say to. Can we eat it now?"

"Yes. Get the plates, at least."

"You mean, get the plates *please?*"

I growled. But she got the plates.

FIVE

A Hedonist's Drink

Callan

IT WAS strange being in Jack's apartment without him. There was so much of his personality in this place, I kept expecting to hear his laughter from another room as he talked to a friend on the phone, or the echo of him singing in the kitchen while he made dinner.

But there would be no more laughter or singing. No more shared meals. He was gone.

I walked through the hallway between the bedrooms and the living spaces, pausing to study the occasional photograph hung alongside the art on the walls. There was an image of Jack as a young man on horseback, mustering cattle on one of the Walker cattle stations. Sending him a thousand miles away into the dusty red heart of Australia had been but one of many attempts my grandfather had made to "make a man" of his gay son.

Jack looked happy in the picture. Free. He'd once told me that being exiled from the family had been his first inkling that there could be a life for him that that didn't involve being ashamed of who he was. He'd moved to New York the following year, walking away from family expectations and obligations.

The next picture showed Jack with the great love of his life, Danny. Taken nearly thirty years ago, it captured the two of them clowning around at Battery Park, hanging off the viewing binoculars in suggestive poses. A well-known jazz musician, Danny had lived with Jack for fifteen years before dying from cancer. During my last visit, Jack had had too much red wine and confessed that his deepest regret was that the law had never allowed them to marry and publicly acknowledge their love.

Emotion burned at the back of my eyes. Time for a drink.

Though I'd spent the afternoon inventorying Jack's private wine collection, I headed straight for the kitchen. Aside from not wanting to have to explain a sudden change of inventory to my mother's lackey, I didn't have a taste for wine tonight. I found what I was looking for in the fridge, as I'd hoped. Despite being able to afford the best, Jack had retained a fondness for the mainstay of his misspent youth, Tooheys New, and I found half a dozen bottles of the beer in the fridge door. Twisting the cap off one, I walked barefoot into the living room and stood at the window gazing out at the many bright lights of Manhattan at night. The bitter, malty taste of my homeland filled my mouth and for a moment I allowed emotion to overtake me. The view became blurry, and I sucked down another mouthful before wiping my free hand across my eyes.

"I'm going to miss you, you fabulous old bastard," I said.

Aware I was in danger of drowning in sentiment, I abandoned the living room in favor of Jack's study. Sitting at his desk, I turned on his computer and sighed with relief when I saw Jack hadn't protected it with a password. Bless his lazy ass.

I spent half an hour running searches through his hard disk and email folders, looking for keywords. It quickly became evident that there was nothing on the computer more than a year old. I checked the model. Sure enough, it was a recent release.

Jack had obviously traded up to a new computer and not migrated his old data across. Damn his lazy ass.

I turned to the built-ins that lined the walls. The top portion of every unit featured open shelves, but the bottom section boasted big double drawers. A cursory examination revealed each one was filled with hanging files. I swore under my breath and sat back on my heels. My gaze ran around the room, taking in the shelving units. There were nineteen in total, meaning I potentially had thirty-eight file drawers to sort through.

Bloody hell.

This definitely called for another beer.

The combination of three beers and jet lag were dragging me down by the time I finished sorting through the fourth drawer. I was tempted to push through, but those four drawers had taught me that my uncle had never met a piece of paper he didn't want to stick in a folder and file for posterity.

This was going to be a marathon, not a sprint.

Rubbing my tired eyes, I collected my empty bottles and dumped them in the kitchen before heading off to bed.

My thoughts drifted to Grace Kerrington as I hovered on the brink of sleep. She'd surprised me a few times today. She seemed to genuinely appreciate my uncle's art collection. And she had a decent sense of humour. She was refreshingly direct, too, not a common trait in the species of ambitious corporate raptor I'd initially taken her for.

She was my last thought before I fell asleep.

———

I'd already been up for a couple of hours when Grace let herself into the apartment at quarter past eight the following morning. She pulled up short when she saw me.

"Hi," she said belatedly, setting her bag and coat on the Le Corbusier sofa. "You're early."

"So are you," I pointed out.

"I wanted to get a head start on things."

"Likewise."

She frowned and I knew she didn't believe me, but was too polite—or, more likely, too worried about my status as a Walker—to call me on it.

"Coffee?" I asked. "I managed to work out how to tame Jack's espresso machine."

She was pulling a battered laptop out of her bag, but her head came up at my words.

"I don't think we should be using your uncle's things," she said.

"Sorry?"

"His kitchen is part of the estate now."

"So are the toilets. You planning on not going all day, too?"

"That's different."

"Trust me, my uncle would want us to be caffeinated." I gave her an assessing once-over. She was wearing another sleek little suit again today, this one navy instead of black. Same shoes, though, and same neat updo. "Macchiato, right?"

Guessing what coffee people drink is my party trick, and I'm almost never wrong.

"Latte. One sugar, please," she said. "If you absolutely insist on using the machine."

I paused, surprised yet again where she was concerned. "Interesting."

"Why?"

"A latte is a hedonist's drink."

"It's just coffee with milk." A wash of pink colored her cheeks.

I'd noticed yesterday that she blushed easily, especially when I flirted with her.

"If you just wanted the caffeine, you'd go for a macchiato or a long black. But a latte is about indulgence. Decadence."

She made a rude noise, her cheeks very pink now. "It's just because I'm too much of a wimp to have straight espresso."

It was tempting to keep teasing her, especially because she responded so spectacularly, but I decided to have mercy and headed into the kitchen to make our coffees.

I was steaming the milk when she joined me. I could feel her watching as I tamped the grinds into the group handle and fitted it to the machine.

"Summer job when I was sixteen," I said.

"What?"

"You were wondering where I learned to make coffee. I worked at the cafe near home one summer."

"Right." One word, dry as dust.

"You don't believe me? How'd you get so cynical so young?" I asked as I handed her coffee over.

"Practice. Lots of practice," she said.

For the second time in two days, her sly humour made me bark out a laugh. She took a sip of her coffee, and I watched as her eyebrows went up with surprise.

I make good coffee. Life's too short for the bad stuff.

"Three months, three hundred coffees a day, minimum," I said. "Still got the scars to prove it."

I offered her my left forearm, where a faded burn mark the size of a silver dollar marred the inside of my wrist, the result of a close encounter with the side of a volcanically hot group head.

A small crease formed between her eyebrows as she tried to work out why a trust-fund kid like me had taken a summer job.

"It's a long story."

"What's the short version?" she asked, licking foam off her lips.

She wasn't doing it deliberately—the gesture was too artless, too unconscious for that—but it drew my gaze to her mouth. Specifically, to her full bottom lip. Despite my determination to focus on the job at hand, I'd had several dirty thoughts about that lip since first meeting her. It fascinated me in a way I couldn't explain.

"I wanted guitar lessons. My mother didn't. So I worked for the money to pay for them."

"So did you get your lessons?" she asked.

"Of course." I gave her a cocky smile. I didn't tell her I'd taken them behind Vicky's back, and that when she'd found out she'd made me give my guitar away. It was far too early in the day for tales of family dysfunction.

"What do you want me to do today?" I asked, leaning against the counter and crossing my arms.

"I've drawn up a schedule," she said.

Of course she had. "Give me my orders and I'll get stuck in," I said.

"Let me go check what I had you down for today." She swallowed the last of her coffee. "Thank you for that, it was delicious."

"I think you mean decadent."

Her mouth twitched into an almost smile. The fact that she was trying not to be amused made my own grin wider, for some reason.

Maybe because I've always liked a challenge.

"Shut up," she said, then she left me standing in the kitchen, grinning at nothing.

Grace

I will not flirt with Callan Walker. I will not flirt with Callan Walker.

He was flirting with me, though. All the smiles and the teasing, and the way he kept looking at my mouth... If I wasn't such a terrible blusher, it would be fine. But I've always blushed at the drop of a hat, and all he had to do is give me one of those half-smiles of his and say something vaguely playful in that delectable accent and I could feel heat burning its way up my chest and into my face.

It was because he was so good-looking, of course, and I hated myself for being so shallow. So what if he had beautifully muscled shoulders? So what if he filled out his Armani jeans to perfection? He was the self-confessed black sheep of his family, and Stephen had all but said Callan was a spoiled man-child. In other words, the very last kind of guy I would be interested in.

Having said all that... I was a little worried by the way my heart gave a distinct high-kick when I walked through the door and saw him this morning. This job could not be more important to me. Not only did I need to keep it, I needed to do so awesomely well at it that Walker Holdings wouldn't have any choice but to offer me a permanent role.

"Hang on to that thought," I muttered to myself as I fired up the laptop Walker Holdings had given me. The Sotheby's modern-art department had asked me to take some shots of the rooms before they sent someone over so they could "marshal resources" at their end. Whatever that meant. And then Stephen had emailed first thing to let me know Victoria Walker wanted me to prioritize packing up Jack Walker's papers. Both tasks were now at the top of my timetable. I was still trying get the stupid software to do what I wanted when Callan entered. He was so quiet I didn't realize he was there until I saw him out of the corner of my eye and nearly jumped out of my skin.

That was when I realized he wasn't wearing any shoes. Why hadn't I noticed that before? His bare feet were long and tanned, with straight toes and not too much hair.

Nice feet, in other words. Large feet.

I gave myself a mental poke in the eye and offered him my brightest professional smile.

"You snuck up on me."

"My other summer job was working as a ninja," he said, absolutely deadpan.

"After the barista thing I'm going to take you at your word."

"Where's the fun in that?"

"I'm not here for fun," I said, more as a reminder to myself than anything else. "I have two things down for this morning—starting to box up your uncle's papers so they can be shipped to Australia, and taking photographs for the auction house."

He frowned slightly. "Why are you shipping all his papers out?"

"I don't know. I guess they want to make sure there aren't any loose ends they need to tie up."

"I'll take the study," he said.

I was thrown for a moment, because I'd expected him to take the easy option, snapping selfies with artwork. "Um. Okay. I've got some archive boxes coming from the office. They should be here any minute."

"I'll go do some recon in the study, get the lay of the land," Callan said easily.

He sauntered from the room, and once again my eyes were drawn to his bare feet. Was taking your shoes and socks off at work a weird Australian custom I didn't know about? And where on earth were his shoes, anyway?

I glanced around, but couldn't see them anywhere.

Then I realized I was wasting precious time standing around thinking about *him* again.

I will not obsess over Callan Walker. Etc.

Pulling out my phone, I got to work. Last night I'd cleared out my photo library so there was plenty of memory on it, and I went into the foyer. It took a while to work out how best to photograph the Corr Danch installation. Once the foyer was done, I moved into the living room. There were so many pieces, I divided the room into sections and started snapping away, pausing only to make a note of artist's names or maker's marks.

I'd just finished when Callan appeared from the study with

hair that looked as though he'd been running his fingers through it.

"I need more coffee," he said as he passed by. "You in?"

I hesitated. But... *Why not me?* "Yes, please."

He was back a couple of minutes later, two coffees in hand and a packet of something tucked under his arm.

"Figured you might be hungry, and all this stuff is just going to go in the bin if we don't eat it." He tore the cellophane off the pack and offered it to me.

I stared at the odd-looking objects in front of me—what looked like a hard, square cookie with stripes of something pink down either side, bisected by a stripe of red, the whole covered in coconut.

"I don't mean to look a gift horse in the mouth..." I said.

"Iced VoVos. They're not nearly as disgusting as they look."

"Is this like Vegemite? Because I've heard about you Australians and Vegemite, how you lure unsuspecting people into having some and their taste buds are never the same again."

"Vegemite is awesome. Iced VoVos are okay. Me, I prefer Tim Tams like most red-blooded Aussies, but Jack was into VoVos. The gayest biscuit ever made."

I blinked at his casual reference to his uncle's sexuality. I'd wondered, obviously. The apartment was hugely stylish, but there was no hint of a woman's presence. And then there was the provocative Mapplethorpe nude on the bedroom wall. Kind of a giveaway.

"All right. I'm going in," I said, taking a cookie from the plastic tray.

Callan watched as I took a bite. Sugar, crunch, squishy marshmallow. A bit of tangy raspberry jam.

"So, O'Malley, what do you think?" he asked.

"It's Kerrington, and I like them," I said. "They're ugly, don't get me wrong. But pretty tasty." Especially by the standards of someone who couldn't afford a dollar fifty for a bagel.

He set the packet down. "Knock yourself out."

"You're not going to have one?"

"I respect myself too much," he said.

Which made me laugh. He watched me, a speculative glint in his eye, and I could feel myself getting warm again. Why did he have to be so good-looking? *Why?*

"Have as many as you want. They'll just go to waste, and we need to clear out Jack's kitchen."

I caught him looking at my mouth again. There was something about his intensity that made me nervous.

Or maybe *self-aware* was the better word. Suddenly I was conscious of the weight of my clothes on my skin, the tickle of a few stray hairs on the back of my neck, the aftertaste of sugar and tartness in my mouth.

"Your uncle had an amazing eye," I said, desperate for distraction.

Callan glanced around. "Yeah. He loved art. He wanted to be a painter when he was younger, but it turned out he sucked at it. So he turned his passion to collecting instead."

"That's tough. One of the hardest things in life is giving up on a dream."

His blue eyes were piercing as he returned his focus to me. "You talking from experience, O'Malley?"

I swallowed the automatic correction that rose to my lips. He had to know my name was Kerrington by now, which meant this whole O'Malley thing was clearly not an accident. No one was that forgetful.

"A little," I said instead. "There are a lot of talented people at design school. It's pretty humbling when you get some perspective on your own talent."

"I thought you said you changed majors out of practicality?"

I was a little surprised he'd remembered me saying that yesterday, which might be why I answered so candidly. "I did. If I could have, I'd have tried to go the distance, seen if I had enough of whatever-it-is to make a name for myself. But things changed for me, so..." I forced myself to stop talking, aware I'd disclosed a lot more than I'd intended to.

"What changed for you?" he asked, his gaze traveling over my face.

It was pretty distracting, having a gorgeous man shine the klieg light of his attention on you like that, but I was ready for him this time.

"You know. Just life." I shrugged. "I should keep going with the photographs."

"Sure. Let me know when you need more black gold," he said easily, indicating the coffee cup with his chin.

He padded out of the room and I felt myself relax a notch. I really had to get a grip on my hormones where Callan was concerned. It was starting to get embarrassing.

I helped myself to another Iced VoVo before finishing my coffee. I wasn't sure where to go next. I'd been avoiding exploring the bedrooms too extensively because it felt like such an invasion of Jack Walker's personal, private space. But it had to be done, so I girded my loins and headed down the hallway.

The first room was clearly a guest bedroom—there were no personal touches, no lived-in feeling. I took a picture of the archi-tectural-looking chair in the corner, then the bed and the bedside table, both of which were French antiques unless I missed my guess. Then I stuck my head into the bathroom to see if there was any art in there I should know about. Jack was such an avid and passionate collector, it wouldn't surprise me if he had a Picasso in there rubbing elbows with a Van Gogh.

I snorted out a laugh when I saw that there was not one but two sketches on the bathroom wall, both of which looked like Toulouse-Lautrec to me. I stepped closer. Yep, they were Lautrecs, and both appeared to be originals.

Unbelievable. Imagine living a life surrounded by all this

beauty and talent. Imagine being so rich you could casually display a couple of Lautrec sketches in the *guest bathroom.*

I was shaking my head at how different Jack Walker's world was from mine as I turned toward the door. Then something registered in the back of my mind and I paused.

The shower was wet.

I stared at the wet glass and tiles for a long moment as the implications of my observation sank in. I glanced at the vanity, and sure enough, there was a lone toothbrush sitting in a glass there, along with a tube of paste.

I retreated to the bedroom. This time my gaze went straight to the pair of men's shoes sitting near the burled-walnut armoire.

No wonder Callan was barefoot. He'd slept the night here in his uncle's apartment. Without telling me.

Just in case I was way off base, I plucked the pillow from his bed and held it to my nose. The scent of smoky wood and warm leather lingered there.

Callan. No doubt about it, that was his aftershave. I'd been trying not to notice how delicious it was ever since we met, and there was no mistaking the distinctive scent.

Dropping the pillow back onto the bed, I turned on my heel and marched for the door. This morning when I'd arrived, he'd let me believe that he'd rushed to be here because he wanted to get an early start.

God, he must have been laughing at me, amusing himself with his private joke at my expense. And to think, I'd been worried about him using the coffee machine. I knew without a doubt that Victoria Walker was not going to be happy when she learned her son was staying in Jack's apartment. In fact, I was already dreading telling her.

Blergh.

I found Callan in the study, on his knees assembling one of the archive boxes. He looked about a million times more approachable today in his plain T-shirt and jeans, and I had to remind myself he was a sneak who had been laughing at me behind my back.

"What's up?" he asked, sitting back on his heels.

I couldn't help noticing the way the denim drew tight across his thighs, which only made me more annoyed.

I braced my hands on my hips. "Why didn't you tell me you were staying in the spare room?"

———

Callan

Grace was pissed with me. I could tell because she had her hands on her hips—the universal signal that a woman is on the warpath. Plus her chin was slightly elevated, as though she was daring me to deny her charge.

"I didn't think it was that big a deal," I said.

"Even though you know I'm supposed to be preparing the contents of this apartment for sale? You didn't think I might be interested in the fact that you're occupying one of the beds?"

"Grace, if I'd thought you were interested in my sleeping arrangements, believe me, I would have kept you up to date," I said.

She narrowed her eyes at me. "No. Don't do that. Don't try and flirt your way out of this."

"Was that what I was doing?"

"Yes, and you know it, so don't pretend you weren't." She spread her hands out at her sides, the picture of exasperation. "Why aren't you staying at a hotel, like a normal person?"

"Because this is where I always stay when I'm in town," I answered honestly. "And I didn't want to be anywhere else, even though I know Jack's not here anymore."

She opened her mouth to speak, then closed it without saying anything.

Sincerity has a way of doing that to people sometimes.

"Your mother is not going to be happy when I tell her about this," she said finally.

"Then don't," I said simply.

"So you want me to lie to her in my report tonight? I'm sure that will work out well."

"What do you mean, your report?"

"Your mother asked for a progress report each night. I'm supposed to load everything I've done each day to the company cloud so she can review it. Or one of her team. I'm not really sure."

"I suppose she asked you to report on me, too," I guessed.

"She wants to know how much progress I've made," Grace said, but her cheeks were pink and we both knew what that meant.

"Fucking hell." I walked to the window then back again, needing to do something to release the tension. Until a couple of days ago, I had managed to go a whole eighteen months without any contact with my mother or her people, because life was simply better that way. Her pathological need to dominate anything or anyone she considered hers was as predictable as it was oppressive, and the only way to avoid it was to avoid her, as much as possible.

So maybe I shouldn't have been surprised she'd instructed Grace to inform on me. And definitely I shouldn't be angry with Grace because she'd been put in the invidious position of being the meat in a fucked-up Walker sandwich.

But I was angry, anyway. There was something about Grace that had made me forget the cardinal rule of being who I am: everyone is out for something, nothing is free. I'd let Grace's sincere appreciation for my uncle's home and her refreshing directness lull me into dropping my guard. Not much, just a little.

I'd started to like her.

After all these years, you'd think I'd know better.

"I'm just trying to do my job here," Grace said. She looked deeply uncomfortable.

"I'm trying to give my uncle a bit of respect. Guess who wins?" I said sharply.

"Listen—"

The sound of the doorbell echoed through the apartment, the chimes resonant. For a moment Grace and I simply stared at each other, then she spun on her heel and headed for the door.

I let out a sigh and swore under my breath. The sooner I could sort out Jack's affairs, the better.

I heard voices as I stepped out into the living room, and when I arrived in the foyer I found Grace talking to a tiny, white-haired woman, her small face swamped by a pair of over-sized glasses. She was dressed in a flowing purple silk tunic over colorful leggings, and a black standard poodle strained at the lead she was holding in a death grip, desperate to get loose and start exploring Jack's apartment.

"Gloria," I said, recognising the woman who owned the only other apartment on this floor.

"Callan! I'm so glad to see you. And so sad. Such terrible news. We've all been so shocked." Gloria's chunky rings flashed on her fingers as she reached out to grasp my forearm in a surprisingly strong grip.

"Terribly sudden," I echoed. *So sudden that nobody bothered telling me.* My gaze fell on the dog, and I was tickled by a memory of Jack saying something about a poodle. I'd completely forgotten.

"This is Jack's Lady," Gloria said. "I kept her as long as I could. But I'm headed to Florida tomorrow and was starting to panic until I saw a light on under your door this morning."

"Lady," I echoed. At the sound of her name, the dog strained on her leash again, this time proving stronger than Gloria. She launched herself toward me and buried her nose in my crotch. I sidestepped, pushing her snout away. "Not very ladylike, girl. Most women ask for an invitation first."

Gloria grinned. "I'm sure you get that treatment from all the girls. Your uncle always said you were quite the heartbreaker."

Grace gave me an unimpressed look before the dog turned her friskiness on her, forcing her to take a big step backward. I grabbed the leash to prevent the animal from mauling her.

And that's how I became the caretaker of an oversized poodle.

Before abandoning me with the dog, Gloria apologized several times for the imposition. "I could call around," she said, wringing her hands. "To ask if anyone else in the building was in the mood to adopt a dog."

"It's all right," I assured her. "You've been amazing, looking after her for so long. Enjoy your vacation, we've got this covered."

"I'm so sorry about Jack," she said, hugging me one more time. "And I'm so sorry I missed the funeral. I kept my eye out for a notice, but I must have overlooked it. I'm not as good at keeping track of things as I used to be."

"You didn't miss the funeral. The family decided not to have one."

Gloria visibly flinched. "But why on earth...?"

"I don't really know," I said tightly. "I wasn't notified, either."

Gloria blinked in confusion, her blue eyes huge and watery behind the lenses of her glasses.

"So many people wanted to say goodbye," she said. "What a terrible, terrible shame."

She continued to look bewildered as she crossed the shared elevator foyer to her own apartment. I waited until she was safely inside before waving a final goodbye and shutting the door to Jack's place.

When I returned to the living room, I found Grace pacing in her heels. *Tap-tap-tap.* The dog's toenails echoed the sound on Uncle Jack's polished floors. *Click-click-click.* I turned the beast loose to see what she'd do.

Grace and I watched silently as Lady took off. I heard the sound of her toenails as she inspected each room, one after another, looking for someone who wasn't there. But then she came back to the living room and stopped in front of me. She sat down and let out a single whine.

"I'm so sorry, girl," I said, my voice rough. Grace looked away as I reached down to scratch Lady on the head. She leaned into my hand, making an inelegant snorting sound.

"She's cute," Grace said. "But I don't think your mother knows about her. She never mentioned a dog, anyway."

"She's not going to the pound."

She flinched. "Of course not. God, Callan. What kind of a monster do you think I am?"

"I wasn't thinking of you. Vicky will tell you to surrender her."

"*No.*"

It took me a moment to realise Grace was offended on my mother's behalf.

"It's not because she's an animal hater," I explained. "It's about efficiency. Expediency."

Grace looked uncertain.

"Don't worry about it. I'll handle Lady. And this way you won't have to kick me out of the apartment."

Grace's lips made a thin line. "I guess not." She didn't look the least bit happy about any of it.

I scratched Lady behind the ears, earning an encouraging nudge. "Did you finish your photography?"

"I finished the artwork," she said. "It will take me all evening to upload it for the auction house. I was thinking of going to the warehouse to check out your uncle's commercial wine stock after lunch."

I'd been there once. "In New Jersey, right?"

She nodded.

"I'll come along."

Her brow creased. "Why?"

"Why not?" I gave her the easy smile that usually got the ladies distracted. If my uncle had another will that I'd be settling, I wanted to know what was in the warehouse before my mother got her hands on it. If it took too long to find the will, it had occurred to me I might end up suing my mother for whatever she'd disposed of before I found the bloody thing.

"All right," Grace agreed, as if I'd asked her to pop into the oral surgeon's for a root canal. She stepped over to my uncle's coat tree and retrieved her jacket. "I'll take a half hour for lunch and we'll leave from here."

"Good plan, O'Malley."

"That's not my name."

"It's a nickname. Consider it part of the rich cultural exchange we're engaging in," I said.

Now she looked confused. "How is you giving me a nickname cultural exchange?"

"Because giving people and things nicknames is an Australian pastime. We can't help ourselves. It's a compulsion. A national obsession."

"Okay, let's just say I buy that. Why O'Malley, then?"

I opened my mouth to explain, then thought better of it. It was kind of fun, keeping her guessing.

"Just because," I said instead. I turned and left the room before I got myself in any more trouble.

SIX

Callan Wrangler

Grace

I ATE my peanut butter sandwich in the frigid park again. As I chewed, I Googled O'Malley on my phone. The mystery wasn't solved until I hit on the idea of Googling Grace O'Malley.

Score.

According to Wikipedia, Grace O'Malley was a sixteenth-century Irish pirate, known for both ruthlessness and competence.

Hmm. Was it a compliment or a slur? Or a little of both? That was the trouble with Callan Walker. He was a maddening combination of outward charm and hidden agendas.

This morning, when I'd gotten my first glance at Jack Walker's study, I could tell Callan had been busy in there well before I showed up. There were stacks of file folders on the desk where none had been the day before, and a few of the drawers were half open.

He was looking for something, obviously. Something he wasn't going to tell me about. Which meant I should probably tell his mother about it.

Ugh. The idea of informing on him—or anyone—did not sit well with me.

On the other hand, I didn't like the idea of being managed, either. He was keeping things from me—like the fact he'd taken up residence in the apartment—and using his charm and good looks to distract me.

It was really annoying, but I filed the problem away to worry about later. My hands were about frozen. This was the cost of my pride, and I needed to get back inside where it was warm.

Once I'd returned to the apartment, I told Callan I was ready to go to New Jersey. "You don't need to go with me," I added. Sitting in close quarters with him on a train sounded like a bad idea. It was bad enough that I experienced a hormone spike whenever he entered a room.

"I'm ready," he said, swatting Lady away from his crotch. "You're staying here, girl." He grabbed a jacket I hadn't seen before and pulled it on. It was one of those waxed Barbour jackets that cost a mint.

"Problem?" he asked, and I realized I was staring. "Yes, this was Jack's, but he wouldn't want me to shiver." *Shiv-ah*. It was irritating the way he sounded hot even when he was goading me. "I'll pose for an inventory photo if you want." He struck a pose, his hand propped against the doorframe, his chin lifted like a model on one of the fashion accounts I followed on Instagram.

He was hotter than most models. Damn him.

"Let's just go," I grumbled.

We rode the elevator to the lobby in silence. When the doors opened, Callan turned to the left while I turned toward the doors to the street.

"Grace," he said, making my name sound far more exotic than it ought to. "The carpark is this way."

"The...what?"

"Carpark. It's Australian for parking lot."

Grrr. "I *know* that. But we don't have a car."

He drew his hand out of his pocket and held up a set of keys. "Not true."

"Oh." I hadn't even known Jack had a car. Another thing to add to the inventory. "I was going to take the PATH train to New Jersey," I argued. "And then a bus."

"Jesus. Why would we do that?" Callan wore a look of horror. As if I'd suggested we hitchhike to New Jersey.

"Didn't know there was a car," I admitted.

"And not just any car, O'Malley."

I followed him into the underground parking garage where he led me to a vintage convertible. "Wow," I said slowly. I'd never seen anything like it. An Austin-Healey, according to the chrome lettering on the trunk. I walked around to the side of the car, admiring the paint, which was sleek and shimmery. Like liquid mercury.

Callan chuckled. "You're not the driver. Not this time."

"No kidding."

"Then your seat is over there." He indicated the wrong side of the car. The left side. Which was when I registered this car had the steering wheel on the right.

"Is this even legal?" I asked him, slowly circling the piece of art that Callan intended to drive. I tugged on the handle and the door swung open. I sat down—the seat was lower than what I was used to.

He laughed, as he usually did whenever I spoke. "It will be fine, so long as I remember to stay on the right side of the road."

"That's not funny." I shut the door and looked for a seatbelt. Thankfully there was one.

Callan got in and started the engine, which was growlier than a modern car. We were even closer together than I'd predicted, cocooned together in...a hundred thousand dollars' worth of antique metal?

Here we were, doing things his way again. I was a very poor Callan-wrangler, apparently.

He reversed out of the parking spot and wound through the garage. Traffic wasn't too bad on our way to the Lincoln Tunnel. It was odd to be seated on the left-hand side. I kept pressing myself back whenever he needed to make a left turn.

"Relax, Grace," he chided.

"I don't have a will," I blurted out.

He laughed at me as we slid into the dimness of the tunnel. "What are you, twenty? I swear you'll make it home safe to your boyfriend tonight."

"Twenty-five. No boyfriend." I shouldn't have added that last bit.

"Girlfriend, then? I'm still convinced you're a hedonist."

I let out an unsexy snort. "I do live with a girl. My sister. So you can hit pause on whatever you're thinking right now."

"I don't know—twin sisters are a staple in porn."

The man could make even the word "porn" sound appealing. Still, I shut him down. "My sister is fifteen. Touch her and die."

"Sorry." He looked over at me quickly. "I wouldn't have said that if I knew how young she was."

"I know," I said. Callan was flirtatious, but not creepy. If anything, I was starting to think his practiced charm was a costume—like those expensive shirts he wore. A slick exterior that disguised his real thoughts. "Don't sweat it."

Callan glanced at me again as our car slid out of the Lincoln tunnel into New Jersey's ugly highway snarl. "So why are you still looking so dark?"

"Is that Australian for grumpy?"

"Pretty much."

"I hate New Jersey."

"Yeah?"

"Can't stand the place." It was usually easy to avoid this side of the river. "I left when I was seventeen and try never to come back."

"Why?"

And there you go again, talking about yourself too much. I wasn't sure why that kept happening with this man. I pointed out the window, at the graffiti and industrial grime. "Would *you* want to revisit this?"

He gave me a curious look, but let it slide.

Luckily, the warehouse was just a few minutes off the highway. "There it is," he said, turning into a giant parking lot, where numbered doors and loading bays appeared to serve many businesses all at once.

"We're looking for number sixteen," I told him.

"It's on the end," Callan said. "I've been here before."

Of course he had. Yet another piece of information he hadn't bothered to share with me until it suited him.

I was the first one out of the car, digging the keys out of my purse. Approaching the door beside the loading bay marked with a big, red sixteen, I pressed the key into the lock. It turned as a lock should, but when I twisted the doorknob, the door wouldn't open. I rattled the knob, then rattled it again. Damn it. If I'd brought Callan and the antique car all the way out here and couldn't get in... I tried the knob again. This was about to become embarrassing.

"Let me have a go," Callan's smooth voice demanded. Even the word "go" sounded sensual to me. He chewed the word, almost.

Frustrated in more ways than were appropriate, I stepped aside.

Callan grabbed the knob and turned it. Then he braced his broad shoulder against the door. With a low grunt he forced it open with a pop. "Bingo."

Two things became apparent when I stepped into the warehouse. One: Wine smells nice even when it's bottled and waiting around to be drunk. The pine boxes stacked up to the ceiling were offgassing the scent of wood and patience. Two: Victoria Walker lied. Uncle Jack didn't have a small, inconsequential hobby here. There were hundreds of cases in this room, in dozens of varieties. This was a serious wine import business, not some rich guy amusing himself bringing in bottles for his buddies.

I allowed myself a half second to feel overwhelmed before I realized this was a positive development. A bigger job meant a longer assignment for yours truly.

Callan wandered off among the rows of wines, running a hand along the labels that had been neatly attached to the tall metal shelving units holding the cases. I spotted a forklift parked against the wall, which solved the mystery of how the wine got onto shelves eight feet above the ground.

"Huh. He's importing Luke's stuff now," Callan muttered from somewhere nearby.

When I found him, he was holding a bottle. Its wooden crate was ajar, revealing eleven more bottles with the same green label. "Do you know this vineyard?"

"It's near Adelaide, in South Australia. My family has a cattle station nearby. One of my mates is the winemaker." He had a distant look on his face. "The vineyard has an amazing ocean view."

I read the label. "Shiraz. There's a lot of that in Australia, right?" My knowledge of wine was minimal. But I knew I'd seen Australian shiraz among the more affordable choices at Astor Wines.

"It's practically the national drink. But Luke's also growing Cab Sauv and Nero d'Avola." My face must have looked blank because he added, "It's a Sicilian variety that does well in red clay soil over limestone."

I blinked. "You know a lot about this."

"Jack was always talking wine. Loved the stuff. Learning to hold my own was a form of self-defense." He shrugged, then tucked the bottle back inside the crate. "And I come from a foodie family."

"Do you know cattle, too? It's hard to picture you roping steers." My gaze wandered, unbidden, down his fine body. It wasn't all that hard to imagine him on a horse, come to think of it. When I looked up again, he was watching me. My cheeks grew warm from the embarrassment of having been caught admiring him.

He made a small noise in his throat I'd never heard from him before, and it made me painfully aware that we were only separated by a few inches. One step and I'd be close enough to touch him. Two, and I'd be close enough to press my mouth to his.

"What? No imagination, O'Malley?" His voice was rough. "I don't find it difficult to imagine you in several different positions."

His words were like a splash of heat—a sensation I hadn't felt in a long time. Visions filled my head—his clever mouth on mine, his hard body beneath my hands, all that playful intensity focused on *me*. A man like Callan Walker would be good in bed. He'd be dirty and adventurous, earthy and bold.

He'd take no prisoners.

Abort! Abort! I took a step backward and looked away. "I'd better start taking photographs or we'll be here all day."

I felt his eyes on me as I walked toward the front of the warehouse. I pulled out my phone with nervous hands and stood against the wall, snapping a picture that would show Queen Vic just how much inventory was here. Then I stood at the end of each individual row and repeated the exercise, often at several angles. Callan moved around the warehouse, too. I glimpsed him, but kept my distance, scared of the way I'd responded to him. I wasn't here to be tempted by him, I was here to work.

Each different label got a close-up photo. I planned to enter the details into a spreadsheet tonight or tomorrow, in preparation for a more thorough stock-take. That would likely take days, given the amount of stock here.

And it was hard to keep track of my photos, because most of the labels were so similar—in a parchment color, with black text. If I had a wine-importing business, I'd design something splashy and fresh.

But no. I was the temp who was meant to keep her opinions to herself. And this business was about to be shut down.

Inevitably Callan and I met again in the pinot noir section. "How did your photos of the warehouse turn out?" he asked.

"Fine, I think. Why?"

His eyes glinted in a way that made me suspicious. "No reason."

I opened up the photo app on my phone and scrolled back through the shots. Since I'd deliberately tried to ignore Callan and focus on my work, I hadn't noticed what he'd done.

"You ass!" In several of my shots, he was posing suggestively. He'd grabbed his crotch in the aisle of white wines. He'd leaned over the forklift, showing off his backside, in another shot.

That picture was actually quite funny, and I let out a bark of laughter against my will.

He leaned in to get a look at the photo. "Some prime beef to go with your cabernets."

"Now I have to retake them all, or your mother will assume that all I do is horse around at work." That idea made me grumpy enough to wipe the smile off my face. "Stay out of my photos, Callan Walker."

"Yes, O'Malley."

And stop sounding so sexy every time you open your mouth.

I will not think dreamy thoughts about that accent. I will not think dreamy...

He smirked as if he could read minds. And it made me want to slap the smirk off his face.

———

As I got ready to leave, I noticed two cases of wine stacked by the door. Callan picked one up and headed outside.

"What are you doing with those?" I asked.

"Putting a couple of cases in the car."

"But my inventory will be off."

"I'll fix it."

"Callan! You can't just walk off with the inventory."

"Jesus Christ. The wholesale value is probably only two hundred dollars. I'll write the estate a check." His fine features were far more irritated with me then they'd been an hour ago.

We got back in the car in silence, not speaking until we reached the approach to the inbound Lincoln Tunnel.

I finally broke the stalemate. "I'm well aware that I sounded like a nag. But your mother is a strict woman and I can't afford to be cavalier about the estate property."

He made a small sound of irritation. "I know. Can you just trust me not to hang you out to dry, though? I'm not about to land you in it."

"Can you let me know if you decide to take any more personal items before I submit my inventory to the wine auctioneer for his estimate? I'd really appreciate it."

"I can't believe Vicky is planning on selling all that stock off at auction. She'll only get pennies on the dollar, you know. Even if the wine was sold to Jack's customers at discount, the estate would earn more."

"Your mother wants things wrapped up quickly."

He sighed, and his next words were like chips of ice. "Right. I keep forgetting her mission is to wipe all trace of Jack from the face of the earth." His expression was bleak, his jaw set.

The bottleneck of cars entering the tunnel cleared up. Callan shifted into a higher gear and stepped on the accelerator. The sports car zoomed forward with a growl. I'd won this round, but the victory felt hollow.

SEVEN

Hi Darling I'm Home

Callan

GRACE LEFT me in the carpark.

"I'm going to spend the evening setting up a spreadsheet so I can do a stock-take of the warehouse," she said. "I'll be back tomorrow at nine."

"I can help with that, if you like," I offered, then immediately wanted to kick myself. Her leaving early meant I'd have longer to search the study. A smart guy would be encouraging her to go, not trying to get her to stay.

Apparently I wasn't particularly smart where Grace was concerned.

"I've got it, thanks. Your mother expects to see progress every day. When she wakes up in a couple of hours, I want her to see all the work I did today. *We* did," she corrected.

She was so fair-minded, so careful, I couldn't help smiling. We both knew I hadn't really helped her, except for forcing the warehouse door open. "All right," I said, since I couldn't think of another reason to make her stay. "See you in the morning."

She headed for the door, and I stood watching as she left. She was such a straight shooter, but there was a little sway in her hips when she walked that drew my gaze to her ass.

It hit me that in another time and another place, I would pull out all the stops to get Grace Kerrington into bed. I'd make it a priority. Maybe even an obsession.

I'd charm her out of her suit and follow the blushes across her skin. I'd unlock the hedonist in her soul and go along for the ride.

But this was not the time, or the place, and Grace was not a woman to treat carelessly. She wasn't worldly and sophisticated, like the women I was used to rubbing elbows with. She was real. Anything I started up with her would mean something, and I'd given up sincerity a while ago.

Turning away, I made my way to the elevator and up to Jack's apartment. When I opened the door, Lady bounded over, rose up, and put her paws on my shoulders.

"Hi, darling, I'm home," I told her. She took this as an invitation to lick my face, so I did an awkward sidestep and nudged her away. "Give me a moment to bring in the wine, and then I'll take you for a run." Not as much fun as making Grace blush, but better than getting all broody and ratting around Jack's apartment again.

Lady must have a large vocabulary for a poodle, because she seemed to get even more excited, tap-dancing in a circle around me as I brought in the wine, then following me into the guest room where I changed into a pair of track pants and a T-shirt.

Then I put on my trainers, found a leash for Lady in the front hall, and left the building.

The beauty of Uncle Jack's apartment's location was its proximity to the park. I liked New York's glamour as much as the next guy, but I couldn't fathom how anyone lived where he couldn't see trees. With the leash in hand, I began to jog, and Lady seemed game to run. Uncle Jack hadn't been much of a runner, so I took the bridle path loop to make it easy on the girl.

Two miles later, my mood had improved. The sky was blue

overhead, and the afternoon sunlight reflected off the grand old Central Park West apartment buildings, warming them to a rosy hue. When we finished the circuit, I stopped at a group of shrubberies just off the Great Lawn, and waited while Lady did her business.

If Jack were still alive, he'd be plotting our dinner plans right now. Together we'd eaten everything from exquisite French cuisine at Bouley to the chewy hand-pulled Chinese noodles at Xian's Famous Foods.

Gone. He was just...gone.

Today while I was browsing his inventory of wines, I'd had a thought. Gloria had made me realise I wasn't the only one cheated out of a memorial for Jack. He had friends. He was loved. People wanted to say goodbye.

I'd nabbed those two cases of wine with a plan. I'd send an email blast to the people listed in the little black address book on the kitchen counter. Surely a few of his mates would turn up if I sent out a general plea to share one last drink in his honor?

His showplace of an apartment made it easy enough. All I had to do was uncork a few bottles and order in some munchies. I could call the tapas place he'd loved. It was in the neighborhood somewhere.

"Come on, Lady!" I said. "Let's go find the tapas place."

She lifted her head and trotted over. She had a regal walk that amused me. We cut west, past Jack's apartment building, to Columbus Avenue. It was busy at this hour with commuters returning home from work. I paused in front of the Housing Works Thrift Shop, which had a cool display of alarm clocks in the front window. When it came time to box up Uncle Jack's clothes, this would make a convenient donation site. I paused to read the hours off the sign in the window.

It was then that my subconscious snagged on a woman inside the store. Her elegant neck lengthened as she raised a hand to point at something hanging on the wall. When she turned her head to talk to the salesperson, I caught sight of her intelligent eyes and pretty face.

Grace Kerrington.

Unseen, I watched as the salesgirl used a hook on a wooden pole to retrieve a clothes hanger from high up on the wall. When she lowered it, Grace took charge, lifting the red suit and holding it up to the light. It was a dowdy thing, like something my grand-mother would have worn to church. Not a garment worthy of Grace's sleek body.

Funny how I assumed I knew Grace's wardrobe choices after a mere two days with her. Noticing her had become my favorite hobby.

I shook my head and walked on, finding the tapas bar on the very next block.

———

Lady and I dined on dog chow and Spanish appetizers, respectively.

I ate my takeaway food at Jack's desk while hunting through yet more files for his will. If there *was* a more recent will. I was starting to doubt my own sanity, though I had a very clear memory of dining at Nobu one night, both of us tipsy on sake, while discussing my mother's support of a prominent anti-marriage-equality lobby group back home in Australia.

I'd been fuming, ashamed of my mother's closed-mindedness, especially given her own brother was gay. The whole reason Jack had made a new life in New York three decades ago was because he'd become tired of being the family's dirty secret.

"She hasn't changed," Jack had said with a shrug. He'd always been much more sanguine about Vicky than me. "If it's any comfort to you, she's going to hate my new will."

"Why? What have you done?" I asked, recognizing the glint of mischief in his eyes.

"I'm leaving it all to charity, a veritable rainbow of gay and lesbian support groups. I wanted to talk to you about being executor, if you're up for it."

"Fuck, yeah. Of course."

We'd had a good laugh about it, imagining Vicky's reaction, not bothering with painful details like the fact that Jack would have to be dead for his will to come into play. As we'd walked home, both of us the worse for wear, he'd told me he'd call the lawyer on Monday. Then we'd never talked about it again.

If only I could remember the lawyer's name.

Although, it was always possible Jack had gotten distracted. Maybe he'd never finished the new will. None of us ever thinks he's going to die.

Either way, my mother would have been the first phone call when her brother died. She was probably listed as next of kin somewhere. And if Jack's New York lawyer wasn't expressly notified of his passing, he wouldn't know to begin the process of executing the newer will.

Long after my food was gone, I flipped through folder after folder. No will. I did locate recent wholesale pricing for the wines in Jack's warehouse, and set those aside for Grace, who would appreciate the help.

Then, thinking it over, I took the prices off the desk and shoved them back into the folder again. Why should I help my mother raid my uncle's estate, especially when her sole purpose was to simply liquidate the whole thing as quickly as possible?

Fuck, but the whole thing was confusing.

Sorry, Grace.

Frustrated, I got up to find my uncle's little black book. Planning his party was more uplifting work than hunting for a will that may or may not exist.

EIGHT

Easy Peasy

_____

Grace

"SO IT WAS JUST HANGING THERE on the wall?" my friend Jasmine asked as I led her into my apartment. "How did nobody else spot it?"

"It was waiting for me, I guess. I might recut the lapels. There will be extra fabric when we shorten the skirt."

I'd called Jasmine after leaving the thrift store to squeal over my lucky find. She was one of the few people I knew who would truly appreciate the joy of scoring a vintage Chanel suit for just forty bucks. She'd insisted on coming over to help me remake my find.

"We can do this tonight," she said, clapping her hands. "Easy peasy."

"I'm supposed to enter a bunch of wines into a spreadsheet," I admitted. My head was full of Chanel, though, and the last thing I wanted was to hunker down over a spreadsheet.

"We can do both," my best friend said. "Who needs sleep? You're wearing Chanel to work tomorrow."

She had a point.

Olivia stuck her head out of the bedroom, her phone pressed to her ear. "I've got to run," she said to whomever. "But I'll see you tomorrow, right?" Then she hung up. "Hey, Jazzy."

I watched as Jasmine hugged and kissed my sister hello. Olivia's gaze homed in on the bag in my hand the second Jasmine stepped away. I swore she had an instinct for these things.

"What's in the bag?" she asked.

I held up the sack in my left hand, the one from Fairway. "Three chicken breasts and a head of broccoli."

But I was instantly annoyed with myself for prevaricating. I had every right to spend a little money on myself. It had been months since I'd been self-indulgent in any way.

"The *other* bag." My little sister rolled her eyes.

Jasmine answered for me. "She found a Chanel suit at Housing Works! And get this—it was only forty bucks!"

"Forty bucks?" my sister screeched. "I *just* asked you for *twenty* for a sweater at F&M. You shot me down. And *winter* is coming."

Good lord. She should audition for Oliver Twist. "The so-called sweater was backless. Not exactly a practical item, Liv. And has that missing MetroCard turned up yet?"

Jasmine looked amused. "You kids."

Olivia scowled. "The point is that when I ask for something, the answer is always no. But you just waltz in with something new whenever it suits you."

Something hot exploded in my belly and all the stresses and confusions of the day boiled up inside me. "You listen to me—I own exactly two suits and spend just as much energy as you do trying not to look like a loser. The difference is that if I look like a loser at work I'll never get a full-time corporate job. Which means that we'll always be two months late on our rent, and the answer to whether or not you can have a new sweater will *always be no*!"

When all the color drained from my sister's face, I knew I'd gone too far. "Two months? Is it really that bad?"

Shit. It really was. But I rarely admitted it. There was no point in both of us being anxious about the state of our bank account. "I'll catch up next week," I promised her. The temp agency would pay me in two days.

"Good," she said, still looking a little uncertain. Then she scowled, as if another wave of teenage temper could fend off the bill collectors. "I have homework," was all she said before stomping into the bedroom and closing the door.

"She's a little ray of sunshine," Jasmine said, eyeing the bedroom door.

"Yeah." I sighed. "She's always so angry at me." I put the groceries on the counter and turned on the oven.

"She's angry with the only person who does right by her, because she can be. She knows you're not going anywhere. If you look at it that way, it's kind of a compliment."

"Wow. I'm feeling so flattered right now," I said, deadpan.

She ruffled my hair playfully then pulled the broccoli from the shopping bag. "What am I doing with this?" she asked, looking at it as though it was a specimen from a space mission.

I took it out of her hands, since she was cursed in the kitchen and could turn almost anything into a charred disaster.

"I've got it. You sit while I get this into the oven. Then we'll look at the suit." The broccoli could be tossed in olive oil and garlic and roasted along with the chicken. I'd put some rice on to simmer, too. "The thing is..." I took a knife out of our only drawer and set myself up to chop the broccoli. "I do care that Olivia feels self-conscious. She never invites anyone over from school, because she doesn't want her friends to see this place. And we can't move, even though there are better apartments in Queens. We can't leave Manhattan because she'd have to change schools."

"Also, you'd live in Queens." Jasmine made a face. "Being a teenager is hard no matter where you live."

"Sure, but Olivia's friends all have more money than us. Not that that's a stretch." I dropped my voice. "I bought her a pair of Citizens of Humanity jeans for Christmas. Two hundred bucks. She'll die of happiness."

"You softie." Jasmine grinned.

"It wasn't in the budget. I shouldn't have done it. But I wanted to give her a boost. She's fifteen and her mother loved drugs more than her. Abandonment issues, anyone?"

"She has a matching set with yours," Jasmine said.

"I'm used to it."

"Uh-huh. Sure. That must be why you always say you'll never look at another man ever again."

"I look. I just don't touch."

"Speaking of not touching, is Monsieur Douchey still calling?" Jasmine asked.

"Please don't call him that." Marcus had done what was right for him, and he hadn't meant to hurt me and Olivia. And truthfully? The guy taught me a vital lesson about independence and reliability.

"Fine. Is Marcus still calling?" Jasmine said it as though it hurt her to say his name.

"He checks in every now and then. Last month he and Olivia Skyped, I think."

I'd made a point of not asking my sister about it, because no way did I want to be the person who brooded over her ex.

Jasmine screwed up her face. "Ugh."

"He promised he'd stay in touch with her, and he's sticking to it. Why is that a bad thing?"

"Because it's about him making himself feel good, not about you guys. If he really cared about you, he wouldn't have taken a job offer that meant he had to move to France."

We'd been over this so many times I couldn't be bothered doing it again. I was hurt that Marcus chose a huge career leap instead of me. And I resented the fact that Olivia and I had been left behind.

Yet if someone offered me great money and the opportunity to secure my place in the world, I would grab it with both hands and never let go.

At the end of the day, we all had to look out for ourselves, because no one else would do it for us.

"Next topic," I said, and—thankfully—Jasmine let it drop.

———

With the food in the oven, Jasmine and I got to work on the suit. She pinned the skirt while I wore it. We took the hem to just above the knee, a flattering length for me, and pinned the waist so I could tailor the waistline and improve the fit. Then I did the cutting while she sat down at my laptop and began uploading all my photos from the warehouse.

This is why I love Jasmine. Her parents might be wealthy, but she knew how to roll up her sleeves.

The oven timer dinged.

"Olivia!" I called toward the bedroom. "Set the table!"

My sister deigned to emerge from her bedroom the third time I called her. I hung the suit up carefully and went to pull the chicken out of the oven.

"Holy heart attack," Jasmine said, peering into my laptop's screen. "Who is this fine hunk of man?"

Olivia glanced over her shoulder as she set a fistful of silverware on the table. "Hello. He's *gorgeous*." She looked at me. "Is this the Aussie guy you're working with?"

"Working *around*," I said, thinking about the cases of wine Callan had requisitioned this afternoon.

"You said he wasn't hot," Olivia accused, sounding aggrieved.

Correction: *more* aggrieved. Couldn't we have one conversation where I was not the evil overlord making her life miserable? Just one?

"I said he was full of himself," I reminded her. "And he is. Way too confident."

"With good reason," Olivia said, leaning over Jasmine so she could scroll through to the next image. "Look at that ass. He is *so* hot."

"He's twice your age, Olivia," I pointed out, feeling distinctly weird about my best friend and sister ogling Callan.

"Hey, I know this guy," Jasmine said, her eyes narrowing as she tried to remember.

"You probably ran into him at a fundraiser or something," I said. "His family is loaded."

Jasmine sat up straighter. "I know where it was."

She brushed Olivia's hands away from the laptop and called up a new search screen. Ten seconds later she was scrolling through the website of a well-known tabloid magazine from the UK.

Jasmine spent three years in a British boarding school when she was younger, and she'd never kicked her addiction to the trashy mags the girls had passed around.

"There he is!" she said with satisfaction, waving a hand at the laptop.

A picture of a group of people on a red carpet filled the screen. Two men, three women, but my gaze immediately went to the man in the middle of the pack.

He was wearing a navy-blue tuxedo with black lapels. The crisp white of his shirt contrasted with his tan, and he stared down the barrel of the camera with a smoky-eyed amusement that suggested he had naughty, dirty things on his mind.

Indisputably it was Callan, looking like a million dollars.

"Is that the Oscars?" Olivia gasped.

"Yep," Jasmine said. Then she turned and gave me a look. "Why didn't you tell me you were working with Callan Walker?"

"I told you I was working for Walker Holdings," I said.

"But you didn't tell me you were working with one of the world's hottest bachelors," she said.

"That's because I didn't know. And he's not *that* hot," I lied. The two of them were already acting like seagulls circling a picnic.

"This man"—Jasmine waved a hand at the screen—"is stinking rich, gorgeous and single. He spends his life going from party to party, hanging out with stunning actresses and models. How can you not know about him?"

"Um... Because I have a life?"

I concentrated on dishing up dinner while Olivia and Jasmine scrolled through the rest of the shots I'd taken today, dissecting every image of Callan like professional stalkers.

"Can we quit the creepy objectification and eat?" I said.

Grudgingly they came to the table, where Jasmine proceeded to pepper me with questions about Callan. What was he like? Was he as good-looking in person as he was on paper? Did he have an accent? Was his ass really that fine?

"You should tap that," Jasmine suggested, and Olivia giggled.

"Listen! I have to work with him every day. And yes, he's really, really good-looking, and when he turns on the charm, I can practically feel my underwear smoldering. But let's be realistic. No matter how much he flirts, he would never be interested in someone like me."

Belatedly I realized I'd left something important out of my declaration. "And I wouldn't be interested in him, either. We have nothing in common. He might as well be from another planet."

Jasmine was silent for a beat, and I hoped my outburst had killed the subject of Callan Walker for good.

"So he flirts with you? Are we talking heavy-duty flirting or just casual flirting?" Jasmine asked.

I glared at her to let her know I wasn't going there.

"She's not going to answer you," Olivia said. "That's the face I get whenever I ask for something."

On top of Olivia's complaints about me buying the suit, her

words were like a slap. I busted my ass trying to give my sister everything she needed, even if she didn't get everything she wanted. For a moment hurt burned at the back of my eyes. I covered by pushing back my chair and standing, even though my plate was still half full.

I busied myself in the kitchen, covering my plate with plastic wrap and running myself another glass of water. The silence was thick behind me, until finally Jasmine asked Olivia about school and they began talking about an assignment Olivia had due soon.

When I felt as though I had a grip on my emotions, I returned to the table and pulled the laptop closer, quickly typing my nightly report for Queen Victoria.

I had to disclose the poodle's surprise arrival. But I wrote that I'd find Lady a new home immediately, and I attached an adorable photo I'd taken of Lady staring up into the camera, her brown eyes wide and guileless.

Who could resist that?

When I was done, I turned to Jasmine and smiled brightly.

"Shall we do this?" I asked.

Olivia was conspicuously quiet as Jasmine and I started ripping seams on the Chanel. Jasmine worked on the waistband and hem of the skirt, and I cut new lapels and tacked them in place. As I'd hoped, there was more than enough fabric to both reshape and line the new-look lapels.

Jasmine and I were about to swap places at the sewing machine so I could start on the jacket when I caught a glimpse of what Olivia was viewing on my laptop screen.

Then I nearly burst a blood vessel.

Multiple images of Callan filled the screen. Callan in a tux, Callan in jeans and a stretched out T-shirt, Callan lying back in a pair of tiny running shorts on the deck of a yacht...

"What are you doing?"

"I found this amazing site—*100 Days of Callan*. He is a serious hottie."

I reached out and snapped the laptop lid down.

"Hey," she protested.

"This computer belongs to his family's business!" I said. "What if they're monitoring the sites I visit? Do you have any idea how bad it would look if I got caught Googling naked pictures of my boss's son?"

"He's not naked. At least, mostly he's not naked," Olivia said.

Jasmine took one look at my face and bounced to her feet. "You know what I feel like? Ice cream. You want to walk to the shop on East Broadway with me and get some?" she asked Olivia.

"I was just having a bit of fun. It's not the end of the world," Olivia said.

"Olivia...!" My anxiety meter was in the red zone.

"Come on, grab your coat," Jasmine said.

When they were gone, I spent ten minutes clearing the cache and search history and anything else I could think of. Then I leaned forward and rested my forehead on the table.

Had I overreacted? Probably. I hated that Olivia and I had been fighting so much lately, and I really wished I hadn't let slip how far behind we were with the rent. We were so busy lurching from one near-disaster to the next, we'd run out of patience with each other. And I didn't know how to claw some back.

One more thing to add to my To-Do list.

———

Jasmine and Olivia came back twenty minutes later, pink-cheeked and loaded down with ice cream. I ate my fair share and then sent Jasmine home.

"But we're not done yet," Jasmine pointed out.

"I can finish the rest. Go on, I know you've got an early start tomorrow. But thank you for being awesome and feeding me ice cream. You're the best."

We hugged goodbye, and, when I shut the door behind her

and turned around, I caught an odd look on my sister's face. She looked almost...jealous.

"You all done with your homework?" I asked.

"Yeah."

I moved to resume my spot at the sewing machine, but Olivia spoke before I could settle in place.

"I'm sorry about before," she said. "About being angry about the suit. I know you do heaps for me."

I blinked, wondering where this had come from. Then I remembered her walk with Jasmine.

"Did Jasmine tell you to apologize to me?" I asked.

Olivia's face immediately scrunched into anger. "No. Believe it or not, it was my idea. Because I'm not a complete spoiled brat, no matter what you think."

Shit. She looked close to tears.

"I'm sorry. I shouldn't have said that. Thank you for apologizing."

Olivia took her time responding. "Okay."

"And for the record, I don't think you're spoiled. I think you put up with a lot, and I wish you didn't have to. I wish things could be different for both of us."

"It's not that bad," Olivia said.

Right on cue, a door slammed next door and loud music started up. Thanks to the paper-thin walls, it might as well have been in our apartment. The timing was so perfect, I began to laugh, and pretty soon Olivia joined in. Then our asshole neighbor started singing along with the song—screaming, really—and suddenly it was so funny I had to sit down because my legs wouldn't hold me anymore.

I laughed until I cried, until my cheeks ached and my stomach hurt. When I stopped, I realized Olivia was watching me, caught between amusement and worry at my hysteria.

"I'm good," I reassured her, wiping the tears from my face with the back of my hand.

"It wasn't that funny," she said.

"I know."

We grinned at each other.

"I can help with the suit, if you like," she said.

"That would be great. I'll dig out the buttons I was thinking of using and maybe you could sew them on for me?"

NINE

The Floor Show

Grace

I FELT like a million dollars when I put on the reworked Chanel the following morning. The vibrant scarlet picked up auburn highlights in my brown hair, and the tailoring Jasmine and I had done meant it fit me like it had been custom made. Which, in a way, it had.

Olivia gave a wolf whistle when she emerged from the bathroom and saw me.

"That looks so cool. Can I borrow it sometime?"

"Of course."

I couldn't help wondering what Callan would think when he saw my new suit, and then I caught myself wondering and froze in the act of booting up the laptop to check my email. Why did I care what he thought of my new outfit? It shouldn't matter to me one way or another.

"Crap," I said out loud.

"What?" Olivia asked, glancing across at me as she buttered toast for breakfast.

I shook my head. My sister didn't need to know I'd been stupid enough to allow myself to be charmed by Callan Walker.

And it *was* stupid. I knew exactly who he was—a guy who had too much of everything, who had never heard the word no in his life. His life was gilded, mine was tin-plated. He slept with super-models and walked red carpets. I hadn't had a boyfriend for six months and my notion of a big night out was a visit to the taco truck on Broadway.

The idea that he'd look at me in my made-over 80s Chanel suit and be overwhelmed with lust was nothing short of pitiful.

I clicked on the email icon on the computer desktop and took a deep breath when I saw Queen Vic had responded to last night's report. I double-clicked and found a terse response in bullet point form. Once I was done with boxing up Jack's papers, she wanted an estimate on how quickly a wine auctioneer could be engaged so they could remove the stock and let Jack's warehouse lease go.

And she didn't want to waste time trying to find a new home for Lady.

I was to call animal control and surrender her as soon as possible and instruct Callan to procure accommodation else-where. *You are authorised to change the locks if he is uncooperative.*

I had to read that paragraph three times before I believed it. Callan had predicted this, but it still made me gasp with shock. The image I'd attached last night was in the email trail below Queen Vic's response. I could see Lady's eyes peering over the edge of the computer screen. The innocent trust I saw there made my gut churn.

I couldn't do it. It simply wasn't in me to hand Jack Walker's beloved pet over to a shelter. Not to mention the fact that Callan would go nuclear if I even raised the subject—and that would be before I told him he needed to find a new place to stay.

It was all too much to deal with before I'd had coffee, so I shut the computer down and tucked it into my bag before gathering the rest of my things.

"I'm off," I told my sister, still feeling a little shell-shocked at Victoria Walker's callous instructions.

The first thing I heard when I entered Jack's apartment was the sound of the coffee grinder from the kitchen and the skitter of claws as Lady rushed to greet me. I'd barely shut the door behind me when she came barreling around the corner, sliding sideways before regaining purchase and aiming herself at me. She was coming in so hot I instinctively braced a hand against the door, just in time for her to skid to a halt and face-plant her snout in my crotch.

"Annnnd good morning to you," I said.

She disengaged and sat back on her haunches, tail whipping back and forth as she looked up at me with unfettered admiration. I couldn't help smiling. Who wouldn't want to wake up to this every day?

"You're a good girl," I said, reaching out to scratch behind her ears. I'd discovered yesterday that this was her doggy G-spot and she closed her eyes and leaned into my hand, a blissful expression on her face.

"Don't worry, sweetheart, we're going to find you a good home," I told her quietly.

Even if it mean lying to the person currently keeping the wolf from my door.

The mere thought of falsifying my reports to Walker Holdings made me sweat, but it wasn't as though I had an alternative. It would be a compound lie, too, because until I found a home for Lady, Callan would have to stay in the apartment to look after her, which meant I'd have to lie about evicting him, too...

This isn't going to end well.

But what else could I do? The thought was still ringing in my mind as I walked into the living room, ready to set up for the day, only to stop dead in my tracks at the sight of Callan walking toward me with a coffee in hand, completely naked except for a towel slung low on his hips.

Holy six-pack, Batman.

I didn't know where to look, because there seemed to be nothing but stupendously hot, hard male as far as the eye could see. The towel hit him a few inches above his knees, showcasing muscular thighs and calves. His belly was a work of sculptural art, all peaks and valleys and firm-looking muscle. I stared at first one flat nipple, then the other. Then—somehow—I managed to hinge my gaping jaw shut and lift my gaze to his face.

"Lady needed to go out, so we're running a little late," Callan said as he handed my coffee over.

I almost forgot to close my fingers around the hot glass, but some self-preserving instinct kicked in at the last second.

"That's fine. Take your time. No rush. No big deal." My voice sounded high and thin, as though I'd just sucked helium from a balloon.

His eyes creased at the corners and he cocked his head to one side. "You okay?"

"Sure. I'm great. Especially now I've got my latte," I said way, way too brightly.

I kept my gaze pinned to his face, even though I desperately wanted to gaze at his body again. He really was a masculine wonderland, lean and ripped and hairy in all the right places and none of the wrong ones.

It figured he had a perfect body to match his perfect face. As if the gods hadn't already smiled on him in every other way.

"Let me get dressed, then there's something I need to run by you," he said.

"Okay," I said instantly. He could have asked me anything right now and I would have agreed to it.

"Back in five," he said. "Don't forget to drink your coffee."

The inevitable heat rushed into my face as he walked away. Of course he'd noticed my stupefied response. The man was smart as a whip, even if he pretended to be a lazy party boy most of the time.

Lady stirred at my side, making a sad sound in the back of her throat at Callan's departure.

I hear ya, girl, I hear ya.

"Come on, then, you big sook," Callan said without turning around, and Lady took off after him, powerful hind legs rocketing her forward.

She was so pleased at being summoned she gave a little jump as she caught up with him, placing her front paws briefly on his towel-covered ass before landing on all fours again.

Everything seemed to slow. The knot at Callan's waist unraveled. He let out an amused whoop, trying to catch the towel before it dropped. One hand found purchase, but the other was hampered by his coffee cup, and the towel slid down his hip on one side, revealing a single, beautifully firm butt cheek and a length of delicious thigh before he caught the towel again.

"Jesus, Lady. Way to scare the horses," he muttered, laughter in his voice. "Sorry about the floorshow, O'Malley."

He threw a smile over his shoulder, and I tried to look as though I hadn't just been taking copious mental photographs for the next time Olivia was out and I had the bathtub to myself.

"Seen it all before, don't worry," I said, waving a hand in the air dismissively.

I will not fantasize about Callan Walker's perfect ass. What was one more line to add to my mantra?

He disappeared through the doorway, and I sagged forward, one hand lifting to press against my chest. Yep, my heart was pounding away like a wild thing, and I was panting a little, like an overheated dog.

How appropriate.

I needed to get out more. Clearly, I had needs that weren't being met. Desperate to normalize the situation, I downed a mouthful of latte and closed my eyes as its rich, heated creaminess filled my mouth. It really wasn't fair that Callan was both hot and capable of brewing such a great coffee.

Like the answer to my prayers, my phone pinged with a notification, which turned out to be a text message from an unknown number. When I unlocked the phone, a photograph of Callan on a sailboat resolved on the screen.

What the...

I squinted at it. He was waving to the camera, his other hand on a thick line attached to a sail. Had Callan sent it himself? I quickly discarded that idea, since I could hear him opening drawers and speaking to Lady in a low voice in the second bedroom.

Who then? Had I conjured him with my little hormone surge?

I tapped in the corner of the message for more info. The sender was listed as "100 Days of Callan." That sounded familiar. In fact, last night one of the websites Olivia and Jasmine had ogled might have had that name.

Olivia! I shook a mental fist at the sky.

She'd be dealt with later. Meanwhile, I deleted the photo. "Focus, Kerrington, focus," I told myself.

The doorbell sounded behind me. I drained my delicious coffee and headed for the door as though I was on a life-saving mission. It was the concierge from downstairs, a long cardboard poster tube in hand.

"This just came for Jack. I wasn't sure whether to sign for it or send it back," the man said apologetically.

"Not a problem. Just send up anything else that comes in," I said.

I made a mental note to make sure Jack's mail was redirected once everything was settled here and took the poster tube from the concierge.

"You have a good day, miss," he said, giving me a courteous nod before moving toward the elevator.

I shut the door and studied the label on the tube. Brindle and Brindle Architects.

Huh.

Had Jack been planning on renovating this place? I couldn't imagine a single improvement that could be made to the apartment, but my standards were probably a lot lower than Jack Walker's. Returning to the living room, I broke the seal on the end of the tube and pulled out a set of blueprints. It took me a few seconds to decipher them enough to find the client name: The Robinson Center. The address was downtown, in Alphabet City.

This must be a project Jack was involved with in some way. I made a note of both the architect's and the center's details so I could add them to the growing list of people I needed to notify about Jack's passing. I was tucking the plans back into the tube when Callan rejoined me, now wearing a pair of dark denim jeans and a soft-looking black sweater.

"Where did that come from?" he asked, gesturing toward the poster tube.

"The concierge just brought it up." I couldn't look at him without seeing his naked butt in my mind's eye, and I cleared my throat. "You wanted to talk about something?"

"I did." He tucked his hands into the front pockets of his jeans and eyed me steadily for a beat.

He looked serious, even a little grim. Unusual for him. I started to get nervous.

"So..." I made a winding motion with my hand to encourage him to spit it out.

"I want to hold a memorial for Jack here tomorrow afternoon," he said.

I was already shaking my head. "You can't. I'm sorry, but your mother doesn't even want you staying here, let alone holding a party. I think a memorial is a lovely idea, though. Maybe you can find someplace else to hold it?"

"It's already arranged," he said. He almost looked apologetic. "I did an email blast to his contacts list and organized the caterers last night."

I genuinely didn't have any response.

A *party*. For everyone on Jack Walker's contact list. Here, tomorrow afternoon, in this apartment full of precious objects d'art and collectibles. All of which belonged to the woman who was paying my wage. A woman who was so ruthlessly efficient she'd rather put a dog down than waste time trying to find it a new home. A woman who expected me to manage her son and execute every order she gave me with perfect efficiency, no matter what.

I was going to lose my job.

The realization made me feel suddenly cold. The moment I told her about the memorial, I would be gone. The weeks of pay I'd been counting on, the money in the bank... All of it, gone. Just when I'd started to think that finally – *finally* – Olivia and I might have some breathing room.

Panic tightened my chest, and tears rushed up the back of my throat. Somehow I held them back. Without saying a word, I turned on my heel and aimed for the door.

"Grace. Wait!"

I ignored him. The front door loomed in front of me, and I wrenched it open. My gaze went from the closed elevator doors to the stairwell beside them. I chose the stairs, and I climbed up. Up and up and up, until I emerged on the roof of the building.

It was cold out there but I didn't care as I walked to the half-height wall that surrounded the roof-top terrace. I stared out at the city. Then and only then did I let give free rein to my anger and disappointment.

―――――

Callan

Fuck.

I started to go after Grace, then stopped as I remembered the look in her brown eyes. Clearly, she didn't want to be around me right now. She'd made that pretty obvious by walking away without a word.

She was pissed at me. I should have seen that coming. I *did* see that coming. What I hadn't expected was the hurt that had flashed in her eyes before she'd made her hasty escape.

Smooth, Walker.

I'd become so used to living in my bubble—insulated from the real world by champagne and a steady supply of leggy beauties. I was out of practice dealing with someone genuine and substantial like Grace.

Planning Jack's memorial had been the right thing to do—for *Jack*. But I hadn't considered the consequences for Grace. She was the one who would have the unenviable task of informing my mother of what I'd done.

Hardened campaigner that I was, even I wouldn't want to make that call.

Regret stung me into action. I pulled on a pair of shoes and stopped by the bathroom to grab a box of tissues—not for nothing had I spent half my life studying the female of the species —then I went in search of Grace. It wasn't until I was waiting for the elevator that I realised she could have gone anywhere. Hell, for all I knew, she'd quit and gone home and I'd never see her again.

It was a disturbing thought, so I ignored it, concentrating instead on formulating a plan of attack. I'd check with the concierge to find out what direction she'd gone in, then I'd search every coffee shop, every bar I encountered along the way.

The doors slid open in front of me at the same time that my gaze fell on the stairwell to the left of the elevator. My feet were moving before I'd consciously made the decision to abandon Plan A.

I didn't know how I knew Grace had gone up instead of down. I just did.

After a hearty climb, I was rewarded by the sight of her slim, straight form, dressed in deep red, standing at the barrier that bordered the rooftop entertaining area.

Deep red. It suddenly struck me where I'd last seen that color —through the window of the second-hand store. Could she have...? I took in the details. A short, tapered skirt. The feminine fit of the jacket. It looked nothing like the dowdy thing I'd seen on the hanger. Grace must be some kind of wizard at the sewing machine.

And now it occurred to me that maybe she needed to be. I flipped back through my memory of the last few days. Her too-thin winter coat. The packet of VoVos that had disappeared after I told her I didn't want them.

The cup of coffee she'd ordered that first morning together, instead of the latte she might have enjoyed.

I felt absolutely hollowed out by where those puzzle pieces led me.

Fuck.

I joined her at the railing. Her eyes were red from crying, her nose pink, her cheeks still shiny with tears. Her arms were crossed so tightly over her chest it was a wonder she could breathe.

"I'm sorry," I said.

"No, you're not." She didn't take her gaze from the city.

"I swear I am," I said.

"Bullshit, Callan. You'd do the same thing all over again because you know it's the only way you'll get your way. Please don't insult either of us by pretending different."

I considered the toes of my shoes for a second, shame licking at me.

She was right. I probably would do it all over again. I'd do anything for Jack, to make sure he was honored the way he should be.

"Let me try again—I'm sorry you're caught in the middle of family crap that has nothing to do with you," I said.

She sniffed back fresh tears and shook her head, rejecting my words a second time. The urge to put my arms around her was ridiculously, inappropriately strong. She looked so...*alone* standing there, holding herself as though if she let go, she might fall apart.

"They didn't even put a notice in the paper," I said, wanting her to understand. "Vicky just ordered them to dispose of his body and sell off his life. As though he didn't matter, as if the fact that he existed meant nothing to anyone."

My throat was tight with grief and anger, and I had to stop talking to clear it.

"Jack was the only person in my family I have ever been able to trust. He never failed to stand by me. Never forgot a birthday or a milestone. He spent his life giving back to people, even though his own family wrote him off because they were ashamed of him. He was a good man, and he deserves to be recognised. And the people who loved him deserve a chance to say goodbye."

Grace's cheeks were wet again and I passed her the tissues. She looked at the box incredulously for a moment before snatching it from my hand.

"God, I hate you."

For some reason her anger made me feel better.

"I'm sorry," I said again.

She blew her nose, then met my eyes. "I understand why you did it. I might even have done the same if I was in your shoes. But I need this job, Callan. And we both know what's going to happen when your mother finds out about this."

"She might not find out," I suggested.

"Of course she will!" She passed the box of tissues back to me. "You said you invited all Jack's contacts. Are you trying to say that *none* of the people on your list have any links with Walker Holdings?"

Shit. Frustration gripped me and I drop-kicked the box of tissues across the roof. The moment it landed I felt like a petulant schoolboy. "You're right. Fuck."

Grace crossed her arms against the cold, and now I had an even better look at her handiwork. It fit her like a glove, hugging her slim hips.

And she'd made it with her own hands. She'd taken that dated, matronly thing from last night and transformed it into something elegant and clean and modern.

"Nice suit," I said.

Her eyes widened with surprise, then she looked away. "Compliments won't keep my job."

She was right. I could marvel at her talent some other time. Right now, I needed to fix this. I pulled my phone from my pocket and hit auto dial. Claire answered straight away.

"To what do I owe this pleasure?" she asked.

"I need to speak to her," I said.

"It's late," came the argument.

But evil doesn't keep regular hours. "It's important."

There was a small silence as my mother's flying monkey digested this. "I'll see if she's available."

I rolled my eyes. "Thanks."

If Claire detected the crapload of sarcasm I squeezed into the single word, she didn't comment on it, and the next thing I knew I was listening to hold music. I expected Vicky to make me wait, but she surprised me by coming on the line almost immediately.

"Callan," she said.

I pictured her sitting at her desk, all of Sydney spread out behind her.

"I know you're busy, so I won't waste your time," I said. "I want Grace Whatever-her-name-is gone."

"I beg your pardon?"

But my mother's surprise was not as violent as Grace's. Her head jerked back as if I'd just slapped her.

I held a hand up to Grace, asking for patience. "I don't care who you get to replace her, but she has to go."

"I see," my mother clipped. "Can I ask why?"

"She's the last person Jack would want going through his things."

"Jack is hardly in a position to care. Is she a drunk? A thief? Incompetent?"

"She's a ruthless pain the ass." I winked at Grace, hoping she'd stay silent. "I told you I'd work *with* someone to pack up the apartment, not *for* them. I'm not taking orders from one of your corporate piranhas."

"Then by all means, absent yourself from the process." She sounded as if she was enjoying herself.

"You know I can't do that."

"The deal was that you could assist with preparing the apartment for sale. You have no authority to hire or fire anyone. And I happen to think Grace is doing an excellent job."

I smiled. *Gotcha.*

"So you won't fire her?" I asked, meeting Grace's angry eyes.

"Not on the basis of what you've just told me, no."

"Fine."

I ended the call then, because that was what she'd expect of me. Despite the fact that I'd just outmaneuvered her on every front, my hands were shaking when I slipped my phone back into my pocket.

It had been so long since we'd spoken I'd almost forgotten the cool distance of her hybrid accent, an odd mix of middle Australian and cut-glass received English. As far as I knew, she'd never spent enough time in England to acquire the latter, which made her a pretentious wanker as well as a stone-cold bitch.

Whatever. It was done.

I took the chance of meeting Grace's gaze. "That should do it, I think."

She looked stunned. "You called me a ruthless piranha."

"Have I taught you nothing, O'Malley? Vicky *adores* a ruthless piranha. I just made you employee of the month. Now when

Vicky gets wind of the memorial, she'll assume I arranged it as a fuck-you to her and to you." *And she'll be half right.*

Grace just stood there, staring at me for a long moment. "That was a reckless little ploy."

"And yet it worked."

"I hope," she corrected.

"Indeed."

She turned away from me and walked to the stairwell. I followed her at a respectful distance.

Back inside the apartment, she made her way into Jack's office. Lady and I joined her. "What are you working on?" I asked helplessly, knowing I'd just damaged our burgeoning friendship. It was a surprisingly painful realisation, because Grace was good people.

"Boxing up files." She didn't even look up. "I don't need your help for this."

Ouch. "Right, then. If I can offer you a word of advice, you should start over there—" I pointed at the filing cabinets I'd already searched. "One of those contains the recent wholesale wine purchases."

She squinted at me. "How did you stumble on that? Just...having a stroll through the file cabinet?"

Fuck. "Just trying to protect Uncle Jack. They say there's no privacy in death. I found his porn stash and disposed of it." This was true, although I'd found it in his bedside table, not a file cabinet. I'd also thrown out some sex toys. The unopened box of condoms I'd kept for myself.

Her stare was laser-like. O'Malley was too smart for her own good. "What else did you find?"

"Nothing." Another truth. "But that wine stuff caught my eye. Thought you should know."

"Thank you," she said slowly. But I was still in the doghouse. I didn't get a smile.

"One more thing? When Jack's friends come round tomorrow,

I'll canvass them to see if anyone wants a poodle. Two birds, one stone."

"Good idea. The sooner I find her a new home, the sooner I can stop lying to your mother about Lady. You're not the only one who's trying hard to get me fired."

"Chin up, O'Malley. The dog isn't going to blab to Vicky about her whereabouts."

Not even a smile.

TEN

Only One Hundred Days

Grace

I AVOIDED Callan for the rest of the day, trying to forget the sick feeling of betrayal that cut through my belly the moment he'd told me about throwing a party in the apartment.

A *party*. When he wasn't supposed to be here at all.

It made no sense that I felt so *hurt*, either. Annoyed, sure. Worried, yes. But Callan didn't owe me anything. We'd only just met. And even if I'd thought we had a growing appreciation for each other, what would that mean to someone like Callan? He was used to getting everything he wanted from life. All he had to do was snap his fingers.

I was just another person on staff. It wasn't a lesson I planned to forget again.

Outside the elegant windows of Jack Walker's private office, the sky became leaden. At one o'clock Callan poked his head in to ask if I wanted anything from Lenny's Gourmet on Columbus. "They make a great turkey sandwich, with cranberry and stuffing. My treat."

My mouth watered just picturing it. "No thanks. I'm all set." A sandwich in this neighborhood was eight or nine dollars. And I didn't want to owe him anything.

Only after he left did I eat what passed for my lunch—an apple and a package of crackers. I'd sent Olivia to school with the leftover rice and broccoli from last night's dinner. In case what's-his-name followed her out of geometry again.

Everything was dreary. But at least I was wearing Chanel.

In spite of my horrible mood, I made progress boxing up Jack's papers. The papers Callan had pointed out were useful, too. I used a scanning app on my phone to store all the relevant wine pricing before packing away the files.

At three o'clock, my phone chimed with a text, which turned out to be a shot of Callan in a Speedo in Cannes. I quickly deleted it. Olivia and I were going to have words when I got home.

Still, the image of him in his tiny swimsuit kept creeping into my mind as I worked, which inevitably led to memories of how good he looked nearly naked in real life. By the time the day was drawing to a close, I had a headache from the tug of war going on inside me.

Callan had put me in a terrible position today. Yes, he'd called his mother and done his level best to retroactively protect my job, but it didn't change anything. When push had come to shove, he'd sacrificed me on the altar of his family feud without a second thought.

My freshly minted, up-close-and-personal knowledge of how much I didn't matter in his world should have made me immune to his undeniable sex appeal.

In theory.

In practice... In practice, I had no idea what was going on with my hormones. It was more than a little galling to be so attracted to a man I had every reason to dislike and mistrust. He might be charming and good-looking, but those things shouldn't matter when he'd proven himself to be an asshole.

I was heartily sick of everything to do with the Walkers by six o'clock. I did a quick tour of the apartment trying to find Callan and say goodbye, only to discover he was nowhere to be found. Probably off organizing things for the memorial. The jerk.

Instant guilt plucked at me. What he was doing for his uncle was admirable in the face of Queen Vic's coldness. Callan was doing the right thing, giving Jack the send-off he deserved.

I walked to the elevator, annoyed I couldn't even hang onto my disappointment and anger for a full day. Talk about a pushover.

The train ride home was crowded and tedious. I was more than ready for my crappy day to be over when I let myself into the apartment and called out to let Liv know I was home.

I unwrapped my scarf and shed my coat, waiting for her to reply. When I got nothing but silence I checked her room and found it empty. Frowning, I pulled my phone from my bag to check I hadn't missed a message from her. Nothing.

Olivia and I have an iron-clad arrangement that she'll always let me know what she's doing after school. No message meant she should be here.

I started to compose a text, but the sound of a key in the door made me stop.

"Sorry. I was hanging out with Tracy," she said.

I swallowed my recriminations. Tracy and her mom lived in the building next door and were good people. Of all the places Liv could go after school, they were my favorite option. I wished Liv had *more* friends nearby.

But you can't have everything.

I made vegetarian lasagna for dinner. Olivia cleared the table and set it without me asking, a minor miracle. We talked about her day, and the fact that Jasmine was coming over tomorrow night for our weekly "Guilty Pleasures" session—bad TV and junk food.

When Liv's phone beeped with a text, I remembered I had a bone to pick with her.

"Hey. You've got to get that thing off my phone."

"What thing?" She grinned.

"Liv," I warned. "Make it stop."

"Why? It's funny. And he's hot."

I slid my phone toward her. "Fix it."

"You are such a spoilsport," she grumbled as she picked up the handset.

I didn't bother explaining how humiliating it would be if Callan found out I was receiving multiple images of him on a daily basis, especially after the way he'd treated me today. I just wanted those pictures gone.

After ten minutes of increasingly frustrated sighing, screen tapping, and typing into my phone, Olivia set it down with a frustrated shrug.

"Can't do it. Sorry."

"*Are. You. Kidding. Me?*"

"I texted a number to start it up. There's no information for stopping it. I guess most people are pretty happy to keep getting pictures of Hotty McHotty every day."

I stared at her, trying to think of a good reason not to lunge across the table and strangle her.

She shrugged, wide-eyed. "It only lasts for a hundred days. What's the big deal?"

I'd probably kill her before then.

ELEVEN

Eloquence Incarnate

Callan

SOMETIMES WORDS SIMPLY AREN'T ENOUGH.

That's the conclusion I came to in the small hours of the night as I struggled to write a eulogy for Jack. Everything I put on the page felt trite and inadequate.

I felt trite and inadequate. Let's face it—the most eloquent thing I'd composed these past few years was a pickup line in a bar.

Meanwhile, my phone lit up again and again with email messages as people responded by the dozen to my invitation. "I'll be there," they wrote. And, "I wouldn't miss it."

Jack had built a life here in New York. He'd arrived knowing only a handful of Australian expats. At the time of his death, he had a thriving business and friends from every corner of the city. There were art-gallery friends and charity friends and neighbors in this old-guard apartment building. He was a vital part of a dozen organizations.

And what, exactly, was I a part of?

The silence pressed in on me as I considered the question. I'd left Australia because I didn't want to waste my life being

Vicky's lackey. Instead, I'd wasted it in a dozen other insubstantial ways.

What a rebel.

Lady wandered over, tucking her chin onto my thigh. She looked up at me, silently asking why we weren't sleeping yet.

"I know it's late, girl. But I'm not done." Taking care of Jack's final wishes was going to be a wakeup call for me. Fucking around Europe and the tonier parts of Asia didn't feel very adventurous anymore. I didn't have a clue what I might do with myself after Jack's estate was settled (and settled *properly*) but drinking champagne on sailboats didn't hold any appeal for me.

Except that I was already screwing things up here. My eulogy was shit. I hadn't found the will. I hadn't even begun to find a good home for his pet.

And *Grace*.

My heart lurched every time I pictured her angry face. I'd made her *cry*, for fuck's sake. She was actually terrified of losing a shitty job temping for Vicky. I hadn't considered her at all when I took my stand for Jack. I'd been so sure of myself.

Tomorrow I'd apologize to her again.

Tomorrow I'd write a decent farewell for Jack. I'd have to.

To Lady's relief, I got up, shut off the light, and got ready for bed.

"Goodnight, girl," I said to my only companion when she followed me into the guest room.

Then she tucked me into bed. That was the only way to describe it. She sniffed my hand as I lay in the bed in the dark. I wondered if we were going to have a disagreement about whether there was enough room for her on the bed. (Spoiler: there wasn't.)

But she was better trained than that. After satisfying herself that I was down for the night, I heard her toenails click on the wood floor as she went to her bed in the corner.

Still, I couldn't sleep. Tomorrow's memorial had me thinking about the other passings in my life. I was five years old when my grandfather died, and just seven when my father was buried. I'd been too young to remember the funerals clearly, even though one had been for Lang Walker and half of Australia's business world had turned out to look solemn and get a head start on kissing Vicky's ass.

I remembered the sea of black suits at my grandfather's funeral, a coffin so shiny I could see my face in it, and my mother's impatience. *Don't do that, Callan. Come here, Callan. If you can't behave, you can wait in the car, Callan.*

She'd brought me to the car to wait. I didn't really understand that my grandfather was gone. The driver bought me an ice cream and Vicky raged when it dripped on my suit.

I don't remember anything anyone said at the funeral itself, just the sense that something bad had happened and that my life was about to change.

It had, too. Vicky had assumed her father's mantle as chairperson of Walker Holdings and been subsumed by the role. She'd been pregnant with Claire at the time, but she'd barely taken time out from meetings to give birth.

The workload had killed what was left of my parents' marriage, and my father had taken his big, fat settlement check and fucked off to somewhere my mother wasn't. He was dead within a year, wrapping his Porsche around a tree. Somewhere in Italy, I think.

His funeral had been more subdued, a hushed, hurried affair. No media, no circling helicopters or extravagant floral arrangements.

I fell asleep wondering why I couldn't remember it more clearly.

———

In the morning, I rolled out of bed and fired up the coffee machine. While it did its thing, I put on my running gear and took Lady for a quick lap around the block. She was starting to get the hang of our routine now, and she only stopped twice to investigate undeniable smells, nearly yanking me off my feet both times.

The memorial was less than twelve hours away. There were a million things to do. Yet I stood there in the park feeling...heavy. As if everything was too much effort.

Lady tugged at the leash, and we left the park.

Grace's key turned in the lock as I stood over the coffee machine. I had the bag of beans in my hand, but I think I'd been standing there in front of the grinder for a long time, just daydreaming.

I shook myself awake as she entered the kitchen. "Good morning."

"Morning," she said coolly, clearly still unhappy with me. She didn't even make eye contact.

I considered my options—more groveling, a shameless charm offensive, perhaps even an attempt at bribery. But Grace was too smart to fall for any of that. I'd have to win back her friendship the hard way—by actually earning it.

Ignoring me, she slid a plastic container into the refrigerator.

"You bring your lunch every day, don't you?" I asked. I'd noticed Grace never went out for lunch, and now I knew it was because she couldn't afford to. It only served to make me feel even more guilty about what had happened yesterday.

"So?" She closed the refrigerator. Then she finally turned to look at me, a fiery expression on her face. And then that fire extinguished unexpectedly. "What's wrong?"

"What do you mean?" She was studying me so intently that I turned away, finally pouring the coffee beans into the grinder, like I'd meant to ten minutes ago.

"Are you okay?"

"Sure," I grunted, throwing the switch on the grinder, filling the kitchen with its loud growl. But she was still watching me when I shut it off again and began to fill the portafilter with grounds. "What's on your agenda today?" I asked.

A beat passed before she spoke. "I was going to head over to the warehouse."

Surprised, I set the tamper down on the counter top. "You're not going to be around for the memorial?"

"Well..." She frowned. "I know you have cleaners and caterers coming. Thought I'd stay out of the way."

Something heavy settled in my chest as I realized I was going to have to get through the next twelve hours completely alone. Not that I should've expected otherwise.

Ask her to stay, my subconscious demanded. She might do it.

No. Grace owed me nothing. I wouldn't ask *anything* of her.

She was staring at me, so I picked up the tamper and compressed the coffee grounds. I fitted the filter into the group-head and turned on the machine.

It wasn't until Grace lunged past me to flip the machine off that I even noticed the problem. No cups. I'd been brewing espresso right onto the drain grate.

In the silence that followed, we held a staring contest. I won it when she sighed and opened the cabinet and took out two cups. She placed them on the grate.

"Go on," she said softly. The gentleness in her voice made my throat feel tight.

I removed the filter, chucked the puck of wet grounds into the trash and turned the grinder back on. Maybe that's a waste, but an imperfect coffee just wouldn't do right now.

When I finally succeeded in making two cups of coffee that were up to my usual exacting standards, I carried them through to the living room, looking for Grace.

I found her in Jack's office, jacket off, digging through a file drawer. Today she'd pulled her hair back into a ponytail. It was longer than I'd ever suspected—well past her shoulders when down, I imagined—and suddenly all I could see in my mind's eye was Grace naked, all that gorgeous dark hair falling over her breasts.

And I wondered why she didn't trust me.

"Here you are," I said, setting her cup down. "Forget something in there?"

She looked up. "No, I just checked my schedule and realized I'd promised more paperwork to Vicky before the wine inventory is due." She grabbed her cup and took a big sip.

"So..." I tried to understand. "What about the warehouse?"

"Another time," she said gruffly.

I chewed on that for a moment. "No, it's okay. Go if you want. The cleaners are coming in half an hour. It'll be bedlam here, and—"

She held up a hand. "It's all right. I'm tackling this instead." She scowled at me, as if to prevent more discussion.

"Um..." Today I was eloquence incarnate. "Thank you."

"It's nothing. Now go get organized. You're not wearing sweatpants to the memorial, are you? Do you have a suit with you?"

I shook my head. "I need to go buy one this morning."

She pulled out her phone. "I have a friend from design school who works at Hugo Boss. Let me see if she's in yet. I'll have her pull some things off the rack in your size."

I wasn't a stupid man. Not always, anyway. So I did exactly what Grace told me to.

———

Grace

There was something very wrong with Callan. The overly charming playboy had disappeared, leaving behind a hollowed-out shell.

I was still feeling burned after yesterday, but the grief on his face was impossible for me to ignore.

The cleaners showed up while Callan was shopping, so I got them organized. And then the caterers were next.

At some point Callan returned, a garment bag over his shoulder. I steered him into the office where it was quiet, and I brought him a plate of the caterers' finger food. When I set it down in front of him, the look I got was so grateful it did fluttery things to my belly.

Shut up, belly.

"What next?" I asked him.

"My speech is shit. I need to finish it."

"All right. After you make us both another cup of coffee, I'll barricade you in here until it's done."

"To think I'd written you off as one of Vicky's raptors when we first met."

"I am," I reminded the both of us.

Then I left the room in order to quiet my Callan-induced endorphins.

My last act of mercy was to move some photographs around. The cleaners had done their thing, and everything was sparkling. So I began to pull the framed photos of Jack Walker off the hallway walls, where few guests could see them, and line them up on the windowsill in the living room instead. Callan might notice, or not. But the mourners would appreciate it.

When I was finished, Callan stumbled out of the office, a piece of paper in his hand.

"Finished?" I asked hopefully. He nodded, coming to stand beside me.

Silently, we admired the line of photographs. Callan's uncle stared back at us in black-and-white and in color—pensive, gleeful, in love, in lust, defiant, playful, adoring.

"Grace," he said, his voice raw. "He was so..."

The sentence died. And Callan swallowed roughly.

And then the doorbell rang. It was the doorman, announcing the arrival of the musicians he'd hired.

"Go," I said. "Shave. Change. I'll handle this."

With another grateful nod, he did.

––––––

Two hours later, the apartment was bursting with people. When I'd panicked about throwing this party, a crowd like this was exactly what I'd feared. But my nerves gave way to awe almost immediately.

Judging by the number of people cramming into the apartment, every last person on Jack Walker's contact list had chosen to come pay their final respects to him. They just kept coming–spilling out of the elevator into the foyer in a unending conga-line of mourners. I appointed myself the job of traffic cop–greeting newcomers and letting everyone know that Callan was somewhere inside, waiting to greet them.

I marveled at the cross-section of New York that had come to bid farewell to Jack Walker. There were fabulous gay men of a certain age. Those were the guests I'd expected to see. There were sober businessmen and a set of elegant women who introduced themselves to me as art dealers.

None of those surprised me.

But I hadn't expected the most colorful mourners—the young men in painfully hip skinny jeans with multicolored hair, the socialites in eveningwear.

And the *mayor*. The freaking mayor of New York arrived to a wave of murmurs. The crowd parted like the Red Sea as he went in to pay his respects.

Unbelievable.

I was just picking up my jaw from the floor when Gloria emerged from her apartment across the landing. She blocked her door open with a stopper in the shape of Buddha. Then she smiled at me. "Hello, darling! I caught the first flight home the second I got Callan's email. You may tell your guests that my apartment is open for overflow business. Jack and I did this all the time." She touched a hand to her chest. "This floor won't be the same without our double parties. An era has ended." She gave a little sniff and went back into her apartment.

It took me a second to understand. But apparently Jack's guests were used to this behavior. Two men standing beside the elevators with glasses of red wine turned to head into Gloria's.

Not only were Jack and Gloria well-loved, they obviously excelled at throwing parties.

"Excuse me," I said several times as I wove through the crowd toward the bar. When I finally reached it, I tapped a bartender on the arm and asked if he could take a tray of wine glasses and a few of Callan's bottles of Australian red into Gloria's apartment.

"Right away, miss," he said, as if I were the hostess.

Okay, a girl could get used to that treatment.

I grabbed a glass of wine for myself, and took a moment to soak in the atmosphere around me. Apparently everyone had a Jack anecdote to tell. A pair of older gentlemen in the corner were laughing about a time when Jack had reenacted the entire "that's not a knife" scene from Crocodile Dundee at someone's dinner party.

The art dealers were giggling about an auction where he'd driven up the bidding on an emerging young artist in order to launch her career. And someone mentioned the *Fuck You, Cancer* party he'd thrown for his partner Danny when his diagnosis had come in.

I spied Callan in a corner hugging a couple of people in pinstripe suits. And laughing. Thank goodness. A smiling Callan was more recognizable.

Our eyes locked across the room, and I felt the flush of embarrassment from being caught staring at him. Again!

He beckoned. The suits moved away as I approached and Callan threw an arm around my shoulders. "I owe you an apology," he said, his voice low in my ear. "This party is clearly out of hand, in the best possible way. If anything is damaged I'll pay for it."

The smell of his aftershave enveloped me—leather and wood and smoke. His arm felt warm and heavy on my shoulders.

"It will be fine," I said. "Where's Lady?"

"Cowering in a bedroom. I've been asking whether anyone knows someone who could adopt her. No takers yet."

We both scanned the room then, as if a dog lover would somehow be obvious. I had an odd, disorienting sense of belonging, standing with his arm around me, surveying the guests. As though we were a couple, hosting a party together. Which was about ten different types of crazy rolled into one.

"Some turnout," I said. "Your uncle was well loved."

"By everyone—except his own family. He was a bloody legend."

We were joined then by a pair of young women in silk dresses and Callan let his arm fall away from my shoulders.

"So sorry to hear!" one of them gushed, tossing herself into Callan's arms.

That's when I made my getaway. I sipped my wine and stole a look at my phone. Tonight was supposed to be Guilty Pleasures Night, a tradition Jasmine and I had started in design school. Trash TV and popcorn with extra butter, me and Jasmine and Olivia squeezed together on the futon.

I texted Jasmine. *This memorial has turned into an Event. I have the feeling it might run late. There must be 300 people here! You guys might have to start without me tonight.*

No problem. We'll eat all the popcorn to punish you, she replied almost immediately. Then she followed up with, *Don't stress, I'll make sure Liv's cool. Have a drink and don't worry about us.*

The press of people had eased now that Gloria's door was open. When I peeked into her apartment, I saw her doing a foxtrot with one of the men in pinstripes, while the other one clapped.

Back in Jack's apartment, the row of photographs I'd helped Callan set out was a popular part of the room. I fetched a box of tissues to set there after noticing how many damp eyes there were as people studied the pictures. Jack had obviously touched so many lives, charmed so many people. And I was sure I was only seeing the surface of it.

After a while, Callan made his way over to a coffee table that had been pushed out of the way for the jazz trio. Their instruments fell silent as Callan stood up on the table.

Okay, fine. A little part of me spent a second hoping the table wasn't a priceless antique. I was still on the job, after all.

Somehow, out of all the people in the room, his gaze found mine for a second. I gave him what I hoped was an encouraging nod. He looked a little frozen up there. His tense smile seemed to say, *I hope I'm not going to fuck this up*.

As if. Nobody had more charm and poise.

He raised his glass, then fished in his pocket for a spoon he'd slipped in there. The ring of metal on his glass cut cleanly through the clamor, and within seconds all heads were turning his way. People began crowding into the big room from elsewhere. He waited a moment before unfolding a piece of paper from his pocket and raising his voice to address the room.

"Thank you all for coming to help honor and celebrate the life of Jack Lang Walker..."

I pressed my hand to my stomach as Callan started speaking. I couldn't believe how nervous I felt for him. Delivering a eulogy is something I hoped never to have to do.

He looked good standing up there, dangerously sharp in his dark suit and bright tie, but it was the genuine emotion in his face and voice that made him truly gorgeous.

"I'll be honest with you, I had a hard time coming up with the right words to say in honor of my uncle. As you all know, he was one-of-a-kind. You never knew what was going to happen next with Jack. One day he was signing up for belly-dancing lessons, the next he was joining the Coney Island Polar Bear club, trauma-tizing half of New York with the sight of his skinny chicken legs in Speedos."

People laughed and wiped their eyes, nodding along in agreement.

"Jack always considered himself lucky to have fifteen great years with the love of his life, Danny, before losing him to cancer, and he was a prominent supporter of marriage equality as well as a number of other causes dear to his heart. He loved art in all its forms, and a gallery opening wasn't complete without Jack showing up to eat more than his fair share of the cheese.

"No celebration of Jack would be complete without the acknowledgement that he was a terrible cook, possibly the worst I've personally experienced. His firm philosophy was that there was no recipe that could not be improved with the addition of yoghurt. I see some people nodding—I commiserate with you. I still have nightmares about Jack's Crème Brulee.

"He could be a stubborn bastard, and he swore too bloody much, even for an Australian. He knew how to laugh, though, and he knew how to love—with his whole heart. Everything I know about being a decent human being I learned from him, and I will miss him more than words can say. I'll miss his quiet courage and his too-loud laugh. I'll miss watching him swan around like Greta Garbo in one of his treasured smoking jackets, and I'll miss his hard-won, take-no-prisoners wisdom."

Callan's voice cracked and he took a quick swallow from the glass of red wine he was holding, buying himself a few seconds to compose himself. I pulled a tissue from my pocket and mopped up my tears, touched by the raw pain beneath his words.

"The last time I saw Jack was in June. We went out for dinner and came back here and drank too much wine. I can't remember everything we talked about, but I can remember the warmth of the evening and Jack's voice and the sense that there was nowhere else in the world I'd rather be and no one else I'd rather be with.

"I won't lie to you—I'm heartbroken he's gone. He was the father I never had, and he deserved many more years. But he *is* gone, and so the best we can do is drink his wine and eat food from his favourite restaurant and share stories about him to make ourselves feel a little better. I encourage you to do just that for as long as you want, and thank you from the bottom of my heart for coming today to say goodbye to a good man."

He paused again, and my hands tightened into fists as I watched him fight for control. He swallowed, then raised his glass.

"To Jack, a truly magnificent fucking bastard."

Laughter swelled as glasses were raised high and a chorus of "To Jacks" rang out. I didn't take my eyes off Callan as he ducked his head and stepped down from the table, quickly disappearing into the throng.

A huge lump of emotion was stuck somewhere between my heart and mouth. I wanted to assure him he'd said beautiful things and that Jack would be both proud and honored. But it wasn't my place to reassure Callan or do anything else a friend would do in similar circumstances. As yesterday had so clearly demonstrated, we were not friends. Technically, we weren't even colleagues.

So instead of searching out Callan, I made myself useful—I checked on the caterers, and made sure there was enough of everything in the bathrooms. And I ducked into Gloria's apartment to make sure she was coping with the crush of mourners. When I spotted her, she was standing in a circle of people, chatting up a storm, clearly in her element.

I glimpsed Callan out in the elevator foyer and made a move toward him. But a sharply dressed man by the door looked so woebegone that I couldn't bring myself to brush past him.

"Are you all right?" I asked, passing him a tissue.

"I..." The man blew his nose. "I still can't believe he's gone. We had a meeting a couple of weeks ago. He looked so well, I actually made a joke about it. He had a new tie, and he'd bought a matching collar for Lady." His eyes filled with tears and I watched sympathetically as he blinked them away.

"How did you know him?" I asked.

"He was a patron of the center I manage. He was our savior, really—he's funding the renovation of a building downtown so we can expand our services."

Something jumped up and down in the back of my mind. "You're not talking about the Robinson Center, are you?" I asked, remembering the name on the blueprints that had been delivered yesterday.

"That's right." He looked pleased. "Not a lot of people have heard of us. We're kind of the new kid on the block."

"A set of plans were delivered to the apartment yesterday," I explained.

I stole a glance toward the foyer. Callan was still there, listening attentively to someone, but there was something about the way he was holding himself that made me frown. He looked...wrong, somehow. Off balance.

"I was wondering if they'd made it. I sent them off before we'd heard that Jack had passed." He shook his head and offered me his hand. "Sorry, I should introduce myself—I'm Gavin."

"Grace," I said. "I'm actually helping sort out Jack's estate. I can return the plans to you, if you'd like. It seems a shame to waste a set of drawings."

"Thank you, I'd appreciate it. I adore our architect, but every time those people lift a finger we get billed for it," he said.

Callan had managed to extract himself from the conversation he'd been caught in and he disappeared from my sightline. I gave Gavin an apologetic smile.

"I'm so sorry, but I really need to try to catch Callan if I can," I said.

"Not a problem. Nice to meet you, Grace."

"I'll put those plans in the mail first thing," I promised as I moved off.

When I reached the foyer, I couldn't spot Callan's dark head in the crowd.

Weird.

And then I remembered the look on his face, and I understood where he'd gone. Squeezing my way past two over-dressed socialites, I started up the stairs. Three flights later, I emerged on the rooftop. At first I thought my hunch at been wrong, but then I saw Callan in the far corner, both hands braced on the terrace wall, his head bowed. His shoulders shuddered and I understood that I'd intruded on a very private moment.

Damn.

I took a step backward, only for my heel to find a crack in the paving, pitching me to one side.

"Shit," I hissed as I flailed, finally catching hold of the doorway to the stairwell. Across the terrace, Callan straightened and looked over his shoulder.

I gave him a feeble wave. "Just me. Sorry. I didn't mean to disturb you."

"I was born disturbed, O'Malley," he said.

He couldn't pull off his usual devil-may-care insouciance, and I took an involuntary step toward him. He was hurting, and it was hard to watch.

"Your eulogy was really beautiful," I said.

"Thanks." He dug in his pocket for something, then shrugged and used the back of his hand to wipe his eyes. It was such a child-like gesture, and my heart gave an odd little tug in my chest.

I'd meant to go, but I found myself moving closer, unable to leave him like this.

"That thing you said about Jack being like your father... That was really special."

"It was true. I can barely remember my father, but Jack was always there. No matter what."

He shook his head and turned away, and I knew he was crying again. I'd seen him angry on Jack's behalf, and I'd caught hints of the depth of his feeling for his uncle, but the wake had clearly loosened something inside him. I guessed that having given Jack the sendoff he deserved, Callan had finally given himself permission to grieve.

I was unable to stop myself from touching him, reaching out to rest my hand on his back. I could feel the power of his emotions as he struggled to get a grip, and I moved my hand soothingly.

"It's okay," I said.

"Jesus, O'Malley. Can't you tell that now is not the time to be nice to me?"

"I think it's the exact right time."

He turned to face me and I let my hand drop to my side. He took a deep breath, then let it out on a long sigh. "Sorry," he said. His eyes were a dark, stormy blue, his lashes spiky from tears.

"Don't apologize for loving someone," I said.

He tipped his handsome face to the side and considered the idea. "I suppose you're right. It's just that the Walkers don't do emotions very well."

"You made it sound like Jack did 'em pretty well." Not that it was any of my business.

He gave me a watery smile. "He's the exception that proves the rule. Jack escaped the family with his dignity intact. None of the rest of us quite managed it."

Callan Walker was one of the most dignified people I'd ever met. But for once I kept my opinions to myself.

"There was this time. I was just a kid in primary school." Callan seemed trapped in a memory. "I had a part in the school play. Can't even remember what it was, probably a shrubbery. But I remember Jack promising he'd be there for the performance. Then he got hit with appendicitis a few days before the big night, and they had to rush him into hospital. I figured there was no way he'd make it, but he checked himself out of hospital and flew sixteen hours to Sydney so he could be there for me. Because he knew that if he didn't, I'd have no one and—" Callan shook his head, unable to finish.

He started to turn away again, but there was no way I could stand by while someone was hurting so much and not offer comfort. I stepped forward, blocking his retreat and wrapping my arms around him. His arms came around me almost instantly, his grip so tight it hurt.

We stood in silence, holding one another, for what felt like a long time. Long enough for the heat of his hard body to seep into mine, and for me to become acutely aware of the tensile strength of the broad muscles beneath my hands.

Maybe it was the wine I'd drunk, or the fact that I hadn't been held by a man in many long months. But I liked it more than I should have. I turned to rest my cheek on the fine wool of his suit jacket. And he turned his head a fractional degree toward mine.

His mouth was right there. I wondered how it would taste...

And then I mentally slapped myself.

Gently, I pulled back from his embrace. The corners of his eyes crinkled, and he gave me a bashful smile that acknowledged how easy it might be for something silly to happen in this glamorous place, under the New York sky, with Manhattan's lights ringing Central Park like a halo.

He felt it, too, my subconscious prodded.

That was all the more reason to keep my distance. "I'll head back downstairs," I said quickly. "Check on the caterers. And Lady." I could hear myself babbling.

His smile grew wider. "Thank you. I won't be long."

"Take your time," I insisted.

And then I got the heck off that roof.

TWELVE

Emotional Cocktail

_____

Callan

AFTER GIVING myself another minute to pull the Walker family mask of indifference back on, I went downstairs to my guests. Some were beginning to make their way toward the exit, and I bid them goodnight.

I shook more unfamiliar hands. "Great man, your uncle," a Mr. Crowley said, pumping my hand. "I did a little legal work on the Robinson Center for him last year."

Legal work. "You never did any estate work for Jack, did you?"

"No." The lawyer frowned. "Just a real-estate contract for the nonprofit. A pro bono job. He talked me into it."

"Of course he did!" I said with a smile, smoothing over my awkward question. "Thank you for coming."

The rest was a blur of well-wishers and booze. By the time there was nobody but Grace and I alone in the apartment, I was weary to the core. The caterers were coming back tomorrow to clean up. But Grace hadn't gotten the memo. She was collecting glassware and stacking mini plates onto the bar.

"Grace, let the restaurant handle that. I'm paying them to do it."

"You can't leave a mess overnight," she said. "This is Manhattan. There could be mice. Or worse."

"Not on Central Park West," I argued. "Mice aren't allowed in these buildings. They can't afford the co-op fees."

She rolled her eyes at me.

"Go home, O'Malley. It's late. I appreciate your help tonight, but I'm starting to feel guilty now. Do you want me to call you a car? I'm in no shape to drive." I wasn't so much drunk as flattened by tonight's emotional cocktail.

"Let me just..." She broke off to rescue another plate from the edge of a potted plant. "The plates are *everywhere*."

I took two steps toward her and grabbed the plate. But Grace surprised me by hanging on. And when I gave another tug, the small abandoned bite of lemon cake leapt from the plate and went airborne. For a nanosecond we both watched its ascent. Then it lodged itself right on Grace's chin.

"Oh, fuck. Hold still," I said. A snort of laughter escaped me. Because Grace—normally so pristine—looked hilarious with icing stuck to her face, and a bit of cake clinging to it.

"Now you're laughing at me?" she asked. Her forehead furrowed. But then I saw her lips twitch. She wiped the icing off her face with her finger. But instead of looking about for a napkin, she reached up and smeared it on *my* face.

"O'Malley!" I gave an unmanly squawk of outrage.

"You deserved that," she said with a grin. "Here, let me..." She reached for my face, but I ducked. "Hey now. I come in peace this time."

Then her slim hand landed on the side of my face, and a gentle thumb stroked across my cheek, coming away with icing on it. Acting on instinct, I opened my mouth and took her thumb against my tongue, licking the icing away.

I felt her go absolutely still.

The air thickened around us. I took Grace's hand in my suddenly shaky one, and I kissed the palm, then looked down, meeting her gaze.

Soft brown eyes looked back up at me, full of wonder.

My self-control was done and dusted. I tugged on her hand to draw her closer, then leaned down. I found the corner of her mouth with my lips and just hovered there, teasing her. Grace made a breathy little sound of surprise, but she didn't pull away.

I pressed my lips against her warm skin, then caught her mouth under my own. Her moan was all I needed. I deepened the kiss, and her lips felt soft and supple beneath mine, as I always knew they would.

Two hands grabbed my shirt, and her touch fed something hungry inside me. I tilted my head and drove on, encouraging her. I wrapped an arm around her body and pulled her up against my chest. She gasped, and I took advantage, tasting her.

That was a mistake. Not because she didn't like it—she liked it very much. When our tongues touched, she moaned again. And when I wrapped my hand around her hair to bring her closer, the contact with her body lit a fire in me.

Now that I knew how good she tasted, my kisses turned greedy. There would never be enough. My tongue gliding against hers brought a throaty groan from my chest. I pushed her up against the door frame, ravishing her mouth with my hungry one. She was warm and solid, her tits pressing against my chest.

It didn't matter that I became a cliché in that moment—life triumphs over death, etc, etc. I wanted Grace and she wanted me. Simple math. The events of the evening fell away as I claimed her mouth over and over again.

My hand slipped between the halves of her jacket to palm her flat belly. When my thumb stroked across the waistline of her pants, she gasped. The sound fueled what was already a raging fire inside me. I wanted her to make that sound again. Preferably as she shattered on my cock.

I slid my hand up her sternum. There was a big heart in there, and right now it beat for me. Overwhelmed with need, I nipped her lower lip. My mind filled with dirty plans for her. I yearned to push her down on the mattress in the guest room and appreciate every inch of her. With my lips and tongue...

I took a deep breath, inhaling her feminine scent. And then I said something that was both true and obnoxious. "See, O'Malley? I knew you were a hedonist."

———

Grace

God damn. As if I hadn't known it would come to this.

Callan's hand did another slow tour of my torso. He cupped my breast before his fingertips danced lower to tease the sensitive skin at my waist. He was only touching me through my clothes, but it was a touch that promised great things. I might combust if he actually got me naked.

When he actually got me naked. Let's be honest. Right now I was one of those frivolous girls in the photos with him—on the deck of a yacht or wearing Gucci on a red carpet. I was trapped in a shimmering, golden moment with Callan Walker.

Why not me. Just this once.

After another bruising kiss he pulled back, regarding me with hungry eyes. And the decision was as easy as taking my next breath. I put my hand in his, silently acknowledging my choice. And that was that. He gave me a gentle tug toward the seat of the Le Corbusier sofa.

But the trip to the couch took longer than it should have, because I put my free hand on his muscular ass and squeezed. If this was my big, foolish moment, I was going to make it a good one.

His response was to whirl around and devour my mouth once

more. Liplocked, we struggled toward the seat. He pushed my suit jacket off my shoulders. It dropped to the plush oriental rug underfoot.

The fact that I didn't worry about wrinkles on my suit should have been the first clue that this was madness.

Fuck it, my heart said. Okay—not my heart. Callan had pushed me down on the couch and climbed on top of me to worship my neck with open-mouthed kisses. Everything inside me buzzed and hummed in tune with his hungry mouth. His weight was delicious. My hips bucked as he pressed his muscular body against mine.

Panting, he raised himself and began to unbutton my blouse, a furrow of concentration appearing between his eyebrows. I didn't help him. Instead, I began to caress his chest through his shirt.

He shuddered under my hands. "You make me insane."

I didn't want to count all the insanities happening here. So I craned my neck to kiss him into silence.

"Fuck," he muttered against my lips, before thrusting his tongue into my mouth to tangle with mine. "First time you walked into this room, you were going on about orgasms," he said when we came up for air.

"Shut up," I said, wriggling out of my open shirt and tossing it aside.

He grinned and then stripped out of his shirt. The glow of expensive lighting illuminated his six-pack. I pressed both hands against the solid muscle I found there, then ran my fingertips through his happy trail.

Then I unbuttoned his pants.

Then I unzipped him.

And when I plunged my hand into his boxers and palmed his erection, he let loose a string of half-intelligible curses. *Bloody-something-or-other-to-hell*. He let me explore his hardened length for about two seconds before he pushed me down and tugged at my pants.

"Watch the stitching," I demanded, and then undid the side zipper myself.

Whoosh! They were gone, along with my panties. And I was lying on the priceless leather midcentury sofa in nothing but a—

Callan unhooked my bra and threw it across the room.

Wearing nothing, then.

He dropped his head and took my nipple into his eager mouth. His tongue sucked another moan from my throat, and I grabbed his dark hair in both hands and tugged him closer.

With a groan, he switched to show my other breast the same love. "Condom. Wallet. Pocket," he grunted.

I hurried to find it, my hands clumsy owing to the fact that I was operating under limited brain power.

When I had his wallet in my hand, he kicked off his pants and boxers, lowering his hips onto mine. "Fucking hell," he whispered, slowly dragging his cock right where I wanted him. We both groaned at the sensation of him gliding so effortlessly against me. "Pity you don't want my cock," he said, clipping the word *cock* with that sexy accent.

"Don't gloat," I panted. *But feel free to hurry up.*

Grabbing the condom out of my hand, he grinned down at me, then sat back to suit up. And no wonder he had an international club of women willing to follow him to the ends of the earth. The sight of Callan Walker naked and rolling a condom onto his dick, the muscles in his tanned forearm flexing as he worked, was almost enough to make me come on the spot.

He gave me a sly smile, then dropped down onto his elbows to consider me. I received a quick, hungry kiss, then he whispered hoarsely in my ear, "You're fucking lovely without your clothes on, O'Malley."

The compliment gave me happy tingles everywhere. He lowered his mouth onto mine and gave me a slow, sensual kiss. And, as our tongues slid together, he entered me with one perfect stroke.

I moaned so loudly the sound echoed off the priceless artwork. With a growl, he began to move. Each kiss made me more breathless. Each thrust of his hips was divine. My heart beat in rhythm with his *So good. So good.*

Hemmed in by Callan and the sofa, I gave myself over to the illusion of being enclosed in a very small world where only leather-scented pleasure existed. The soundtrack was made up entirely of my whimpers and the gentle click of teeth as he kissed me. And Callan's ragged breathing as he picked up the pace.

A hungry, desperate sound escaped from his chest, and suddenly I was tumbling toward climax, my muscles clenching as if trying to hold him in this perfect moment forever.

But all good things come to an end, and I gasped into his mouth as I shuddered around him. I gripped his body with all four limbs and moaned one last time.

"Fuck," he panted, his rhythm stuttering. Then he planted himself one more time before burying his face in my neck and shuddering happily.

And then all was quiet. Or, it should have been. Except Callan began to chuckle against me. "Jesus, O'Malley. That was something else."

I did not share his humor. My body was still doing a happy dance, but my eyes were jammed shut against the very real possibility that the regret train would roll into the station before Callan and I even got off the sofa.

The naked hottie spread out on my body suffered from no such worries. Still chuckling, he disengaged himself and then lay down again, half on the sofa and half on me. He kissed my neck leisurely. He pushed a lock of hair out of my face. "What a mess I've made of you."

He reached an arm around me and gathered me up, making more space for himself on the sofa, probably so he wouldn't crush me.

But I wasn't ready for eye contact. Needing another moment

to recover my bravado, I pressed my face against his perfect chest and sighed. He smelled like expensive aftershave and man. I took a deep breath of him, trying to memorize the scent.

This must be how all his dates ended—with a stunned woman trying to put a brave face on the end of an episode with scorching hot and clever Callan Walker. Other men paled by comparison.

Hell, I wasn't even a *date* like those women in the *100 Days of Callan Walker* photos. I was just a convenient body at the end of an upsetting evening. A balm for the ache of his loss. And I'd signed up for the part, knowing it would be just a walk-on role.

Right.

Lifting my face, I made myself smile at him. Awkwardness be damned. "It's late. I should get home now that I've performed all my duties."

I was trying for light and breezy, but I may have missed the mark, since Callan's smile died. "Not so fast, O'Malley," he whispered. Running a hand up my back and holding my gaze, he kissed me again.

The scrutiny was more than I could really bear. But the kiss made up for it. His lips were firm and knowing. He took his time kissing me, and then kissing me again. I felt myself give in, damn it. Melting against him, my feet tangled with his larger ones, and I tilted my head for a more perfect connection.

"That's a girl," he said quietly, idly stroking my skin. "Don't run away so soon."

It was hard to argue when his chest beckoned me closer, and his kisses turned sweet.

———

I never meant to have fast, crazy sex with Callan Walker on the sofa.

So it goes without saying that I also never meant to have a slow, luxurious second round on a stool in the kitchen. I was pretty sure there was an impression of the granite countertop's edge in my back.

I was also pretty sure it was worth it. If only briefly.

The next time I protested the lateness of the hour, Callan had no choice but to agree with me. "Let me call you a car," he said. "You can't take the subway in the middle of the night."

Although it offended my frugal heart to accept, I did anyway. I hated leaving Olivia home alone, even though she'd probably been sound asleep for hours. And, at two a.m., a car would be faster than waiting for trains running on a late-night schedule.

There was a steamy kiss goodbye, which I thoroughly enjoyed. But then I got the hell out of there, wondering how on earth I'd face him tomorrow morning.

The car dropped me in front of my building. I ran up the stairs and quietly made my way into the apartment. I nearly had a heart attack when someone said, "You are so busted," from the sofa.

"Jasmine," I gasped, putting a hand to my chest. "You're still here?"

She sat up. "Olivia was a little weirded out at the idea of being home alone. She said it was okay, but I told her I was going to stay because I'm too lazy to go home."

"Oh. Shit. I'm sorry," I whispered. She was such a good friend. I didn't deserve her.

Jasmine only grinned. "Spill, sister. You slept with him, didn't you?"

"Um..." I walked slowly around the futon couch to sit beside her. "It was an accident."

"You slipped and fell on his dick?" She cackled quietly.

"More or less."

"That good, huh?"

I put my head in my hands. "It was amazing. And I'm not sorry I slept with him. But now he needs to go back to Australia so I don't do it again."

"But why wouldn't you?" she squeaked. "Amazing sex doesn't come around very often."

"No kidding." I managed to look her in the eye. "Every time he opens his mouth from now on I'm going to imagine him whispering into my ear."

You're fucking lovely without your clothes, O'Malley.

Jasmine fanned herself. "The accent, right?"

"Right," I lied. The accent was hot, don't get me wrong. But unfortunately I was attracted to the whole package—the sensitive Callan, the clever Callan.

The *dirty* Callan. In the kitchen he'd bounced me on his hips while whispering filthy things into my ear...

I shivered, and Jasmine grinned. "You have it bad for Mr. Crocodile I-Done-Did-Him."

"Stop," I hissed. But she wasn't wrong. Wanting Callan was just a given. Anyone would. But there were lots of things I wanted that were out of the question. It was already a pretty long list. "It won't happen again."

Jasmine sagged. "Ah, well. Happy to hold down the fort while you had a night of fun. You deserve fun."

I gave her a poke in the hip. "Go home. Sleep. Should I get you a Lyft?"

She was already pulling out her phone. "No waiting at this hour. Huzzah."

After she left, I unfolded the futon and went to bed, trying not to be stirred by the memory of Callan smiling at me while he made me see stars.

———

Callan

I expected to sleep like a baby after Grace left. It had been a huge day, and I'd just had epic sex with a woman I'd been lusting after pretty much since the moment I met her. Once I'd seen her out the door, I went to bed, but instead of slipping into satisfied sleep, my brain kept throwing up memories from the day.

Grace offering me a plate of food before the circus started.

The tight strength of Grace's arms as she'd hugged me after I'd delivered my eulogy.

The hazy, slightly confused look in her eyes after I'd made her come so hard her whole body had clenched around mine.

Damn, but I was proud of myself for making her look like that.

I've had plenty of sex in my thirty-one years. Some of it had been great, some of it ho-hum. Sleeping with Grace had been...

Something else.

I didn't know how else to describe it. I'd been studying her body surreptitiously since the moment we'd met. In some deep, dark, primitive part of my brain I'd been rehearsing touching her, imagining the scent of her skin, fantasising about the slide of my cock inside her.

She'd been every bit as luscious as I'd imagined. But there had been an extra element to the sex, and it took a full hour of ceiling-staring for me to put my finger on what it was.

I liked her.

Fucking Grace hadn't just been about getting off or scratching an itch. It hadn't just been about satisfying my animal curiosity. It had been compelling. And funny. And fucking hot.

Because it had been Grace, and because I'd felt connected to her.

It had been years since I'd had sex with someone I genuinely enjoyed being around. For a long time now, I'd limited my sexual partners to women I'd met on the party circuit. Beautiful women. Sexy women. Bold, adventurous women. Did I remember their names? Some, but not all. Did I lose a wink of sleep after I'd sent them home or rolled out of their beds? Nope. Not for a second, because the whole point of having sex with someone I didn't know was that it was safe.

Not in the traditional sense of the word, obviously.

I kicked off the covers and rolled out of bed. Naked as a jaybird, I prowled around Jack's apartment until I finally came to a halt in front of a Gerhard Richter portrait. But even the spectacular artistry of Richter's brushstrokes couldn't stop my thoughts from turning to the last woman I'd slept with who I'd liked.

Jana Butler and I had met at the University of New South Wales. She'd been warm and sexy and a little crazy. I'd been drawn to her from the moment I met her, and it hadn't taken us long to tumble into bed.

I'd fallen for her, hard. For the first two years of my degree, she'd been the mainstay of my life. We'd studied together, vacationed together, partied together. I'd eaten numerous meals around her family's scarred kitchen table, joining in long, torturous games of Trivial Pursuit and always insisting on doing the dishes at the end of the night. It was so different from my own home.

At the end of our second year, Jana and I had started looking for a place to live together.

That was when Vicky started paying attention. She'd invited Jana to the Point Piper mansion that had been her father's home and treated my girlfriend to a full interrogation while I did my best to run interference. Afterward, she'd told me Jana seemed "sweet."

A month later, Jana had broken it off with me. She'd made half a dozen excuses—we were too young to be so serious, she wanted to travel, I was crowding her...

In my gut, I'd known there was more. When I confronted Vicky, she hadn't bothered to deny that she'd strong-armed the love of my life into leaving me. Jana was not someone I wanted to get "entangled with" at twenty, and so Vicky had asked Jana to make a choice—her relationship with me, or enough money to cancel out her student debt. Jana hadn't hesitated, apparently.

It had been more than ten years, but I could still feel the sting of shame. I had loved Jana with the impetuous, whole-hearted fervency of someone who had had precious little unconditional love in his life. She had been my life-raft and my true north. Spending time with her family, watching their easy interactions, their warmth and laughter, had fed something in me.

And yet Jana had deemed my love to be worth around thirty thousand dollars, give or take.

Abandoning my restless prowling, I made my way through the dark apartment to bed.

———

Grace

I was on my way to Jack Walker's apartment the following morning when my courage deserted me.

I'd given myself a pep talk when I woke, telling myself it was time to put on my big-girl panties and face up to the repercussions of last night's craziness. Then panic kicked in when I was just two stops away, and I realized there was no way I could hope to face Callan with even a hint of composure when my lady parts were still feeling tender after last night.

It simply wasn't going to happen.

Also, I was terrified I'd take one look into his smoky blue eyes and come on the spot.

The sex had been that good.

I couldn't be around him. Not yet. I needed a buffer. Some time to get my shit together. The second the train pulled up at the next station, I got out and started the long journey to New Jersey. I'd do all the things at the warehouse that I'd planned on doing yesterday before opting to help out with the memorial, and hopefully it would seem like I was simply catching up on delayed work instead of avoiding Callan.

And there *was* delayed work to do. The memorial had been a big time-suck, and I hadn't uploaded any data last night. When I scanned my email this morning the first thing I saw was a one-sentence note from Vicky asking what I'd done the day before.

Good thing she hadn't asked *who* I'd done.

It took over an hour to get to the warehouse, and this time there was no Callan to help shove the swollen door open. I rammed it with my shoulder half a dozen times before it finally gave. I could practically hear Callan giving me grief over needing six attempts to achieve something he'd achieved in one, and before I knew it my mouth was curling into a smile.

I snorted impatiently. For a smart person, sometimes I could be really stupid. I was not going to spend the day thinking about Callan. I wasn't going to have imaginary conversations with him in my head, and I wasn't going to wonder if he'd miss not having me around today, or if what had happened between us had registered as more than a blip on his personal radar.

Sleeping with Callan had been a one-off. He wasn't looking to strike up a thing with a cash-strapped temp who acted as guardian to her teen sister, and I was not looking to have a fling with a playboy ladies' man I found way, way too charming and likeable.

I had enough insecurity in my life without starting up something with someone who already had one foot out the door. I'd had my fill of being left behind, thanks very much.

I'd turned on the warehouse computer and was searching my phone for the text Stephen had sent me containing the password, when the phone rang in my hand. I didn't recognize the number, but then I'd been calling a lot of new-to-me people over the last week. Distracted, I switched the phone to speaker mode as I took the call.

"Why don't I have your number?"

Callan's voice echoed off the concrete walls, his tone tinged with impatience.

"Good morning," I said as heat rocketed up my chest and into my face. Thank God we weren't on Facetime.

"I had to call Stephen to get your number."

"Is there some kind of problem?" I flapped the neck of my shirt, hoping to vent some of my unwelcome body heat.

"Where are you?" he asked.

"At the warehouse, doing the stock-take I was supposed to do yesterday."

For a moment all I could hear was the faint sound of traffic. I was about to ask if Callan was still there when he spoke again. "I was worried when you didn't show up."

There were a lot of unspoken questions beneath his words, but no way was I going to answer them. "Sorry. Maybe you should give me your email so I can let you know if anything comes up in the future." Email was much, much safer than texting. More arm's length and professional.

"You've got my number now," he pointed out.

"Oh. Right. Of course." I huffed out a nervous little laugh. Having his voice in my ear again was triggering hundreds of sense memories, each more explosive and heated than the last.

"What does your work schedule want me to do today?" he asked.

Come to New Jersey and do me on the forklift.

"Maybe you could start packing up the linens and things for Goodwill?" I suggested.

Another long pause.

"I'll get right onto it," he finally said.

"Great. I'll probably be here all day. So I guess I'll see you next week. Have a great weekend, okay?"

"Yeah. You, too," he said.

I ended the call and let out a ragged sigh. My armpits were damp with sweat. It wasn't the only place I was wet, either, proving that putting some distance between us had been a good decision. The state I was in, Callan would only have to say something mildly flirtatious and I'd be naked on my back, begging for more.

More would only lead to disaster. I firmly believed this, no matter what my body wanted. So I needed to stick to my self-imposed Callan-ban until I could be trusted around him again.

Or at least until Monday, when—hopefully—I'd have a tighter grip on my self-control.

I threw myself into studying Jack's spreadsheets, noting that the prices his various customers had been paying were considerably higher than the auctioneer's estimates for the same stock. I remembered Callan had said something along the same lines, and I fired off a quick email to Stephen pointing out as much and suggesting it might make more sense to do the rounds of Jack's customers and try to off-load the stock at wholesale prices instead of auctioning it off en masse. It only took an hour for him to get back to me.

It's a good idea, Grace, but Ms Walker isn't interested in prolonging this process. Please direct your energies into progressing matters with the auctioneer.

So much for taking the initiative and showing I could be an asset for the company. Then I remembered all the ways I'd strayed already—lying about Lady, allowing Callan to stay at the apartment, the unauthorized memorial, the crazy monkey sex with Callan on Jack Walker's genuine Le Corbursier LC3 sofa...

There was no way I was landing a permanent job with Walker Holdings when this assignment was over. Not in a million years.

I made sure to leave on time at the end of the day, guilt eating at me for having abandoned Liv the previous night in order to do the wild thing with Callan. It wasn't like me to let my sister's needs slip from my mind while I indulged myself.

In the cold light of day, it was hard to justify last night's lapse.

I was the only person keeping Olivia from becoming a ward of the state. I couldn't afford to forget that. Ever.

Liv was in the kitchen cutting up onions when I let myself into our apartment, and it was such an unusual sight I stopped in my tracks. I could count the number of times she'd voluntarily cooked dinner on the fingers of one hand and still have a couple of spares.

"Yeah, yeah, I know, it's a miracle," she said self-deprecatingly.

I must have looked as surprised as I felt.

"It's awesome, is what it is," I said. "What are we having?"

"I had a craving for chili con carne. Like Mom used to make."

I saw a packet of meat on the counter and realized my sister had even sprung for ground beef. Again, she guessed my thoughts.

"I found some change in one of my coat pockets," she said. "Enough for beef and beans."

I peeled off my coat and scarf and dumped them on the futon. "What can I do to help?" I asked, because no way was I looking this gift horse in the mouth.

"Um...you could open a can of tomatoes," Liv said.

For the next ten minutes we worked side by side in the small space. Liv's knife-work was slow, but she was meticulous in measuring out the various spices and adding them to the pot..

"I can't believe you remember how to make this," I said, shaking my head as she added our mother's secret ingredient—dark chocolate—to the pot. "It must be five years since we've had this."

"I used to watch Mom make it all the time," she said with a shrug.

Her words dredged up a memory—Liv sitting on an orange vinyl stool at the kitchen counter in the faded New Jersey row house where we'd both grown up, chattering away while Mom cooked. Me at the kitchen table, cutting up clothes I'd bought from the thrift shop, fabric and thread and pins everywhere.

That had been back in the days when Mom had still been

functional, her binges confined to the weekends. She'd still been volatile at times, but she'd held down a job and tried to look out for us, in her own messed-up way.

I shook off the memory. Liv might be in the mood for nostalgia, but I wasn't.

"We probably have time for me to make some cornbread," I suggested.

Liv's smile took up her whole face. "Yeah?"

"Hell yeah."

An hour later, we sat down to a meal we'd both prepared, the vibe between us warmer and more relaxed than it had been in ages.

"This is really good, Liv," I said. "Plus there's enough for tomorrow, and it's always better—"

"—the next day," Liv said, and we laughed at the same time.

The line had been one of our mother's favorites, and for the first time in a long time I felt a bittersweet ache when I thought of her. She'd let us both down in the worst possible way, but there would always be a part of me that loved her. Like baby ducks imprinting on the first thing they see, kids are programmed to love the people who raised them, even if those people don't deserve love.

"Do you ever think about her?" Liv asked.

"Not really. I try not to," I said honestly.

"I think about her, all the time. I wonder if she's happy. If she misses us."

I nodded, even though I couldn't relate. I knew our mother didn't miss us. She was far more invested in her addiction to drugs and alcohol than in her daughters' happiness. The way she'd been using when Olivia came to live with me, she was probably dead by now.

"What would you do if she came to the door right now, clean and sober?" Olivia asked.

I reached for my water glass and swallowed a big mouthful

before answering. "Never going to happen."

"But just say it did. What if she apologized and said she wanted to make amends?"

There was a fervent thread beneath her words and I felt a pang for her. She was only fifteen years old. Of course she wanted her mother to be around. Of course she wanted her mother to love her more than she loved oblivion.

"She won't," I said, even though it felt as though I was killing unicorns and stomping on rainbows.

"But just say she did," my sister said stubbornly.

"Then I'd tell her to go, because it's too late."

Olivia flinched, her face stiffening.

"I'm sorry," I said, because I knew it wasn't what she wanted to hear.

"It's okay. I know you hate her." She stood and started clearing the plates.

I watched her downturned face, trying to understand what this was really about. "I don't hate her, Liv. I just... I ran out of hope. All those times she was going to be better, and things were going to be different. And they never were. All I want now is for us to be okay, to make sure you're all right."

She nodded, her face still downturned. "I get it. It's okay."

She took the plates to the sink and turned the tap on. The need to go to her and put my arms around her was almost overpowering, but I sensed she'd probably push me away. I stood and wrapped the remainder of the cornbread. Then I used my hip to bump my sister away from the sink.

"The cook never cleans," I told her when she opened her mouth to protest.

"You always cook and clean," she pointed out.

"Yeah, but I can dream," I joked.

She almost smiled. "All right. Thanks."

She left me at the sink, elbow deep in bubbles, feeling as though I'd just missed an opportunity.

THIRTEEN

I Can't Unremember That

Callan

GRACE WAS AVOIDING ME. There was no other explanation for her escape to the warehouse on Friday and her determined brightness on the phone when I called. It wasn't what I'd expected after the hours we'd spent in each other's arms, and I spent half the weekend brooding over it and the other half digging grumpily through Jack's office looking for his will. With no luck.

The only pleasant distraction came on Sunday when my old school friend Luke called with belated commiserations over Jack.

"You should have told me. I would have been over there for the funeral like a shot," he said.

I sprawled out on Jack's sofa—now forever immortalized as the sex couch—to let my old friend's voice comfort me. It would have been good to have him here. He and Jack had always had a lot of time for each other, and Luke was one of the few people I counted as a true friend.

But I explained about the twisted events after Jack's death, and he had a few choice words to say about my mother. And then

—maybe it was the couch—I found myself asking for a second opinion on my situation with Grace.

"So, am I being paranoid, or do you think she's avoiding me?" I asked.

He was silent for a long moment.

"You still there?" I asked.

"Yeah. Just trying to remember the last time you talked about a woman and actually remembered her name."

"Funny."

"Here's a thought for you—maybe she just wasn't that into it."

I remembered the look on Grace's face afterward, the sounds she'd made, the way she'd dug her fingers into my hips and ass. "She was into it. That's not the problem."

"Then I guess it's just your personality she's avoiding."

He laughed at his own joke and I rolled my eyes. "Thanks. That's beautiful. Remind me to reach out to you in my time of need again."

"Any time. But let's ask ourselves why this is your time of need."

"What? Mourning my only worthy family member isn't enough?"

"That's not what I mean. This temp... Is it possible you're thawing out some? That maybe all that crap with Jana didn't put you off women forever?"

"I'm not off women."

"Correction. You get onto them, but then you get off of them immediately."

There was an unspoken criticism behind his words.

"Jana took a payout to get away from me," I reminded him.

"That was at least half Vicky's fault," Luke argued. "Jana was young, staring her student debts in the face. You can bet Vicky would have made sure she believed your breakup was inevitable."

I grunted.

"Not everyone is Jana, mate," he said.

I did some generalized grumbling about his big theories, but the truth was he was right. Playing it safe wasn't as fun as it used to be.

Shooting the shit with Luke was a good distraction. But it didn't stop my thoughts from gravitating once again to the subject of Grace the moment I set down my phone. Specifically, what I was going to say when I saw her tomorrow.

Except I didn't. See her, that is. She didn't come to the apartment on either Monday *or* Tuesday. Instead, she sent a jaunty little text each day, letting me know she was busy at the warehouse, or visiting the East Side art auctioneers.

This was not the way my mornings-after usually proceeded. Usually I had to step carefully around an emotional minefield while lunging for the exit.

Seemed Grace was doing the lunging this time.

Wednesday morning found me pacing the kitchen, wondering if I should make myself a second espresso or wait to see if Grace was going to put in an appearance. All the while, a certain barstool mocked me.

She wasn't going to turn up, was she?

I made another espresso while pondering my own reactions. This was the first time in a decade that I'd given a flying fuck about a girl and it wasn't going well. Then I started thinking about the lengths she'd gone to avoid me and the prospect that she might actually quit because of what had happened between us.

Grace needed the money. She'd said so. Guilt weighed down my shoulders.

Fuck.

Just as I reached the bottom of my coffee cup I heard a key turn in the door. I actually sagged against the countertop with relief. That should have been a big hit to my playboy cred, but I didn't give a shit.

"Grace," I called out. "Can I make you a latte? I just shut 'er off, but the machine is still hot and ready." Then I laughed because everything sounded like sexual innuendo all of a sudden.

But no echo of laughter came from the foyer.

Hmm.

I flicked on the machine and poured fresh beans into the hopper despite the lack of encouragement.

A minute or two later, Grace came into the kitchen wearing her killer red suit and carrying a stack of boxes, a roll of tape the size of a dinner plate, and bubble wrap. "Morning," she said briskly. "You don't have to do that."

I looked down at the shot I was tamping. "Did you already caffeinate? This shot could wait."

She shook her head.

So I fitted the group handle into the group head and kept at it. "Are you all right?"

"Of course."

But she hadn't made eye contact yet. "Do we have a problem?" I asked, stepping back from the machine to make her my full priority.

"No." Grace actually flinched. "But the other night shouldn't have happened, okay? Let's just forget about it and go about our business. You don't have to make me coffee or be extra nice or whatever."

Fuck.

I took a moment to gather my thoughts, so that I could say my bit delicately. "That's a load of bullshit, O'Malley." All right, so I didn't do delicate very well. "In the first place, I can't unremember that, even if I wanted to."

Her gaze snapped to mine, and I saw heat in it. But then she quickly looked away. "Well, you're going to have to forget it. I have a job to do here, and Thursday night wasn't my most professional moment."

"We don't work together, Grace." Jesus. "Our behavior had absolutely nothing to do with professionalism." And everything to do with chemistry. I wanted to sit her right back down on that bar stool, hook my hands beneath her knees and...

Fuck. I was getting hard just remembering it. Grace, for her part, was already taping a cardboard box together.

Right.

I finished making her the best bloody latte this side of Rome. I set the cup on a saucer and added two mini muffins I'd picked up while out on Lady's morning walk, and set the cup down beside her.

She looked up. Her gaze was a little more frazzled than the cool, professional air she was so determined to project. And since I'd never meant to make her nervous, seeing those darting eyes really got to me. If she needed me to be casual about Thursday night, I could do it. For now.

"Enjoy," I said, pointing to the coffee. "I'll leave you to it. I'm sure you'll feel more at ease after you check a few things off your list."

"Okay," she said shakily.

"I'll be in Jack's office if you need anything. Another coffee. A quickie..."

"Callan!"

"Joking." I held up my hands in submission. But all good jokes are based in truth. Then I made myself leave.

Since I'd been ransacking the place all weekend, Jack's office was a tip. I surveyed the mess, knowing Grace wouldn't like it. So I took a fresh file box and began putting folders into it. These files concerned Jack's art purchases, so I labeled the carton when I was through and put it aside, in case Grace and the auctioneers found it helpful.

Then I started in on another.

An hour or so later I was sifting through a file drawer when I unearthed some material that was legal in nature. Finally! The deed to Jack's co-op apartment was there. And then I saw something on top of a document which stopped my heart. *Last will and testament*.

I let out a whoop of victory.

And fifteen seconds later, a growl of defeat. I was holding a will in my hands. But it was Danny's will—Jack's lover—from fifteen years ago.

"Listen!" I dropped the file onto the desk and addressed Jack in heaven, if there was such a place. "I'm doing my best. But could you put down your martini glass and lend me a hand? I'm running out of time."

"Who are you talking to?"

I swiveled to find Grace in the doorway, one hand on her hip, her warm eyes taking me in. It was not a face that asked me for jewelry and commitments. Not O'Malley. She wanted this shitty temp job more than she wanted my cock or my platinum card.

And the appraising expression on her face was sexy as fuck.

"I was just, uh..." I sighed. "Looking around a little. And putting files in boxes."

She stepped in and lifted the legal folder where I'd dropped it on the desk. "A will?" She arched a brow in my direction.

"Danny's will," I said quickly. "From years ago."

Grace frowned. "I'm not stupid, Callan. You're looking for something in Jack's files. You have been this whole time."

Uh-oh. The question shouldn't really have surprised me. She was smart as a whip and I hadn't exactly been covering my tracks.

"Yes," I said. My days of lying to Grace were over, I realised.

"What is it you're looking for?" She crossed her arms under her amazing tits and waited.

"A will," I admitted, hoping she wouldn't blow her stack. "The will that Vicky is executing dates to 1983. I think there's a more current one somewhere."

She visibly blanched. "You're accusing your mother of trying to *steal* Jack's estate?"

"Well..." I scrubbed my forehead with my hand. "She might

not know there's a more recent will. Or there might not *be* one. But about two years ago, Jack told me he wanted to redo his will. He said he would."

Grace tapped one of her sleek shoes on the floor. I could almost see her gears grinding. And not the good kind of grinding. "You think the newer will is materially different from the old one. Who inherits in the new version. You?"

I shook my head. "Charities. Philanthropy was a huge part of his life. He always said that we'd been born lucky and it was our duty to try to spread the luck around. He talked about making sure he could keep doing good once he was gone."

"Oh," she said slowly. The antique clock on the mantel ticked while she tried to digest this idea. "So if he made a new will, why is it so hard to find?"

Smart girl. My perusal of Jack's contacts hadn't turned up another lawyer. Every now and then, I'd run a new search on his computer or waste a sleepless hour in the dark of the night trawling through his hard disk, but I'd still turned up nothing. "Because there are a thousand file folders in this office? If you help me in here, we could figure it out quicker."

"You want me to help you find the will. And therefore fire myself?"

I opened my mouth to argue the point and then shut it again. She owed nothing to Jack, I reminded myself. She'd never met him. "I suppose the will isn't really your problem. But you could leave the study to me while you get on with the rest of it. I'll do good work, and at least I'll be satisfied if nothing turns up."

Grace wore a more guarded expression than I'd seen on her face since the first day we met. "Okay," she said quietly. "I'll be in the kitchen."

———

Grace

When would I stop being surprised when things went sideways? You'd think I wouldn't even blink anymore, especially where this job was concerned. From day one it had gone wrong, so there was really no excuse for how shaken I felt as I returned to the kitchen and started boxing up Jack's possessions.

My hands trembled as I found a set of kangaroo-shaped egg cups and put them into a box, tucked into a sheet of bubble wrap. The hours I'd spent in Callan's arms last week had been too good for me to fully regret them…But I would by lying if I pretended I didn't feel stupid now I knew how much he'd been playing me.

I'd always known Callan had an agenda. I'd known he was managing me, and I'd had ample evidence he would do whatever he needed to do to achieve his goals – and yet I'd still allowed myself to feel for him, to be sucked in by his considerable charm to the point where I'd gotten naked with him and had some of the best sex of my life.

The moment Callan confessed to organizing the memorial, I should have started hedging my bets. I should have been *prepared* for the fact that this job could disappear at any second. Instead, I'd thrown myself into helping him send off his uncle and wound up naked and moaning on the couch.

I wouldn't make the same mistake twice. Tonight I was scouring the employment sites and applying for anything that looked remotely achievable, and tomorrow I would touch base with my agency to let them know this gig was likely to end sooner rather than later.

It was time to be smart again.

After a few minutes the prosaic task of packing away Jack Walker's kitchen worked its magic, easing the worst of my agitation. Every pot and pan was nicer than any I owned. The folks at Housing Works would wet themselves with excitement when they found an entire Williams-Sonoma's worth of kitchenware in these boxes.

It's just a job, Grace, I reminded myself, and such were the soothing powers of bubble wrap and repetition, it almost felt true by the time I got to the coffee cups.

There were a dozen of them, and I packed them all away except for the two we'd used this morning, which were waiting to be washed in the sink. Then I registered what I was doing: still making assumptions about my job – about Callan – that common sense told me were not supportable.

The odds were good I would be pounding the streets looking for a new job in the next few days, while Callan would probably be boarding a flight to Australia or wherever the next big party was being held.

I would never see him again, and all this – the lattes, the flirting, the awesome sex – would be history.

The splash of reality chilled me enough that I washed my coffee cup. Then I dried it carefully and packed it away in a box. Callan could keep the cup he was drinking from, but I was done.

"O'Malley," he said from the doorway.

Speak of the devil. I wished he'd stop with the cute nickname spoken in the hot accent. It gave our situation a false sense of affection and intimacy that it didn't have. "Yes?"

"Don't worry about the will, okay? Even if the whole thing blows up on Vicky, the estate still needs someone to look after it."

Af-tah in Callan-speak. Grrr.

"Right," I said, refusing to be charmed by him.

"Grace," he whispered, coming closer. I steeled myself as he approached, his eyes soft. "I didn't mean to panic you."

"I'm not panicked." His nearness was a problem, though. I felt my neck heat with awareness. I could smell his aftershave. And because he was taller than me, my eyes were drawn to the V of his shirt collar and the smooth skin visible there...

You're being smart now, remember?

My phone gave a little burp on the counter beside me—the sound of an incoming text. Both of us turned at the sound, our eyes drawn to the screen, which suddenly lit up...

With a photo.

I grabbed for the phone, but too late. "What's this?" He snatched it off the countertop.

"Holy God." He laughed. "Who's texting you a photo of me on the beach in... Hawaii? That's Diamond Head, right?"

Where was a trap door when a girl needed one?

"Give me that," I stammered, grabbing for my phone, but he held it out of reach.

"This photo is a few years old, O'Malley." His eyes were laughing at me. "I could find you a fresher one. Maybe a skinny-dipping shot."

I made a noise of fury, and he handed me the phone. "It's from that website, right? 100 Days of Stalking. Didn't figure you for a fan, O'Malley, especially now we're keeping things 'professional.'"

"This," I said, stabbing at my phone, "was not my doing. My fifteen-year-old sister thinks she's funny."

His smile only widened. "You talked about me with your sister?"

"No! She just wanted to know who I worked with. She added that thing to my phone. I can't shut it off."

"Ah." His brow furrowed. "And it's caused you irreparable psychological harm. You feel sick each time I show up half-naked on your phone?"

"Well, not *sick*," I argued, wondering how the morning had gotten away from me.

"I see." He chewed his lip. "So the photo wasn't *that* bad?"

"Of course not," I babbled. "Not a thing wrong with it. But..."

He smiled so suddenly I didn't see the kiss coming. Warm lips met mine, cutting off whatever idiotic thing I was going to say next. I knew I should push him away, but instead I found myself grabbing fistfuls of his shirt and pulling him closer, every sensible, pragmatic thought leaving my head.

Hypocrisy, thy name is Grace.

He made an approving sound, stepping closer, his body pressing mine against the wall. He tasted so good and felt even better. All I could think about was getting my hands on his bare skin again.

He seemed to have the same idea, his hands slipping inside my suit jacket. He tugged my shirt from my skirt, and I found myself holding my breath. When he smoothed his palm up my ribcage and onto my breast, fireworks went off in my brain and my underwear.

I wanted him naked now. I wanted him inside me. I wanted everything he had to offer and more. I wanted—

Callan broke the kiss, his expression distracted. "Ignore it, it'll go away," he said.

I had no idea what he was talking about—then the resonant gong of the doorbell echoed through the apartment and I realized I must have missed the first round.

Lust-induced selective deafness. Apparently it's a thing.

"What if it's something important?" I said, very, very reluctantly. I was addled with lust, unable to think beyond the man pressed against me.

"They can come back," he said, his thumbs sweeping across my nipples.

My whole body swayed toward him, wanting more, but it was too late. My brain had finally kicked in, and it had noticed that not only was I once again being a terrible, terrible employee, I was also reneging on my commitment to myself to be smart about this man and my situation.

"God," I groaned, hating the sensible part of myself. Then I grabbed Callan's wrists. "We need to stop."

"It's probably just someone selling encyclopedias," he said.

I could feel his erection against my belly. So, so close.

The doorbell rang a third time, and this time he let out a heavy sigh.

"Okay, all right. Fuck you, doorbell," he muttered.

He stepped back and the loss of his touch made me want to protest.

I was so messed up where this man was concerned.

"I can't answer the door like this," he said.

We both considered the substantial bulge in his jeans. What a tragic waste of a truly excellent erection. The sad thing was, there would be no encore performance, because this was never happening again.

"I'll get it," I said, already turning away.

I started tucking my shirt in as I left the kitchen. By the time I was crossing the living room I was almost grateful for whoever was leaning on the doorbell. If they hadn't arrived, I'd be compounding Thursday night's mistake by now.

This was why I'd stayed away from the apartment as long as I could. I had no self-control where Callan Walker was concerned. The worst thing was, he knew it, too. I was going to have to do something to counter that.

I paused before the front door, taking a moment to make sure I was tucked in and presentable. There was nothing I could do about the heat I could feel in my face, so I just plastered on a smile and opened the door.

"Hello," I said, surprised to find the charity guy from Jack's memorial standing in the foyer. It took me a moment to dredge his name from my memory. "It's Gavin, right?"

"It is. I'm sorry for cold-calling like this, but I didn't have any other way of making contact. I'm really hoping to talk to Callan Walker, if he's available?" Gavin looked stressed, the tendons in his neck standing out as though he was struggling to keep a grip on strong emotion.

"He's here," I confirmed. "Why don't you come in and I'll get him for you?"

"Thank God," Gavin said, stepping into the apartment. "I've been pulling my hair out, trying to work out what to do."

I led him into the living room and gestured toward the sofa. "Take a seat, he won't be a second."

Gavin nodded tightly and sat on the edge of the couch. I headed straight for the kitchen, where I found Callan staring out the window, arms crossed over his chest.

"Better be someone with a cure for cancer," he said darkly.

"It's a guy called Gavin, from the Robinson Center. The people with the blueprints for the big renovation," I explained. "He wants to talk to you. He seems pretty upset about something."

He frowned. "He came to the memorial, didn't he?"

"That's right."

He let his arms fall to his sides, his expression marginally less frustrated now. "Am I decent?"

I risked a quick glance at his crotch. The situation there appeared normal. "You're cleared for take-off."

His mouth kicked up at the corner. "Funny." He headed for the door, then turned back when he reached the threshold. "This conversation isn't over, by the way."

"What conversation?" I asked.

"Exactly," he said, then he disappeared through the door.

FOURTEEN

One Tightly Wound Dude

Callan

GRACE HAD BEEN RIGHT—GAVIN was one tightly wound dude. He popped up from the sofa when I entered, practically leaping forward to shake my hand.

"Gavin Tomic," he said. "We met at the memorial last week."

"I remember. You're with the Robinson Center, right?" Bless Grace for making me look as though I had a steel-trap memory.

"That's right. I'm the director. Your uncle was our foremost patron."

"He supported a lot of charities," I said neutrally. My spider-senses were tingling, telling me I was about to be hit up for a donation. Sadly for Gavin, all my available funds were already allocated for the quarter. It was tempting to cut straight to the chase and tell him as much, but he was so wound up I didn't have the heart. "How can I help you?" I asked instead.

"I'm sorry for barging in like this," he said, "but I didn't know where else to go. Jack always talked about you with great fondness... I hoped maybe you'd be able to intervene on our behalf."

I waved toward the sofa. "Grab a seat and tell me what's happened."

Gavin resumed his seat on the sofa and took a deep breath before diving into his explanation. "Your uncle had been working with us for some time on relocating the center from its current site in Brooklyn to a new, larger building on the Lower East Side. We found a building on Avenue B last June, and we had plans drawn up to renovate the new location. Jack committed to funding almost the entire project, and the work was supposed to commence next month. But I just heard back from the lawyers handling his estate that the remainder of the payments Jack had committed to won't be honored."

I closed my eyes for a brief, weary moment. *Ah, Vicky, you've done it again.*

"How much is outstanding?" I asked.

"Just under a million dollars," Gavin said.

Fuck. If it had been less, I might have been able to shuffle my own finances around, but there was no way I could put my hands on that kind of money easily in the short term. My grandfather had made sure his grandchildren had substantial trusts, but the bulk of my assets were preferred shares of Walker Holdings stock.

"I don't suppose you had anything in writing from Jack, stipulating the amounts he planned to donate? A sponsorship agreement, something like that?" I asked.

With something in writing, I could lean on Vicky. Make the case to honor Jack's wishes.

Gavin shook his head, then spread his hands helplessly. "It was Jack," he said, as if that explained everything. "He's helped us out so many times in the past. We've got minutes from board meetings where his donation was discussed, emails, that sort of thing. But there's no formal legal commitment. We simply didn't think it was necessary."

I ran a hand through my hair, trying to think. I could try talking to Vicky, even without some kind of binding document to make her toe the line, but the odds of her listening to anything I had to say on Jack's behalf were somewhere between slim and none.

"Forgive my ignorance, but what does the Robinson Center do?" I asked.

"We're a support center for LGBQTI youth. We offer counseling, crisis accommodation, courses for kids coming to terms with their sexuality, training for educational professionals..."

I smiled grimly. It sounded like the sort of thing Jack would be all over, given the lack of support he'd received as a young gay man. It also sounded like exactly the kind of touchy-feely foundation my mother would roll her eyes over. She'd made no secret of the fact she'd donated to the anti-marriage-equality movement in Australia.

Gavin was watching me anxiously, clearly waiting for me to perform the miracle of the loaves and fishes.

"When do you need the money?" I asked.

"The next stage is the first progress payment for the construction crew. Three hundred thousand at the beginning of next month."

Which meant I had two weeks to either shame my mother into doing the right thing or find some other way of raising three hundred thousand. Fuck.

"Okay. Leave it with me. I'll make some calls."

Gavin visibly paled, and I realised he thought I was fobbing him off.

"That doesn't mean I'm blowing you off, mate, don't worry," I told him quickly. "Jack wanted this to happen, so I'll make it happen. You have my word on it."

I offered him my hand, and he shook it, a wary expression in his eyes. He didn't know whether to trust me or not, but that was okay. I wasn't going to let him down. My search for a more recent will might have been fruitless so far, but this was a part of Jack's legacy I could act on right now.

"Give me a couple of days. We'll get there, I promise," I said.

Gavin and I covered a few more details before he left, offering me his business card on the threshold. The moment he was gone, I fished my phone from my pocket.

"Is everything okay?"

I looked up to find Grace in the entrance to the living room, a pensive look on her face.

"No, but it's going to be, if it kills me."

I filled her in quickly, my mind racing.

"Surely if your uncle intended to donate money to the Center, his estate should honor that commitment?" she said when I was done.

"Come on, Grace, get with the program. Why throw good money at a charity if you don't have to? Especially a charity that supports a minority group Vicky has no time for."

She frowned at my sarcastic tone. "But it's what Jack wanted. That's pretty clear. Your mother has to honor his wishes."

"Why?" I challenged.

She blinked. "Because he's not here to do it for himself. This is his legacy."

"Legacies don't count on the balance sheet, baby."

"No one is that cold," Grace said.

Right on cue, Lady click-clicked her way into the entrance hall, tail wagging faintly as she looked from me to Grace and back again. I lifted an eyebrow, daring Grace to deny my mother's ruthless streak when we had a living, breathing reminder of her callousness standing in front of us.

"Okay, point taken," Grace conceded. "What are you going to do?"

"I'm going to make Vicky honor Jack's commitment," I said.

"But... Didn't you just convince me she'd never do that?"

"Not voluntarily. But there may be a work-around." The idea had been forming in the back of my mind ever since Gavin had laid his predicament at my feet. "My sister has some influence with Vicky. If I can get her on board, she might swing things."

"You have a sister?"

"In theory. In practice, not really. You've dealt with Claire before, haven't you? Part cyborg, part heartless corporate crusher of dreams?"

I watched understanding dawn in her eyes. "Claire is your *sister?* She's been reviewing the stock-take files I sent her, sending me queries."

I bet she had. I could just imagine Claire examining everything Grace sent in with forensic detail.

"So you've had the pleasure, then" I chuckled uneasily. Exposing the worst of the Walker family skeletons to Grace embarrassed me.

"She's..." Grace chewed on her lip.

"A cold-hearted bitch?" I supplied helpfully. "She's drunk deeply from the Walker family Kool-Aid."

My sister had always been more worried about pleasing Vicky than I had. I almost pitied her for that, because Vicky was a harsh taskmaster and an even harder marker. My guess was that there were precious few pats on the backs in my sister's world, and a lot of "must try harder."

"I'm sorry," Grace said quietly.

And that's exactly why I never talked about these things. Pity was unnecessary. I had a big life whether my family was in it or not. There were a lot of people in the world with a lot more to cry about than me.

"Don't lose sleep over it—I don't. I'm going to call Claire in..." I checked my watch. "Five hours. Maybe this'll be the day she listens to me."

Grace checked her own watch and looked startled. "Crap. I've got to go. I've got a follow-up appointment with the art auctioneer across town."

She backtracked into the living room to collect her coat and bag. I wondered if she'd organised the appointment to get away from me. Then I remembered the way she'd responded in the kitchen before we suffered Gavin interruptus.

Grace wanted me. She might not *want* to want me, but there was no denying our sexual chemistry. I wasn't above exploiting that if I had to, but I wasn't just in this for a quick fuck. Grace was special. I was interested in her mind as well as her body. She deserved to be wooed, not just seduced.

I cleared my throat as she shouldered her bag, then slipped my hands into the front pockets of my jeans.

"Before you go... You up to anything tonight? I managed to score a reservation at Le Coq Rico. I hear their rotisserie chicken is insane." I tried to play it casual, but it came out sounding as though I was reading from a script.

Grace blinked. Then she frowned. "Are you... Did you just ask me on a *date?*"

"I asked you out for dinner, yes." I fought the urge to shuffle my feet like a schoolboy.

It had been so long since I gave a shit about my personal life, I'd forgotten what it was like to put myself out there. *Uncomfortable* was the word that leapt to mind, closely followed by *exposed*.

"I can't have dinner with you, Callan," she said. She looked very serious.

"If tonight's not good, I can probably swing another night."

Grace considered the tips of her shoes for a second. When she lifted her gaze to mine again, she looked determined and a little embarrassed.

"I know I probably gave you the wrong idea in the kitchen just now, and I'm sorry about that. But I'm not sleeping with you again."

I held up my hands. "Three courses and some wine. No nudity, I swear."

"I can't afford it," she said.

My social graces clearly needed some serious work if Grace thought I'd been suggesting we go Dutch.

"It's my shout," I said. When she frowned, I remembered we sometimes spoke a different version of the Queen's English. "Which means 'I'm paying' in American."

She shook her head. "I wasn't talking about money."

It was my turn to blink. She gave me an apologetic smile, then brushed past me on her way to the door. The sound of her exit sounded pretty damn final in the small space.

I thought about what I knew about Grace—her thrift-store shopping, her concern for her job, her diligence and determination. Then I thought about what she knew about me—that stupid 100 Days bullshit, all this crap with my family, my own behaviour. From the moment we'd met, I'd tried to play her, keeping my search for Jack's will a secret.

Was it really a huge surprise she'd turn down the opportunity to spend quality time with me?

"Fuck."

Lady appeared around the corner, head cocked quizzically. *You rang?*

She almost made me smile.

"Come on, girl. Let's get back to it," I said, leading the way to the study.

* * *

I was the short-tempered owner of three new paper cuts by the time Grace returned from her appointment. I heard the door open and close, then she appeared in the study doorway, eyebrows raised in question.

"Still no luck," I reported. "How did your meeting go?"

She peeled off her coat and threw it onto one of the red leather couches.

"Depressing."

"'How so?'

"It's all about money. I thought there'd at least be a little respect for the art. Maybe even some appreciation and awe."

"Everything's about money, especially when people pretend it isn't," I said.

"Speaking of money, have you called your sister yet?" She parked her butt on the arm of the couch.

I had to fight not to get distracted by the way her skirt stretched across her thighs, outlining them in faithful detail. I was trying very hard not to put pressure on Grace, but it was tough now I knew how good we were together.

"Another hour. She usually gets to the office by seven."

Grace pulled a face. "Early."

"Vicky starts at five."

Now Grace looked appalled.

"She's one of those titans of industry who only need two hours hanging upside down in their bat cave each night," I explained.

Grace pushed herself to her feet. "I've got some spreadsheets to update, so I'll be in the kitchen if you need me."

I went back to packing files into boxes, feeling more upbeat than I had a right to, considering all the open-ended questions in my life right now. The world was a better place when Grace was nearby.

I'd set an alert on my phone to let me know when it was seven in Australia. It went off when I was elbow deep in a heavy file drawer, wading through banks statements and invoices for everything from cleaning services to dog grooming. The paper this man kept... It was doing my head in.

I silenced the alarm, then took a moment to think through how I wanted to approach this call.

Staying calm was a given. Claire and I had a history of pissing each other off, but I couldn't afford to let my temper come into play this time. Whatever her faults, Claire had loved Jack. She hadn't spent a lot of time with him in recent years, but Jack had been a good uncle to both of us, despite Vicky's disapproval. I needed to appeal to my sister's sense of fairness—if she still possessed such a thing after so many years as my mother's understudy.

I figured I was as prepared as I'd ever be, so I dialed her direct line and listened to it ring half a world away.

"She's in a meeting," was Claire's opening gambit.

"That's all right. I wanted to talk to you, anyway."

There was a brief silence while Claire tried to imagine what for and came up blank. "Why?"

"I need advice." Flattering her was *my* opening gambit. "Uncle Jack was funding a charity, a youth center here in New York. They're terrified they'll lose the building they're redeveloping unless I can help keep Jack's promise to them."

"And you think I'm going to help you?" she asked. "Why would I do that?"

Given the state of almost constant acrimony between us, it was a fair question.

"You wouldn't be helping me," I said quietly. "You'd would be helping teens in crisis. And you'd be honoring Jack's wishes."

I could hear her gears turning from nearly ten thousand miles away. A businesswoman like herself couldn't say aloud that she didn't give a fig for at-risk youth.

Even if she didn't.

"You're not supposed to be mucking around in Jack's affairs," she tried.

"I'm not *mucking around*," I snarled before I could catch myself. "He was trying to do some good, Claire. And now it's all hanging by a thread. Even if his will leaves everything to Vicky, there's no reason why his intentions shouldn't be fulfilled. They need a million dollars."

She snorted. "How can you be so sure of his intentions? Maybe the charity is trying to take you for a ride."

My sister's cynicism was deeply ingrained for someone only

twenty-six years old. Then again, she'd been trained by the master. "His name is on one of the rooms in the plans. This was a big project for Jack. He'd want us to finish it."

"So I'm supposed to sweet talk Mum around?"

"Yes," I said simply. "If I ask, she'll never say yes."

"There's a *reason* for that, Cal. She's given you opportunity after opportunity, but you never show your face. You never lift a hand. You're traipsing around Europe and Asia on the yacht circuit while we do all the work. Why on *earth* would Mum say yes to something you asked for?"

It was such a fucked-up, distorted version of history my blood boiled.

"To be a good person!" I thundered. "She chased me off, Claire. You forget that bit when it suits you. She bought Jana off and then *both* of you shat all over my business start-up because *she* had other plans for me."

"Because your venture was in direct competition with the family business," she said heatedly. "Don't pretend it wasn't, Callan. That whole start-up was just an exercise in trying to stick it to Mum, as always."

I had to hold the phone away from my ear for a second before I loosed a string of profanities into it.

I mentioned my sister and I were good at pushing each other's buttons, right?

"Please point me to the organic-beef division of Walker Holdings," I said when I could form complete sentences again. "I'm all ears to hear about this fictional business conflict."

My start-up had been all about small producers, capitalising on the local-food movement. It had been about good food, respectful animal husbandry, ethical food supply. In other words, the antithesis of everything Walker stood for—mass production, feed lots, live export. There had been no market crossover whatsoever. My mother was even on the record saying that organic beef wasn't an area she was interested in.

That had been the whole point of the damned business I'd started up with two mates from university—to do things differently.

And like most good things in my life, once Vicky found out about it, she'd reached out and killed it before it even had a chance, buying off my partners with the offer of a quick cash grab. The whole ugly incident had served to underline the lesson I'd learned with Jana: Everyone has their price.

"You could have gone into any industry," Claire said. "But you chose to compete with Walker Holdings. That makes you an ungrateful asshole as well as a traitor."

This conversation was going so well. Lucky I'd taken the time to prepare for it.

"Jesus, Claire. Is Vicky's hand up your ass, making you parrot this shit, or do you really believe what you're saying?"

"Fuck you, Callan. You think I could care less what you think of me? You live the most pointless life I've ever seen, and you want to judge *me?*"

We both fell silent then, the only sound our angry breathing. After a few seconds the red haze cleared, and I took a deep breath.

"This isn't about us. This is about Uncle Jack, about how he wanted his estate dealt with."

"What he wanted is clearly stipulated in the will—everything goes to Mum."

"That will is thirty years old, Claire," I snapped. "You really think it accurately reflects his current wishes?"

"Then he should have written a new one, if that was the way he felt. But he didn't, so you need to—" My sister broke off with an audible gasp. When she spoke again, her voice was low with accusation. "Oh my God. You think there's another will, don't you? That's why you insisted on sticking your nose into Jack's affairs. That's why you're over there in New York, pretending to help out."

Fuck. I wanted to punch myself in the face. Only a dumbass would throw shade on Jack's will before he'd finished searching for a more recent version.

"I'm trying to give Jack the dignity he deserves," I said carefully. "It's clear he wanted to support the Robinson Center, and I just want to make sure his wishes are honored."

"Do you have any grounds to believe there's another will?" Claire asked, refusing to be distracted.

I considered denying her accusation outright, but the odds were good she was going to go straight to Vicky with her suspicions anyway. Which meant things were about to get ugly, fast. My only hope was to appeal to her sense of decency. If she still possessed such a thing.

"He mentioned he was drafting a new will a couple of years ago. He talked about leaving his estate to charities. That's all I know."

"There's no record of another will on file with our lawyers."

"So? He probably used a local firm here in New York. He'd want to deal with someone who is across US law."

"Then why hasn't anyone come forward with the new document?"

"I don't know! It's not like there was a funeral notice, let alone a funeral," I said bitterly.

Even though she was thousands of miles away, I sensed my sister's discomfort. She was still human enough to know that denying Jack a sendoff was wrong, at least.

"It was a difficult time. We were jammed with meetings here in Australia. No one could get away…"

"Bullshit. Vicky has always been ashamed Jack was gay. Don't pretend that's not the truth, because we both know it. Now he's dead, she wants to sweep his life under the carpet and pretend he never existed."

"How can you say that?" Claire asked hotly. "Jack was her

brother. Of course she was upset he died. Of course she cared, even if they haven't been close for years."

I started to pace, frustrated by my sister's mindless loyalty.

"Oh, come on. She hired a temp to pack up his apartment. A complete stranger who is being paid by the hour. Vicky had him cremated without giving his friends a chance to say goodbye. You tell me—are those the acts of a loving, grieving sister?"

There was a long pause while my sister tried to come up with a convincing counter-argument and failed.

"There are two sides to every story," she finally said.

It was time to put my cards on the table. All or nothing.

"Are you going to help me make this right?" I asked.

"How on earth am I supposed to do that?"

"Don't tell Vicky about the will until I've had a chance to finish looking for it. And convince her to honor Jack's intentions with the Robinson Center."

I heard the sound of papers being shuffled on the other end of the phone. "She's in the middle of an export deal right now."

"So?"

"She's stressed, it's not a good time." More paper shuffling. My sister had always tidied her personal space when she felt anxious.

"We don't have the luxury of waiting for a better time. The Center is supposed to start work on their renovation next month, and the second probate is granted, Vicky's going to start selling off Jack's life."

"Look, the will is one thing, but why should I put myself on the line for a US charity that I've never even heard of? They can find someone else to fund their Center. Surely there are other rich old queers out there willing to hand over big fat checks."

Rage exploded in my brain, white-hot and deadly.

"That's *Jack* you're talking about," I said, my voice shaking with anger. "He taught you to ride a bike. He's the person who made sure we had Christmas every single year. And you think *I'm* a traitor? Jack had more humanity and decency in his little fucking finger than—"

The dial tone sounded in my ear.

I threw the phone at the wall, unable to contain my fury any longer.

Out of the corner of my eye, I caught movement, and when I looked over my shoulder I saw Grace in the doorway, eyes wide, face pale.

I took a deep breath and let it out on a harsh sigh. Then I scrubbed a hand over my face.

"Sorry. I didn't realise you were there." My hands were shaking. Adrenalin will do that, when the dose is high enough.

"I heard you yelling."

I laughed humorlessly. "I'm betting half of Manhattan did."

Feeling stupid now the moment had passed, I crossed the room to pick up my phone. The case had done its job protecting the body of the phone, but the screen was a crazed mess.

"You weren't joking about not getting along with your sister," Grace said.

"We know how to piss each other off," I said.

"I guess that means she isn't going to help with the Center?"

I thought about Claire's parting comment and a fresh acid capsule of anger fizzed in my gut.

"Let's just say it isn't a priority for her," I said flatly. "And she's probably going to go straight to Vicky and tell her I think there's a more recent will."

"What do you think your mother will do?"

"I don't know. She'll be keen to hang on to Jack's stock, which is set to go to her at the moment. But trying to bury a more recent will is a bad look, legally speaking. She won't want the heat she'd get from that if the media got wind of it." I looked around the study. Over the past ten days, I'd combed through almost every file folder in this room, painstakingly checking every document. "I need to find that fucking will."

"Is there a chance there isn't one?" Grace asked quietly. "I don't want to be a doomsayer, but it's a possibility, isn't it?"

I sighed heavily. "Yeah, it is. Which means getting the Robinson Center over the line is even more important."

The realisation gave me new energy, and I crossed to Jack's desk and pulled a fresh legal pad and a sharp pencil from one of the drawers.

"But if your sister won't push it with your mom, what can you do?" Grace asked.

"I'd fund it myself if I could, but my money's tied up. It'd take too long to shift things around." Not to mention being hugely wasteful, since I'd take big hits for pulling funds early. "I'm going to have to find the money somewhere else."

I hit the home button on my phone. I was half expecting it to remain dead, but the screen lit up. I navigated my way to my contacts folder.

"What do you mean, you're going to find the money?" Grace asked, approaching the desk.

I looked up at her. "I gave Gavin my word I'd make this happen."

I started writing. It was going to be a long night.

FIFTEEN

Sex for the Charitable

Grace

I WATCHED as Callan scrolled through his contacts folder and jotted down names and numbers every few seconds.

I wasn't sure what to do. He was upset, a barely visible tremble in his hands, his face still flushed with anger. I'd heard enough of the conversation with his sister to understand why.

What an ugly business.

Olivia and I had our moments, but we'd never gone at each other the way Callan and his sister just had. We cared about each other too much to use our understanding of each other's flaws and weaknesses as weapons.

Thank God.

I moved closer and sat on the chair in front of Jack's desk.

"How can I help?" I asked simply.

Callan glanced up, the pencil stilling on the page. "Seriously?"

"Yes. I want to help, if I can."

For Jack, but also for Callan. What he was trying to do for his uncle was a good thing. The right thing.

"Okay." He considered the page in front of him, then tore it off the pad and held it out to me. "We're going to be making a lot of calls. Half these people are going to be travelling, unavailable, whatever. If you get onto them, pass the phone to me. Otherwise, leave a message telling them you're calling on my behalf and asking them to call me ASAP."

"Okay." I reached out to take the paper, but Callan didn't release it immediately.

"Use the landline, okay? I don't want you running up your phone bill."

"That was my plan," I said with a smile.

He smiled in return, and I was pleased to see his eyes had lost the distant, glittery look they'd had when he ended the call with his sister.

I took a few minutes to set myself up, getting my own pad and pen and clearing a spot on the corner of Jack's desk where the phone was located. Then I checked the name at the top of the list and made the first call.

Over the next two hours, I called and left messages for dozens of people. Some numbers were busy. A couple simply rang and rang. Enough people answered that I was able to see Callan in action, and it was nothing short of a revelation.

I'd seen him sincere and emotional at his uncle's memorial. I'd been on the receiving end of one of his charm offensives. I'd seen him angry, I'd seen him grim. But the Callan who came to the fore during those two hours was someone else entirely.

He started all the calls in the same way, slipping into playful, friendly banter with whoever it was, recalling the last time they'd met, asking after business or family members or mutual friends. He made jokes. He laughed. He mentioned upcoming events, hoping to see them there. Then he charmingly, naturally, easily segued into talking about the Robinson Center.

He touted the Center's achievements eloquently and thoroughly. He spouted statistics. He talked of Jack's involvement, and every time there was the husky gravel of emotion in his voice.

At first I thought he must have been bullshitting, but a surreptitious search on my phone revealed he'd done his research and that every word he'd said was true.

Halfway through hour two, I went and made tea for us and raided Jack's pantry, cracking open the last packet of Iced VoVos. It was getting toward dinnertime, and I texted Olivia to let her know she should eat without me and that I might not be home for a few more hours.

Every time Callan ended a call, he made a note next to the person's name. I got pretty good at reading his looping scrawl upside down, shaking my head when I saw the numbers he was recording. By the time we'd nearly reached the bottom of the list, he had firm commitments from ten people and he paused to do a tally.

"Two-fifty. Okay. We're close. We only need three hundred to keep things ticking over at the Center in the short term." He ran a hand through his hair for the hundredth time since we'd started making calls. The dark strands sat up in spikes and clumps, giving him a rumpled, just-got-out-bed look.

"You've left a lot of messages," I reminded him.

"Yeah, I know. We'll get there."

It was stupid, but I felt a warm wash of pleasure at his use of the plural pronoun.

He sat back in his chair, one leg stretched out in front of him. "You give good phone, O'Malley," he said, his gaze warm on me.

"Me? You're the LeBron of phone. I swear, the way you work that thing..." I shook my head slowly. "Your mouth should be registered as a dangerous weapon."

A slow smile curved his lips. "I think that's the nicest thing you've ever said to me."

"I didn't mean it like that," I said, rolling my eyes. It was too late, though—I was already remembering the way he'd worshipped my breasts with his dangerous mouth. Among other things.

"Neither did I," he said, eyes wide with faux-innocence.

Refusing to be drawn into flirtation, I asked the question that had been burning in the back of my brain for the last two hours.

"You've done this before, haven't you?"

He shrugged a shoulder negligently. "Not on this scale. But I help out occasionally, if I can."

I knew him well enough by now to guess he was bullshitting me again. "I thought you were supposed to be a party-loving playboy?"

"So?"

"One of these things is not like the other," I pointed out.

He shrugged again, then glanced down at the desk. It took me a moment to recognize the expression on his face as shyness.

Callan Walker was *embarrassed* because I was recognizing his philanthropy.

That was when I realized I was in big, big trouble.

"How many charities have you 'helped out'?" I asked, acting on a hunch.

"I don't know. Jack has hooked me up with a few. I stumbled over a couple of causes on my own..." He looked genuinely uncomfortable now.

"Let me guess how this works," I said, putting the pieces together. "You go to parties with your rich friends, and you shoot the shit with them, then you charm them into digging into their deep pockets and supporting a good cause."

He shrugged again. "It's not as calculated as that."

"You're a fraud," I said.

He looked startled.

"You walk around in your designer clothes with your perfect tan. You act as though you don't have a care in the world. You call yourself the black sheep of the family. You let your mother and sister think you spend your days lying around on yachts. And it's all a front, isn't it?"

He frowned. "I spend plenty of time on yachts, O'Malley.

Don't go turning me into Mother Teresa because I made a few phone calls."

Jesus, now he was being modest *and* humble. How on earth was I supposed to resist that? It had been bad enough when I thought he was feckless and too charming for his own good, but now I knew there was substance beneath all that masculine beauty...

I'd just watched this man—this beautiful, sexy, *humble* man—pace and cajole and charm hundreds of thousands of dollars from his peers for a great cause. Two hours of watching his big, hard body walk back and forth. Two hours of hearing his laughter and clever wit.

Two hours of truly torturous foreplay.

I was officially done.

I stood and reached for the button on my suit jacket. Callan's eyes followed the movement as I flicked it open. Holding his gaze, I slipped it off my shoulders. Dropping it onto the chair behind me, I reached for the top button on my shirt and pushed it free. Callan's gaze sharpened as I went after the next button.

"What's going on, Grace?"

"What do you think is going on?"

"I'm really, really hoping you're taking your blouse off for me," he said.

My shirt parted as I loosened the last button, and I let the silk slide down my arms.

"Good guess," I said, reaching for the zip at the small of my back.

The lining hissed against my stay-up stockings as my skirt slid to the floor, leaving me in nothing but my ankle boots, stockings, and underwear.

"Fuck me," Callan breathed as I walked around the desk toward him.

"I don't see any other men here," I said.

The way he was looking at me gave me the confidence to place a hand on his shoulder for balance before straddling his lap. I could feel his cock beneath my backside, hard and hot, and everything inside me tightened with anticipation as I wriggled closer.

"If I'd known philanthropy turned you on this much, I would have told you about it a long time ago," he murmured, his hands sliding up my thighs to my waist. His pupils were dilated with desire, and a pulse was visible at his neck.

"No, you wouldn't," I said.

That was why I was sitting in his lap, breaking my own rules where he was concerned. He'd just shattered my last protection against him. He was a good man, and I was old enough and wise enough to know how rare and valuable that was. This wasn't going to last—he was going to leave—but suddenly that didn't seem as important as it should.

Sliding my hand to the nape of his neck, I leaned in and pressed my mouth to his. He groaned happily as his arms settled around my back. Our lips slid hotly together, and then he smiled. "How much money do I have to raise to get the rest of your clothes off?"

None. I'd already fallen off the Callan wagon. "Name some other good deeds you've done, and I'll consider it."

His hands rose to cup my breasts over the lace of my bra. "Sometimes I help old ladies cross the street."

"Do you now?" I ducked my head and kissed the underside of his jaw. Then I reached back and unhooked my bra.

"*Ungh*," he said, lifting my hips and ducking his head for a lick of my right nipple. He carried on making me crazy while I tried not to think about what a dumb idea this was. But it was hard to worry too much when his tongue was doing wicked things to my breasts.

I closed my eyes and ran my fingers through his fine, thick hair. But I opened them a moment later when I rose suddenly into the air as he stood, taking me with him. Too bad I also let out an unladylike noise of surprise.

"Hang on, O'Malley," he said, as I wrapped my limbs around him.

"Where are we going?" I asked.

He began walking toward the back of the apartment. "Somewhere more comfortable. I'll tell you more of my good deeds, and you can reward me appropriately."

SIXTEEN

Always Leave a Tip for the Barista

Callan

I DEPOSITED Grace on the bed. I knew her life was complicated, and she was reluctant to give in to me. So I planned to make it very much worth her while.

Grabbing my shirt, I quickly shucked it over my head. Grace lay there watching me, an appreciatively hot look in her eye.

And that did something to my insides that I hadn't felt in a long time. Her craving for me had a different flavor than that of the girls on the yachts and in the European clubs I visited. It was the gaze of someone who was getting to know me and liked what she saw.

"You know," I said, "I once saved a turtle who was crossing the road."

"Oh. Well." Grace winked and reached down to tug off her panties. She shimmied out of them and my mouth went dry at the sight of her lying there in stockings, no underwear in sight.

I dropped my trousers and boxers and palmed my erection. When I gave myself a slow, hungry stroke, her eyes darkened.

"And..." But, fuck. I was running out of good deeds to name. And brain cells. "I always leave a tip for the barista."

Grace sat up. "A tip?" She reached around to palm my ass, and squeeze. "Mmm, a tip is nice." She licked the tip of my cock while I about died from excitement. Her soft hair brushed my belly, and I cupped her head as she took more of me.

I made a noise as she enveloped me in her mouth, giving me a hearty suck. "Christ, O'Malley." I gathered her hair into my hand. "You're bloody good at that."

Grace hummed and tongued me and teased until I was shaking with eagerness and beginning to sweat. "If you don't stop now, I'll..."

She groaned on my cock, and my balls tightened dangerously. I put a hand under her chin and nudged her off me and then onto her back.

She pulled off her ankle boots, then hooked her thumbs into the top of her stockings and slowly slid them off while I watched hungrily. "Grab the headboard," I demanded.

Her eyes widened slightly, but she reached up and took hold of two of its wooden spindles.

My hands were actually shaking as I opened the bedside drawer and fished out the box of condoms I'd found in Jack's stash. If this was my inheritance from his estate, I considered it a fine and timely bargain.

I suited up slowly, for both our benefits. As Grace watched me touch myself, her hips shifted in anticipation. And I needed a few extra seconds to settle.

But even an hour might not have been enough. As I lowered myself onto Grace's body, coming within inches of her espresso gaze, I felt as eager as a teenager, and just as lucky. *You're so beautiful to me*, I wanted to say. But it sounded sappy in my own head, so I kissed her instead.

Our tongues tangled, and she moaned. I nudged her knees apart, and she practically purred with anticipation. I was enjoying torturing her, though. So I dragged one hand up the inside of her thigh until she shivered.

"You are..." She gasped as my fingers taunted her again, not quite reaching the apex of her legs. "Such a bastard."

"Ah, the truth comes out." I dropped my head and kissed her between her breasts. "Not so generous now, eh, Grace?"

She let out a little growl and kicked my leg.

Laughing, I kissed my way down her lithe body, parted her thighs, and then kissed her right where she wanted me.

"Oh!" she cried, arching up to me. "Yes."

I gave her a long, luxurious lick and heard panting. Payback was sweet on my tongue. Fingers gripped my hair, and I lifted my head quickly. "Thought I told you to grab the headboard."

She whimpered and groaned, and then did as I'd asked. I worked her over with slow kisses until she sobbed my name.

The sound of it made me a greedy man. I sat up quickly, fitted my cock against her and pushed my way home. Her muscles rippled with pleasure, and I felt like the horses at the Melbourne Cup—mad for it and unstoppable.

She gripped my hips and lifted her chin. I crushed my mouth onto hers and gave it everything I had. It was sensory overload— her sweet tongue in my mouth, and the tight grip of her body. I made myself slow down as I neared the finish line. Who would want this to end?

"Grace," I whispered hoarsely so she'd open her eyes. "So fucking lovely."

She tipped her head back and gasped, pulsing around me.

And I was done and dusted. I gripped her knees and poured myself inside-out in two soul-stealing bursts. And when I couldn't stay upright anymore, I came to rest on her chest, my nose in her sweet-smelling hair. She sighed beneath me.

"Jesus God," I panted when I could speak again. "How are you still single?"

"Asked the single thirty-year-old of the single twenty-five-year-old."

I snorted. "I know why I'm still single. It's because of my piss-poor attitude, underpinned by a healthy dose of dysfunctional family dynamics. Which you do not share." I rubbed her back and she wiggled appreciatively under my touch.

"Who says? There's more than one way to be dysfunctional."

I lifted my head so I could see her face. "Tell me." I wanted to know everything about this woman.

She held my gaze for a beat, then closed her eyes. "I'm single because of Marcus."

"And Marcus is...?"

"My ex. We were making plans to live together when he got an amazing job offer in Paris. A couple of weeks later, he waved goodbye and hopped on Air France."

"When was this?" I asked, because there was still hurt in Grace's eyes.

"Nearly seven months now. So I'm over it. Over him. But it taught me a lesson—fool me once, no more dating for me."

"Only sex for the very charitable?"

"Right."

"How long were you two together?" I asked.

"Four years." She pleated the sheet between her fingers for a beat. "It's hard for a girl to compete with a promotion and a view of the Seine."

She smiled to show she was being plucky, and I wanted to punch her ex in the face. I'd seen the Seine a thousand times, and I'd pick Grace over a muddy-brown river without thinking twice. Clearly, Marcus was a tool of the highest order.

"Your turn," Grace said.

Worried I was getting too heavy for her, I rolled to one side, then slid my arm around her shoulders and encouraged her to rest her head on my chest.

"My life is an open book," I said. "Fire away."

"Who's Jana?" she asked.

I tensed, and I knew she felt it because she lifted her head to look at me.

"You mentioned her when you were fighting with your sister," she said. "But if you don't want to talk about her, it's cool."

"It was a long time ago," I said.

"Because you're so much older than me," she said, deadpan.

I craned my neck so I could kiss her sassy mouth. Fuck, she was delicious. She opened to me, her tongue stroking mine with lazy sensuality. My cock stirred and I rolled toward her.

"Wait a second. Are you using sex to distract me?" she asked, breaking our kiss.

I blinked at her, more than a little dazed. "I thought that was what you were doing."

An adorable wrinkle appeared between her eyebrows and I realised I needed to get Jana out of the way before she started thinking my ex was more important than she was.

"Jana was my first girlfriend. We met at University. She was pretty wild, different from anyone I knew. And she had a great family." I shrugged. "I fell pretty hard. Not a lot of dignity involved."

"First love always cuts you off at the knees," Grace said.

"I think mine made it all the way to the hips," I said. "After a while, my mother realised we were serious, and she decided it was time to get to know Jana. Long story short, a few weeks later, Jana told me she didn't think we were going anywhere."

Grace's eyes got wide, and I could see her putting two and two together.

"Tell me Vicky didn't," she said, her voice hushed with awe at the awfulness of her suspicion.

I smiled tightly. "She offered to pay off Jana's student debt if she ended things, and Jana took it—after much careful considera-tion and discussion with her parents, you understand. When I confronted Vicky, she told me she didn't think we were suited. And she wanted to prove something to me."

"That she was an asshole?"

This time my smile was genuine. "That everyone has their price. Even the people you think are only in it for you."

"That's so twisted."

"I'm pretty sure that's what happened with my parents. He saw dollar signs when he married her, meanwhile she was crazy in love. What was it you said before? One of these things is not like the other."

"You never talk about your father."

"Neither do you. Or your mother, for that matter."

"I don't have a lot to do with either of them," she said carefully.

There was a story there, but I was learning that Grace was protective of her secrets.

"My father's dead," I offered.

"I never really knew mine."

We stared at each other across a few inches of rumpled sheets. "This is the best therapy session I've ever had," I said.

"It's about to get better." She pushed me onto my back and crawled on top of me.

———

Grace

Even though it was nearly nine and I needed to get home to Olivia, I had a quick shower before I left. My sister was not worldly in that way, but after the crazy-good sex Callan and I had enjoyed, I felt as though I reeked of satisfaction.

I was pushing my feet into my shoes when I realized Callan was pulling on a pair of jeans.

I gave him a querying look and he threw me a quick smile. "I'm taking you home," he said.

"You don't need to do that."

"I know. Traffic won't be bad at this time of night. Where are we heading?"

"I'm fine with the train," I said, feeling my shoulders start to tense up. So much for afterglow.

He considered me for a moment. "O'Malley, are you secretly married with five children and a mortgage?"

I smiled, couldn't stop myself. Callan could always make me laugh, even when I didn't want to.

"No. It's just dumb for you to do a round trip for nothing."

I felt stupid, because I'd turned taking me home into something bigger than it was. I genuinely didn't want him to have to go to the trouble.

And I didn't want him to see where I lived.

Ugh. Is there anything worse than realizing you're more fucked up than you think you are?

He cocked his head, studying me some more. "Can I at least walk you to the station?"

"Sure. That sounds good."

We finished dressing and gathering our things in silence, because I'd made it weird. Yay me.

In the privacy of my own head, I reminded myself that Olivia and I had nothing to be ashamed of. Yes, our apartment could fit into the bathroom at Jack's place. And yes, one of Callan's shoes probably cost more than my monthly rent. But being poor wasn't shameful.

It wasn't.

It just felt that way.

I didn't want him to see the sleazy check-cashing business downstairs from the apartment. I didn't want him to smell the pee-soaked foyer. And I really didn't want to see the sympathy in his eyes as he looked around the tiny space I shared with my sister.

This *thing* between us belonged here, in this gilded apartment, surrounded by priceless art and all the good taste that money could buy. I didn't want to invite him into my world. As I'd said to him not so long ago, I couldn't afford the fantasy he represented. I simply couldn't.

If I let myself think that this could be real, that it had the potential to mean something... It would kill me when Callan jetted out of my life. As he would. It was inevitable. Guys like him did not wind up with women like me. Not in real life.

I'd failed at keeping out of his bed, but I needed to succeed at keeping him out of my life. I needed to hang on to some scrap of self-preservation. Somehow.

He took my hand as we left the apartment, and once we were in the elevator he used it to pull me close and wrap his arm around my shoulders.

"How long do you think it will take you to raise the rest of the money?" I asked as the elevator did its thing.

"I'm not sure. I've got a few hot prospects on my call-back list. Maybe today or tomorrow?"

"When are you going to tell the Robinson Center you solved their problem?" I asked.

"I've only solved it temporarily. I still need to find the rest of the money to complete the renovation."

"You will."

He looked down at me. "I love the way you say that with utmost confidence."

"I am confident. I know how much you want this."

He kissed me as the doors opened, a hot, lush kiss that stole my breath and had me sliding my arms around him, searching for more.

The sound of the doors sliding shut again made us pull away

from each other. Callan's look was heated and a little wild as he looked at me.

"What you do to me, O'Malley…"

He tucked me against his body as we exited the building, which was just as well because it was bitterly cold and my coat way too thin. It was nice having his hard, warm body against mine. Too nice. Too easy to get used to.

I waited until we'd arrived at the steps to the station before I turned to face him.

"I need to ask you a favor."

"Anything."

"I need for this to not happen between us during work hours." I'd given up on pretending I could stay away from him, but that didn't mean I couldn't contain whatever was happening between us.

"Okay," he said slowly. "I can do that."

Relief washed through me. "Thank you."

I already felt as though I was serving two masters—my growing feelings for Callan and my actual employer, his mother. Knowing he would respect my working hours gave me the illusion that I could continue to juggle the two.

"Am I still allowed to flirt with you?" he asked, reaching out to turn my collar up against the sharp wind.

"As long as it's just flirting."

"So no touching?"

"Nope." There was no way I'd be able to keep a grip on my already frayed self-control if he touched me. Not now that I knew how hot it could get between us.

"What about lunch?"

"What about it?"

"You have to eat lunch. Technically, that would be your time, yes?" he asked.

He'd moved closer, crowding my body with his.

175

I frowned, trying to think. It was hard when his mouth was just inches away. "I don't know."

"Let's just see how it goes," he said easily. There was a glint in his eye, and I suspected I'd just ceded important territory to him.

"Okay."

He kissed me then, and for long, molten seconds he was my whole world. His arms around me, his lips against mine, the thud of his heartbeat vibrating through my body. Then someone jostled us, because we were doing all this at the head of the stairs, blocking half the walkway. Like idiots.

"I need to get home," I said.

"I know."

He walked me down into the station and we kissed goodbye again at the turnstiles. Then I went through and headed for my platform. When I looked back, he was still standing there, waiting. Watching over me.

It was scary how safe that made me feel. How much I appreciated his silent presence and desire to be there for me. *Don't get used to it. This is only temporary,* I reminded myself as I pushed through the turnstile.

SEVENTEEN

My Share of Decadence

Grace

I WILL NOT GET NAKED **with Callan Walker during business hours.**
I will not get naked with Callan Walker during business hours.

This was my mantra as I went in to work the next day. I entered the apartment cautiously, nervously, but Callan was nowhere to be seen. I made my way into the study and set myself up at Jack's desk. I was ready to do battle with all the data I'd collected during the stock-take at the warehouse.

Callan brought me a latte ten minutes later, along with a giant apple muffin with a crumb topping. My mouth watered just looking at it. That wasn't my only source of hunger, either. He delivered these gifts wearing a dress shirt which was completely unbuttoned, displaying his fabulous six-pack between the shirt's halves. A tie hung loosely around his neck.

After setting down the cup and the plate, he proceeded to button the shirt slowly, hiding each glorious inch in a subtle reverse striptease. Then he looped the tie and proceeded to tie it. "Eat up, O'Malley. You'll need your strength later."

"For wh—" I bit back the rest of the question as he began to grin. That devil.

"I'd demonstrate, but I'm meeting Gavin for a tour of the Robinson Center site. But I'll be back for lunch."

He made lunch sound like the most decadent event in the history of the world. My dazed expression probably gave away a few of the naughty thoughts he'd just inspired in me. I had a brief memory of Callan grinning down at me on the sofa while his hips—

Gah! *I will not get naked with Callan Walker during business hours.*

"I don't think 'lunch' is a good idea," I said, desperately fighting a rearguard action. "I could manage an early 'dinner,' though."

"Lunch *and* dinner. I like your thinking, O'Malley." Before I could protest, he winked and disappeared.

It took me a while to get my heart rate back to normal and settle in to business. But there was plenty to do. I spent the next several hours wrangling with numbers and spreadsheets. I started to get twitchy around lunchtime, waiting for the sound of Callan's key in the lock. I debated whether I should give in to what we both wanted or not. Technically, I was entitled to a lunch break. It was my prerogative how I used that time. Right?

Callan took the question out of my hands by texting at twelve thirty.

*Held up. Late lunch? Early dinner? *Very* hungry.*

It was a little pathetic how disappointed I felt. Feeling like a hypocrite—an increasingly common phenomenon where Callan was concerned—I ate my paltry lunch in the apartment.

At three thirty, my sister texted to say that she'd taken the subway uptown after school, and was downstairs in the lobby of the building. *Can I come up?*

Oh boy.

I'm working, Liv. Just because this apartment looks like a public museum doesn't mean it is one.

It was a terrible idea for Olivia to meet Callan, and he was due back any second. She tended to get attached to people. And Callan would never be a permanent fixture in our lives.

You and I never go to museums anyway!

Great. Now my sister and I were arguing again. So I gave in. *Callan isn't here,* I said. Hopefully it would stay that way, too. *You can come up for five minutes.*

No response.

Olivia?

Nothing.

I sat there for a couple of minutes, marinating in guilt, wondering if my reluctance had set her off again. But then I heard keys in the door and the mystery was solved.

"Knowing your sister, I'm pretty sure you'll find Grace toiling away in the office," Callan said, his voice echoing through the apartment. Jumping out of the desk chair, I ran to the doorway. Sure enough, Olivia was just entering the apartment, looking pretty damned pleased with herself. She must have spotted Callan coming into the lobby, and turned on the charm.

So much for keeping the two parts of my life separate.

"Well, hello there," I said, my voice a lot calmer than I felt inside.

"Hello to you, too, O'Malley," Callan said with a wink. "Your sister was downstairs, looking for you."

Sis-tah. It was disturbing how much I loved that accent.

I turned to Olivia, feeling oddly exposed now Callan had met her.

"Don't you have homework?" I asked. "You should be at home taking care of that."

"It's not much," she said gaily. "I could sit with you and polish it off in no time." She had turned the charm dial all the way up to eleven, obviously. Usually when I brought up homework, she'd give me an evil look and stomp away.

"Who wants a coffee?" Callan asked. "Lattes are on offer."

"I'd love one," said Liv with a megawatt smile. "Can I watch you make them?"

Jesus. When had my sister become such an accomplished flirt?

"Grace?" Callan asked. "Can I fondle Uncle Jack's Italian espresso machine for your benefit as well?"

"Fondle away," I grumbled, not quite making eye contact, too afraid my very astute sister would pick up on the vibe between us.

"She means, 'Yes please,'" Olivia said with a smirk.

I suppressed a growl of frustration.

A few minutes later, Olivia carried a latte into the office and set it beside me. It occurred to me that Callan must have unpacked the dishes I'd already stowed away. Sigh.

"What are you up to?" I demanded in a whisper. "You shouldn't be here, Liv."

She plopped down on a tufted footstool. "Just curious, Grace. Geez. Why should you have all the fun?" Her eyes widened. "And why don't you want me around, anyway? Do you prefer to be alone with the Hot One?"

Ack! If she only knew. "Once your coffee is finished, and your curiosity satisfied, you can go home."

"He is so hot," she mouthed, her eyes sparkling.

Yes, I noticed.

I turned my eyes back to my spreadsheet, but the numbers no longer made any sense at all.

———

Callan

I found Grace's sister perfectly hilarious.

Someday Olivia would be beautiful like her sister. For now she had gangly limbs and none of Grace's ability to dissemble. She was as eager as a puppy, with a pleading face and big brown eyes.

I thought she'd settle down in the study, but instead she made a pest of herself. "What's the oldest thing in the apartment?" I heard her ask Grace, who, being Grace, was trying to work. "Which one was made by the most famous artist?"

"Olivia!" Grace warned. "Go home. Or read your book. One or the other."

"You are no fun."

"I'm working," Grace said as I eavesdropped from one room away. "You need to make yourself scarce. Go home."

"I can't!" Olivia hissed. "The MetroCard you gave me is kicked."

"Already! Are you freaking kidding me?"

"Come out here, you troublemaker," I called from the living room. "I'll show you the oldest thing in the joint."

She galloped into the room and skidded to a stop in front of me. "I *love* this fireplace. It looks like a bunch of Vikings are going to walk in and roast goats inside it."

"I've thought the exact same thing many times," I said.

"Really?"

"No," I admitted, and she laughed loudly. "But it really is a big fireplace."

I showed her an ancient urn my uncle had in a niche off the kitchen. "My knowledge of Roman history isn't so great, but that's got to be a thousand years old."

"Two thousand," Grace said, entering the room. "And it's Greek, not Roman."

"Know-it-all," Olivia said under her breath.

"Good thing Vicky put you in charge of the art," I said.

"Can I see you for a moment?" Grace said to her sister. The subtext was: *Get back here before I murder you in cold blood.*

Olivia pulled a face and followed her back to the office, where I could hear Grace whispering fiercely.

"Grace," I called when she'd stopped tearing into her sister. "Could I ask you a favor privately?"

She came out of the office looking like she might burst a

blood vessel. "Yes?" She wandered closer to me, and I reached out to take her hand. Grace balked, as if terrified that I'd do something untoward.

Since teasing Grace was like breathing for me, that only made me bolder, and I smoothed a hand down her shoulder to her waist and onto her hip. She glanced over her shoulder, biting her lip.

"Lady hasn't been out for a good walk today. What if I ask Olivia to walk her in the park while you finish up your work? She'd be helping me out, and I'd pay her, of course."

She squinted, as if trying to see through me. "Um. I suppose. She'll love the idea."

"But you don't?" I was starting to get the sense Grace and her sister didn't have a typical sibling relationship, and I didn't want to step on Grace's toes.

"It's fine." She tugged at the hand I was still holding. "Can you...?"

I let her go and she took a big step backward before glancing toward the study doorway again.

"What's wrong?" I asked.

"I don't want the third degree from my nosy little sister," she said.

I could understand that. I'd only met Olivia half an hour ago, and I already knew she'd be a tireless interrogator.

"Fair enough. I'll ask her now, before it gets too late."

"Thank you," she said, throwing me a small smile before disappearing into the office again.

Olivia came bounding out. As predicted, she loved the idea of walking Lady. "Do you need anything else while I'm out? Coffee? Tea? M—"

"*Olivia*," her sister warned.

"Some people have no sense of humor at all," she said. "Where's her leash?"

After the door closed on Olivia, I went to find Grace. She looked up from her work when I entered the room.

"I just realized—doesn't the co-op have dog walkers?" she asked.

"Maybe? I didn't check. But Lady needs a good run, and you looked like you needed some quiet."

Grace made a small noise that meant either *thank you* or *mind your own business*. One or the other. Then her phone rang, and she pounced on it. "Hello! Yes! Thank you for returning my call. I was hoping you could take a look tonight. Your partner said—okay, sure. I'll hold." She turned to me and mouthed, *Rare-book dealer*.

Ah. I waited.

"Okay, great. See you then." She hung up. "He's coming at seven thirty. Hope that doesn't cramp your style?"

"I'm Australian—I have no style." I moved some folders off the other side of the small leather sofa where Grace was seated. "But Lady told me she's having a party tonight. It could get crowded, but she'll clean up afterward."

"Bet she won't," Grace said, her eyes on the folder in her lap.

I sat down beside her. "Did you miss me today?"

She didn't look up from the file she was scanning. "It's not five yet."

"Flirting is allowed before the five o'clock cut off," I said, leaning close to kiss the soft-looking skin beneath her ear. Her skin smelled amazing—soap and perfume and Grace.

She angled her head away. "That's kissing, not flirting."

"You say tomato..."

I kissed her again, and this time I felt the little shiver that went through her.

"You didn't answer my question," I said.

"What question?" She sounded dazed, and her breathing was starting to get ragged.

Fuck, I loved how responsive this woman was. I slid my mouth upward until I could tug the small, juicy pad of her lobe into my mouth. I bit it gently, and she gasped.

"Did you miss me?" I asked.

"Yes," she said, as though the word had been dragged from her.

I soothed her earlobe with my tongue, then went exploring, trailing kisses across her collarbone. Even though I could feel her need rising with each passing second, she held herself stiffly until my kiss wandered hotly beneath the collar of her blouse. Then she seemed to melt into the furniture. "What are you doing?" she asked feebly.

"Nothing," I said between kisses. "Don't mind me." I undid one of her buttons and kissed the swell of her breast.

From this angle I could see the tight bud of her nipple beaded against the pale pink lace of her bra. My cock pressed against my zipper.

"We had a deal," she said. Then she pushed me away by the forehead.

I wasn't really surprised, since Olivia would return at some point and Grace was determined to be professional. Still, my cock gave a throb of disappointment. Like me, it was wild about Grace.

She pushed herself to her feet and quickly re-buttoned her shirt.

"You're breaking the terms of our agreement," she grumbled.

"It's not my fault you're irresistible," I said.

She gave me a scornful look, convinced I was using a well-worn line on her, but I meant every word. When it came to Grace, I couldn't get enough.

Not so long ago, that realisation would have had me on the first plane to somewhere with blue skies and girls in bikinis, but for some reason I was perfectly content with where I was right now, sharing a study with Grace.

"How long have you been taking care of Olivia by yourself?" I asked. It was a guess, but I was almost one hundred percent sure I was reading the vibe right.

She looked up quickly, a guarded expression on her face. "Did she *tell* you that?"

I shook my head. "No. But you seem pretty stressed out." I waited a beat. "Seems like a big job."

She sank onto the arm of the couch with a sigh. For the first time since I'd met her, she looked defeated.

"It's not something I talk about a lot. I don't have legal custody of her."

She shot me a look as though daring me to question her ability or authority where her sister was concerned.

"I'm guessing that makes a complicated situation even more complicated," I said. "How long has it been?"

If Grace's wary eyes hadn't already told me I was treading on delicate ground, her tense posture would have done the trick.

"It depends how you count," she said slowly. "When I started design school, my mother was more or less holding things together. By the time I finished the second year, things had gotten pretty bad."

"Drugs?" I asked, even though it felt as though I was intruding.

"Sure. And the unsavory dirtbags who provide them. I switched to a business program my second year, because I didn't think I could make it through design school before she imploded. And a few months in, Olivia called and asked if she could come and stay with me. It took me a long time to graduate because I had to work and study at the same time."

"Olivia's lucky to have you," I said.

Grace hadn't had an older sister to look to when things had gone to hell. She'd had to cope with every turd life threw her way on her own.

"She'd be even luckier if her mother wasn't a junkie and her father a piece of shit who disappeared when she was two."

Those things had happened to Grace, too. But I knew without asking that she didn't have a lot of sympathy to spare for herself. Grace was not a wallower; she was a fighter.

"How old is Olivia? Fourteen?"

"Fifteen going on thirty-five." There was weariness in her tone, but also a certain pride. I'd seen for myself that Olivia was a character.

Her phone buzzed on the coffee table. Guessing what it might be, I grabbed it before she could.

"A skinny-dipping shot. Nice. You can print this one out for your wallet." I pretended to study the image filling her phone screen.

She rolled her eyes.

"That shot doesn't really do my ass justice," I said. "I'm happy to stage a live reenactment any time you like, though."

I watched as the tension left her shoulders, her mouth lifting at the corners.

"Look at you, with your self-esteem issues," she said.

"I'm glad you can see I need help."

She stood and looked at her watch. "Four thirty. Still too early for what you're thinking."

"Put me to work, then. Where are we up to?"

"All of those need to be taped up for the couriers coming tomorrow morning," she said, indicating a stack of archive boxes I'd already been through with a fine-tooth comb.

"Consider it done."

———

Olivia came back with Lady as I was taping down the lid on the last box.

"We did a lap of the bridle path and I swear she smelled every single tree."

"I forgot to mention she has a tree fetish. Thanks for indulging her," I said, passing her a ten-dollar bill.

"Thanks!" she said, eyes bright. "I'm available to walk her at any time. Just say the word. Day or night."

Like I said, a character.

"Noted."

She turned toward the study. "Grace! Isn't it time for dinner? I'm starved," she hollered.

"I have to wait for the rare-book dealer," Grace called back.

Olivia made a disgruntled sound. "Fine. If you give me your MetroCard, I'll head home."

"You have ten bucks in your hand," Grace said, appearing in the doorway. "Use that, or wait for me."

"This is extra money. I'm saving this for a rainy day."

"Your choice," Grace said with a supremely indifferent shrug I guessed had been honed in the fires of many a sisterly argument.

Olivia gave her sister an evil look. "I guess I'll wait."

She walked over to a plush rug in front of Jack's monstrous fireplace and sat down. Lady trotted over and rolled onto her back beside Olivia, offering her belly.

It was heading toward six o'clock. So I went into the kitchen and opened Jack's menu drawer, which I'd found last week. There were so many menus the drawer didn't close easily. I sifted through them until I found the one for pizza. Everyone liked pizza, right?

I ordered two large pies and a family-sized salad. For the first time since I'd landed in New York, I would not dine alone.

When the food showed up, I called the two of them into the dining room, where I'd set the Biedermeier table with plates and paper napkins and water glasses. Grace stopped on the threshold, taking in the scene with a worried frown.

"You unpacked the plates as well?" she asked.

"We can eat directly off the table if you like...?"

She gave me a look.

"Yum, pizza." Olivia brushed past her sister, racing to pull out a seat.

"Thank you," Grace said quietly, making a point of catching my eye.

Olivia ate like a wolf after a hunt. Maybe all teenagers are good eaters, but she seemed especially gleeful. "We can never get pizza. I love this." Then, "Ouch."

I guessed Grace had just kicked her under the table.

"Salad?" I asked, ignoring the family drama. "This would all be better with a bit of grapey red wine..." I got up and found a bottle. I opened it and poured two glasses.

"Where did you get that?" Grace asked.

"Leftovers from the catering," I promised her. "Even I wouldn't open a Chateau Lafite-Rothschild with pizza, O'Malley."

The corners of Grace's mouth turned up, and I caught myself smiling at her until I noticed Olivia staring at us.

Whoops.

Olivia's phone rang in her pocket. After checking the number, she jumped out of her chair and left the dining room. "Hello?" she said from the distant foyer.

A little food had made Grace look more serene than usual, so I moved my chair closer to hers. When she turned to see what I was about, I closed my eyes and kissed her. She tasted of red wine, and I couldn't get enough.

"Errhmph," she said against my lips. But then she opened to me and our tongues tangled.

This woman. I couldn't stop thinking about her.

She pulled back suddenly, her cheeks pink. "Olivia."

"She's as light-footed as a rhino." There was no way we'd miss her coming back. Grace looked tense, though, so I moved my chair a respectable distance away. I figured she had enough stress in her life without me adding to it.

"I met some of the Robinson kids today," I told her.

"Did you?" She took a sip of wine, looking like a movie starlet with her red suit and her red wine and those kissable lips.

I leaned forward as if pulled by a magnet. "Most of these kids are homeless before they find the place. Thrown out by their parents when they're Olivia's age. Did you know that perhaps forty percent of homeless teens are LGBT?"

"No." Grace tucked her perfect cheek into her hand, her big brown eyes on me as she waited for more.

Her attention made me feel giddy. "I want to do this, Grace. I want to make that Center happen."

"You're cute when you're all fired up," she whispered.

Olivia's voice could be heard drifting in our direction again, saying goodnight to her caller.

The moment was broken, so I got up to pack away the leftovers.

———

Grace

The rare-book dealer was a half hour late. But when the man arrived, he was sharp and focused on the task, making assessments and taking down information at lightning speed.

He reminded me of me. Or rather—the old me. The new Grace kept sneaking looks at Callan, half listening to the book dealer. My libido was suddenly stuck in the "on" position. I was supposed to be listening to an explanation about Dickens volumes and instead I wanted to scale Callan like a tree.

Forty minutes later the book dealer was on his way out again, promising to call me tomorrow with an outline for a plan of action for Jack's collection.

"Can we please go home now?" Olivia begged. "My homework has been done for hours."

"The TV-withdrawal symptoms are kicking in hard, huh?" I teased her.

"I'll drive you," Callan said pulling his keys from his pocket.

"You really don't have to do that," I argued immediately. He sure as hell couldn't spend the night, if that's what he was thinking.

He held up the keys. "It's just a ride, O'Malley. It would be

189

nice to get out of the house for an hour. You've kept me slaving away since late afternoon. I'm not used to so much hard labor." *Lay-bah.* "My usual workday is approximately twenty minutes, give or take."

We both knew his playboy routine was an act, and I rolled my eyes.

He turned to my sister. "You are going to love this car," he said, heading for the door.

She followed him like a goddamn puppy, and I gave up the argument.

I let Olivia take the front seat. Not only did it make her happy, but it let Callan know which one of us he was humoring right now. His generosity tonight was so lovely, but I didn't want to get used to it, and I really didn't want my sister to get used to it. She'd been very attached to Marcus, and we'd both been left with broken hearts when he left.

This little fling between Callan and I was going to be as fleeting as a firework on the Fourth of July. Loud and bright and wonderful. Then gone in an instant.

As predicted, Olivia oohed and ahhed over the car, marveling at its retro cool. Since it was already nine o'clock, the traffic moved well and only became stop-and-go through the Times Square district.

I so rarely saw this over-bright part of the city. New Yorkers knew to avoid it. We traveled underground, past the blinking chaos, the buskers, and the tourist foot traffic. But tonight I relaxed against the old upholstery and let myself be briefly dazzled by the shimmering lights.

Tonight I was a tourist in Callan Walker's life, and it was a fine place to be. He and Olivia chattered in the front seat while I floated happily along behind them.

Inevitably we pulled up in front of our building. I cringed inwardly as he looked up at awful little building. And then I cringed outwardly when our skanky neighbor emerged from the front door and lit up a cigarette.

"Oh goody," Olivia grumbled. "Just who we need to run into."

"Is he a problem?" Callan asked, killing the engine.

"No," I said at the same moment Olivia said, "Yes."

"He's our neighbor," Liv explained. "Most of the time he's drunk. He plays loud music half the night. And last week he got all up in my face. Wouldn't let me go up the stairs until I answered his questions."

This was news to me and my spine chilled. "What kind of questions?"

"Did I have a boyfriend. And when I said no, he said it was a waste."

"And then what happened?" I asked, even though I'd prefer to have this conversation without Callan listening in.

"The mailman opened the front door, and Mr. Skank gave up and went inside his own place."

"You have to be fucking kidding me." Callan opened the door and climbed out.

"There's a hydrant," I pointed out, scrambling after him. "You can't park here."

But Callan didn't listen. He stalked toward Mr. Skank. Before I could stop her, Olivia jumped out, too.

"Hey baby," our awful neighbor said with a smirk as he eyed my sister. "Got a boyfriend after all? Nice car. Bet that back seat sees some action."

Callan moved so fast I didn't even register it. One minute he was standing a few feet in front of me on the sidewalk. The next he'd shoved Mr. Skank up against the wall, a forearm at his throat, one knee in his groin. "Don't touch her. Don't talk to her. Don't make eye contact with her."

Mr. Skank made a choking sound.

"She's a minor. Anything happens to her I'll send the police right to the door of your shithole."

Later I would remember that Callan could make even the word "shithole" sound exotic. But as this went down, I was terrified. My heart crawled into my throat and I choked on the warning I wanted to give him.

Callan stepped back as quickly as he'd attacked, leaving Mr. Skank to double over, his cigarette falling to the sidewalk, where Callan ground it out.

"Ladies," he said tersely. "He speaks to you again, let me know. Day or night."

"That was *so* hot," Olivia whispered, gaping.

My jaw was still somewhere in the vicinity of my ankles.

"I'll walk you upstairs," Callan said.

That jolted me into action. I didn't particularly want to share the sorry details of our living space with him. "You can't leave the c-car," I stammered. "Thank you for the r-ride home."

"My pleasure."

Mr. Skank stayed there—his butt parked against the wall, his head dropped in defeat.

Olivia unlocked the door, gave a cheerful wave to Callan, and carried the leftover pizza upstairs.

I followed her at a brisk pace.

An hour later I found a text on my phone. *Are you okay? I meant what I said. If he bothers you I want to know. I'll rip his head right off.*

Was it wrong of me to feel a shimmy of desire? My inner feminist loved to take care of situations like this herself. But my inner bad girl would have liked to jump on his dick in gratitude.

I didn't take you for the physical type, I replied, trying to lighten the tone.

Usually I'm manhandling cattle, not wankers. But the moves are the same.

I doubted that. But any more chatter about Callan manhandling things was going to get me even more hot and bothered than I already was. *Thanks for the show of force. Olivia really appreciates it.*

You can thank me in person tomorrow. After hours, of course. Or before work? Maybe I'll sleep naked and pray for the sound of your key in the lock at seven thirty.

Great, now I was going to picture naked Callan all night long. *Good night*, I said to excuse myself before I lost control and typed something risqué.

Night O'Malley.

EIGHTEEN

Sleep Starkers

Callan

I DID SLEEP STARKERS. Because a man can dream.

But before I went to bed, I wandered around Jack's apartment feeling lonely. Grace took such good care of her sister. Even if Olivia made her crazy, there was a closeness there that was unfamiliar to me.

My own sister was nearly ten thousand miles away. But I knew in my gut that the miles between us weren't really the issue. In the war between my mother and I, everyone must choose a side. Claire was still at university when I broke with my mother. I'd made no space for half measures. My struggle was black and white.

Or so I'd thought.

The result was that I had a sister I barely knew. I was five years older than Claire, and had made myself scarce these last few years. Even if she'd wanted a relationship with me, I hadn't exactly made it easy.

There's something about a death that makes you aware of your own petty follies. With Lady on my heels, I scanned Uncle Jack's collection of photographs for clues to what to do. What to think.

Not every photograph had made it onto the windowsill for his memorial party. One of the ones left on the wall in the hallway was of my sister and Jack in Central Park, smiling at the camera. They were sharing a hot pretzel. Claire had a balloon tied to her wrist. She must have been about six at the time. I'd taken the picture myself.

I turned the hall light on to get a better look at it. And then I snapped a picture of it with my phone and, before I could think better of it, I texted it to Claire. Hopefully she wouldn't take it as a comment on her behavior, but rather a friendly gesture.

Maybe it was the loneliness talking, but I missed what Grace and Olivia had—a partnership.

It got late, and I got too broody. So I finally went to bed.

———

I woke up the next morning when Grace sat down on the bed. Without opening my eyes I reached for her.

She kissed me once on the forehead. "It's ten to nine. I already took Lady outside to pee. Get up already."

"Mmm," I said, pulling her down on top of me. "Show me some skin, and I'll be up in no time."

She slapped my shoulder. "That's not what I meant. Business hours start in ten minutes. No—nine."

"I'll work fast," I mumbled, kissing her neck. "Take pity on a man, O'Malley."

"You don't need my pity."

She sounded determined, and I knew I should let her go. I couldn't resist the weight of her on my body, though. I hugged her close.

"Your phone was ringing when I walked through the living

room," she said, propping herself up on an elbow. "What if it's another donor trying to give money to the Robinson Center?"

I groaned with frustration. "I don't want to talk to donors right now. I'd rather do the donating." I lifted my hips to give her a sample.

She looked away, taking a steadying breath. "Callan. Stop tempting me."

"Fine." I sighed. "But I really need to get you alone for a night."

"We can't always have the things we want," she said simply. Then she kissed me quickly and walked out. "I'm turning on the espresso machine," she said from the hallway.

"Uh, we might be out of milk. Decadence requires a trip to the grocery."

"I brought some," came the answer from elsewhere in the apartment.

Jumping into my jeans, I smiled to myself. Typical Grace, always on top of the details. Still pulling on my shirt, I headed for the kitchen. But when I spotted my phone on the sofa, I made a detour to grab it. If I couldn't have a tumble in the sheets with Grace, I supposed a new donation was the next best thing.

"Hmm," I said, noting the last number to call me. "My sister left a message. I may need coffee before I can handle hearing what she has to say."

Grace got the cups off the drying rack and set them on the counter. We'd come a long way from the morning when she'd been scandalized that I'd use Jack's machine.

"Fuck it. How bad could it be?" I hit the button to play Claire's message, setting it to speaker so that I could pour coffee beans into the grinder at the same time.

"Hey." My sister's voice sounded far more tentative than usual. "I've been thinking about what you said. You were right, I was out of line. I shouldn't have said that about Uncle Jack, and it's not what I think or feel. But that doesn't mean you're right about everything. Anyway, I remembered something, and I thought it might put your mind at ease to check it out. Uncle Jack has a safe in his closet. I used to play with it when Mum brought me to visit. I pretended I was discovering ancient mysteries in there..." She sighed through the speaker, and it sounded like a great gust. "Anyway. You probably know about it already, but it occurred to me that maybe you don't, so... Look after yourself. And please don't throw out that photo you sent. I'd really love to have it."

She may have said a few more words after that, but I didn't hear them. Grace and I were staring at each other with wide eyes. For a long beat we just stood there, jaws slackened by surprise. The words "*a safe*" hung there in the kitchen, stunning us.

Then I gathered my wits and ran out of the room. Grace was right on my heels. We tore past the great Viking fireplace, causing Lady to bark with excitement. The sound of toenails on the wood floor told me that she'd added herself to the exploration party.

Jack's room was dark, as it faced the back of the building. I threw on the light switch and darted for the closet.

"I was going to clean out this room last," Grace said as I opened the door. "I thought it would be the least important."

"No kidding." I'd been avoiding it as much as I could. Too much of Jack in here.

When I flipped on the closet light, all we saw were rows of clothing. I'd opened this closet a couple of times to borrow clothes—the jacket for the cool weather, and a tie for the memorial. The space had been set up to maximize clothing storage, and Jack's wardrobe hung neatly on all three sides of the little room.

Quickly, Grace and I began lifting hangers off the double-height racks, checking the walls behind them.

I saw nothing but plaster.

"Omigod, these silk fabrics," Grace breathed. She'd found Jack's smoking-jacket collection.

But I'd spotted something. So I lifted an armload of clothes off the rack and handed the whole lot to her.

And there it was—a metal safe, bolted into the wall. It had a keypad lock.

Grace sent up a cheer. She disappeared for a moment—probably to lay the clothing on the bed. "Any guesses at the combination?"

I was already kneeling down, tapping in a combination. "Jack's birthday didn't work," I said a moment later, when the safe failed to open. "But that was probably too obvious, anyway. And I don't know Danny's birthday off the top of my head..."

"Try yours," Grace said.

"Mine?"

"You're his closest relative, the son he never had."

I blinked, my throat suddenly tight.

"Try it," Grace said gently.

I tapped it in and held my breath. After what seemed like a very long time the safe made a single beep and the door clicked open.

"Eeep!" Grace said, her hand on my head. "How smart am I? Maybe I should be a private investigator."

I nudged the door aside. The interior of the safe was smaller than I'd expected. Inside was a stack of very few items. Jack's passport on top. Then a thin envelope marked simply "Insurance." Under that, another envelope—fat and unsealed—containing a pile of various currencies—Euros and Aussie dollars, primarily. He must have stored that money for convenience of travel overseas.

I reached for the final envelope with a shaking hand. It was labeled, "In the event of my death."

"You found it," Grace whispered, dropping to her knees beside me on the closet floor.

Grief picked that moment to hit me hard. *In the event of my death.* "Fuck." I just stared at those words, which Jack had printed in a tidy hand one day when he was feeling fine. Had the possibility seemed remote to him that day? Or was he smarter than I would ever be? I'd just been drifting through my life, trying not to feel anything too deeply.

Wordlessly, I passed the envelope to Grace. I needed a moment to take a deep breath.

She put a fingernail under the flap and opened it carefully. Then she slid out several sheets of paper folded together. She cleared her throat. "'The last will and testament of Jack Lang Walker. Executed on April seventeenth, 2015.' There's a list of witnesses, including the lawyer."

Flipping the page, she read on. "You're named as the executor, like he said." She offered me the pages.

I took them and began scanning. I recognized the lawyer's name from my invite list to the memorial. That begged investigation. Where the hell was he? Why hadn't he contacted us the moment he learned of Jack's death?

Skimming the will, I saw that Jack hadn't wavered from the ideas he'd floated in his conversation with me all those years ago. All his assets were meant to endow a charitable organization that would carry on his good work. *The executor may exercise his discretion at the speed and order of selling art and other properties for raising cash.*

In other words, I could take my bloody time.

The last page was handwritten, which surprised me until I saw what it was. A letter from Jack to me. *My Dear Callan*, he wrote.

Fucking hell. My eyes got hot just reading my own name.

If you're reading this, then I've reached the end of the line. I hope you aren't too irritated that I've made you the executor of my will. I wasn't joking when I threatened it. And it gets worse, kiddo. I want you to actually manage my foundation. If you loathe this idea, you can hire someone after the foundation is funded. But please consider the job. I know you'd be bloody good at it. You are such a capable, loving man, and I fear nobody in your life tells you that as often as they should.

The words got blurry.

Grace removed the pages from my hand. Then she climbed into my lap and hugged me. "He loved you so much."

I nodded, my chin on her shoulder.

"You were right the whole time. The Robinson Center is going to get their renovation now. Gavin will be so relieved."

That was all true, but nothing could make up for the fact that Jack Lang Walker no longer lived and breathed. His laughter and brashness were gone from the world, never to return. I would never again feel the wiry strength of his arms around me as he kissed me hello. I would never again receive one of his pithy emails.

It wasn't like any of this was news to me—after the memorial, the reality of Jack's death had been set in stone. But reading Jack's last letter had brought home that the one person who had always believed in me and loved me unconditionally was gone, and it fucking hurt.

Grief—the gift that just keeps on giving.

"I am going to miss him so much," I said, my voice thick with emotion.

Grace didn't say a word, her arms tightening around me. She was so good and warm and real. So strong and determined. It was a constant wonder to me that so much grit and guts could be contained in her slim form.

The day we met, I'd been disgusted by my mother hiring a temp to dispose of Jack's life. Now I understood that hiring Grace had been her greatest gift to me. My mother didn't know it, but she had changed my whole outlook on life.

Overwhelmed by grief and gratitude, loss and lust, I found Grace's mouth with my own. She opened beneath me and I stroked my tongue into her mouth. God, she tasted so good. Fisting my hands in her shirt, I pulled her closer, losing myself in the sweet heat inside her.

Very quickly it wasn't enough. It never was with Grace. I tugged her shirt free from her skirt, sliding my hands beneath it.

Warm, silky skin, the ragged expansion and contraction of her ribcage, the thump of her heartbeat, the smooth satin and lace of her bra... I groaned, already hard as a rock, need tightening my balls. Grace responded by breaking our kiss, pulling back a few inches so she could see my face.

I waited for her to tell me we were breaking the rules, but she simply gave me a small smile before reaching for her top button. So much compassion and heat in her eyes... She understood I needed this, and she wanted to give it to me.

Pure Grace, generous to a fault.

The moment her shirt slid down her arms to the floor, I reached for the clasp on her bra. Her breasts tumbled free, her nipples already puckered with desire. The lace had left a faint imprint on her skin and I cupped her in both hands and soothed her flesh with my thumbs. She gave a little shudder, her hands tightening on my shoulders.

The urge to bury myself inside her and seek the oblivion of release was like a hand gripping the base of my skull, but I didn't want to rush this. I wanted to prolong her pleasure as long as I could. I wanted to push the outside world away and lose myself in her arms.

Ducking my head, I pulled a nipple into my mouth and bit it gently. She shifted in my lap, grinding her ass down onto my cock. I sucked firmly on the hard peak and she made a guttural noise, the sound so primal I felt myself grow even harder.

I devoted myself to her breasts for long minutes, biting and licking and sucking, my hands mapping the smooth skin of her back and sides, tracking the soft undercurve of her breast, exploring the tender hollows beneath her arms.

I lost myself in worshipping her, adoring her, and only when she was trembling and pleading for me to give her release did I lower her to the carpet and push up her skirt. Her panties were visibly damp with want for me, a discovery that almost made me disgrace myself. Unable to resist, I lowered my head and pressed my face into the wet silk of her panties.

Her fingers wove into my hair as I nudged her sex with first my nose, then my chin. Then I reached for the waistband of her panties and dragged them down her legs. When she was bare to me, I kissed her smooth inner thighs and lost myself in the intimate valleys of her flesh. She quivered and bucked beneath me, and just when I could feel her starting to fall apart, she used the hands fisted in my hair to pull me away.

"I want you inside me when I come," she said.

It was what I wanted, too, more than anything, and I fumbled at my waistband to loosen my belt before attacking my fly. I kicked my jeans off, only remembering the condom in the back pocket at the last second. The foil packet shook in my hands as I tore it open. I lifted my gaze to Grace's as I smoothed the latex down my shaft and caught her watching what I was doing with an avid, greedy intensity.

I took myself in hand and moved over her. She spread her legs wide to accommodate me, one hand reaching to wrap around my hips before settling on my backside, drawing me closer still. I notched my aching cock into place, ready to begin the sweet slide inside her. Then I paused, making conscious note of the moment. Of the way she looked, sprawled beneath me in pink, panting abandon.

This is what salvation looks like.

It was the last thought I had before I plunged inside her.

———

Grace

The first slide of Callan's cock inside me was so needful, so necessary I almost came on the spot. Pure greed held me back—I wanted this to last and last. I wanted to wring every last second of pleasure from being in Callan's arms.

Especially since there was a very high likelihood it might be the last time.

But I didn't want to think about any of that, I just wanted to feel. And so I did. I traced the broad width of his shoulders with my hands. I tasted his mouth, his neck, the skin of his chest. I tested the resilience of his ass muscles as he pumped into me. I wrapped my legs around his hips and lifted mine to meet each of his thrusts, maximizing the friction between us. When he lowered his head to my breasts, I keened my pleasure, unable to express it any other way.

My climax took me in great pulsing waves, radiating out from my core, taking over my body. My back arched, my thighs tightened. I gasped out Callan's name and a dozen filthy words of praise for what he did to me and how he made me feel.

He came mere seconds after me, his mouth finding mine in a hard, demanding kiss. The shudders that ripped through him were seismic, almost violent, and when it was over he collapsed on top of me before wrapping me in his arms and rolling to one side.

We lay panting on the carpet for a long time, our bodies still locked together intimately. I felt him grow soft within me, and, when he finally moved, the loss as he slid free made me murmur a protest. He soothed me with tiny kisses across my cheeks, his hands smoothing up and down my back.

"You're amazing," he said. "Thank you."

His words made my eyes feel hot. I'd fought a losing battle with my desire for this man every step of the way, but I refused to lose the final battle. I couldn't give him my heart. I couldn't afford to, and I told myself that it was a good thing that finding Jack's will meant that I no longer had a job. This was the last time I would lie in his arms and feel as though I was home.

The distant sound of a phone ringing drew a curtain on our timeout. I stirred in his arms, recognizing the ring-tone.

"That's Stephen," I said.

I had enough integrity left to feel a hot rush of self-consciousness as I disentangled my limbs from Callan's. I was pretty sure Victoria Walker wasn't paying me fifteen bucks an hour to receive mind-bending orgasms from her estranged son, and even though getting naked with Callan had felt necessary half an hour ago, right now it felt as though I'd crossed a line.

It doesn't matter. It's all over, anyway, I realized. My shot at impressing the New York branch of Walker Holdings was about to come to an end once Queen Vic heard about what we'd just found in Jack's safe.

"He can wait," Callan said as I threaded my arms through the straps of my bra and hastily did up the back clasp.

I let the call go to voicemail. But my face must have given me away, because Callan reached out to catch my hand. "All good, O'Malley?"

"Yes. Have you thought about what you're going to do next?"

"Well, I was a little preoccupied just now," he said, his mouth curving into a knowing smile.

He was so irresistible I found myself smiling back. Like a doofus.

"But you must have a plan," I said, determined not to be distracted. "You've been looking for the will for nearly two weeks now." I didn't believe for a second that he didn't have a strategy mapped out in advance.

"True." He pushed himself to his feet and turned toward the bathroom, presumably to do something with the condom. "First port of call is contacting Jack's lawyer. Before I talk to Vicky, I want to know why he hasn't come forward."

I watched his perfect ass disappear into the en suite bathroom.

"Maybe he hasn't heard about Jack's death," I called.

"I invited him to the memorial," Callan explained as he returned to the room.

Huh.

"Then I'm out of guesses," I said.

"Me, too." He pulled his jeans on and a part of me noted that this was probably the last time I'd have the pleasure of watching him dress. And it was a pleasure—the ripple of muscles, the interplay of tendon and sinew. He was beautiful.

"No time like the present, I guess," he said, and I blinked at him, momentarily forgetting what we'd been talking about.

The power of hormones.

Then he reached for the will and I remembered. He found the page with the law firm's contact details, and I crossed my arms over my chest as he punched the number into his phone.

"Good morning. I'd like to speak to Richard Trask, please." His tone was business-like and crisp. If only they could see him, standing barefoot in nothing but his jeans.

"I see. In that case, I'm going to need to talk to someone else in the practice." Callen watched me as he talked, his expression giving nothing away.

I fidgeted impatiently as Callan explained the situation, then I heard the distinct sound of hold music.

"He's on paternity leave," Callan explained the moment he was free to do so.

"And not screening his email, apparently," I said.

"Yeah. I think— That's right, Callan Walker. My late uncle Jack Walker was a client of Richard Trask's, and I'm trying to verify the status of a will I've found amongst his papers."

There was more back and forth, then I saw Callan's shoulders drop and I knew he had the confirmation he needed. Jack's will was legitimate and sound, which meant Callan now had the authority to take over the management of Jack's estate.

He ended the call and we looked at each other.

"Are you going to call her now?" I asked.

He checked the time. "It's past midnight over there."

"So I guess we have to wait until tonight." Was it selfish of me to be relieved that the time difference meant I'd have another full day's pay in my pocket before my job went poof?

"She's probably awake. She barely sleeps," he said.

I watched as he tapped in a text message to his mother. *Need to talk about something important. You still up?*

Callan's phone started ringing almost immediately, and I could tell from his face who it was.

"Do you want me to go?" I asked, because the likelihood of things getting ugly was pretty high.

"No, stay. You may need to throw a bucket of cold water on me." He took the call, lifting the handset to his ear. "Thanks for getting back to me so quickly."

There was a great deal of careful reserve in his tone.

"You said it was important," Victoria Walker said, her voice clear despite the fact Callan wasn't using the speaker function. The woman was loud.

"It is. While going through the Jack's files today, I found a more recent will. I've checked with Jack's lawyers, and they've confirmed it was properly executed about two years ago."

There was a long, long pause. I imagined his mother sitting up in bed, trying to absorb this new twist.

"I'll need a copy of the new document," she finally said.

"I'll ask the law firm to send you a copy straightaway. But I can tell you the relevant bits. Jack named me executor, and he leaves his estate to fund a charitable foundation to continue his philanthropic work."

Another pause, this one much shorter.

"My legal team will go over everything first thing."

"It's legitimate. There's no doubt about that," Callan said stiffly.

"We're talking about a great deal of money, Callan, not to mention shares in Walker Holdings. I wouldn't be doing my job as head of the family or the business if I didn't do due diligence on this new document."

I hadn't taken my eyes of Callan's face and I saw the small, cynical quirk to his lips.

"You do whatever you need to do, Vicky. But you can't steamroll Jack's wishes. I'm hitting pause on all the auctions you've set up until I can be sure I've maximized the value of his estate for its charitable purposes."

"Now hang on a moment," Victoria Walker said, her voice even louder. "I see no reason to halt progress until the will has been validated."

Callan's jaw worked. "There's no way you're picking holes in this thing. It would be a huge waste of Jack's resources to have to go to court, but I will if that's necessary."

"You always jump to the most dramatic possible conclusion, don't you? I simply want to ensure Jack wasn't taken advantage of in any way. It's my last act for him."

There was a distinct crack of emotion in Victoria Walker's voice and for a moment Callan seemed nonplussed. "You can talk yourself into anything, can't you? But if you knew Jack at all, you'd understand this document reflects his wishes far more than the piece of outdated crap you've been working from," Callan said.

The crispness was back in his mother's voice when she spoke again. "You'll be hearing from my lawyers."

There was silence on the other end as she ended the call, and Callan made a rude noise before sliding the phone into his back pocket. "I wonder how many times Vicky has said that over the years?"

I rested a hand on his bare chest. His heart was pumping speedily, a reflection of his heightened state.

"Do me a favor and take a deep breath," I said.

He looked into my eyes and did as I asked before letting it out again.

"Better?" I asked.

He nodded. "Yeah, thanks. She just gets me worked up."

"I get it. But you've won, Callan. You've got the power to enact Jack's wishes now."

"It's going to take a while for that to sink in. I was starting to think I'd never find this bloody will."

He contemplated the document in his hand, and I knew his formidable brain had kicked into gear.

"I should go see this mob today, if I can. And go through this document with a fine-tooth comb so I know what's what."

"Okay..." My mind was already jumping ahead a few hours. I needed to let the temp agency know I was available again, so they could reassign me. Maybe the next company on the list would be the magic one.

"Coffee," Callan said suddenly. "We didn't get our coffee."

"What?"

"I can see your wheels turning. And that's not healthy if you're under-caffeinated." He slipped my hand into his and gave me a gentle tug toward the kitchen.

Following him was easy. After all, this was probably my last decadent latte with Callan Walker.

The thought made my chest tight, even though I'd been anticipating this moment from the start. We had always been temporary. No one had made any promises or commitments. Saying goodbye had been inevitable.

And yet despite all that excellent pragmatism, I was finding it hard to maintain my equilibrium as I watched him tamp down the grounds, muscles flexing in his forearm.

I had worked so hard to go into this fling with him with my eyes open, but it hadn't stopped me from liking him more than was wise. And I did like him, so much. His wit, his cheeky sense of humor, his generous heart... The way he'd fought so hard for Jack had won my admiration, and the more I'd learned about him and his fractured, toxic childhood, the more I'd come to understand just how much of a miracle it was that he was as warm and personable and good as he was. No one knew better than me how hard it was to rise above a shitty beginning to forge your own path.

Maybe that was why I'd gravitated to him so powerfully. Maybe, right from the start, we had recognized the damage and determination in each other. Maybe that was why being with him felt so right.

I gave myself a mental shake as he handed me my latte. This was not the time to dwell on our connection, not when we were on the verge of ending it. There would be plenty of time for that sort of maudlin self-indulgence later.

When he was gone.

The coffee was as spectacular as always. Everything about Callan Walker was a little more glamorous than what I was used to. A little brighter, a little more perfect. I was never going to forget this brief moment when we'd enjoyed each other's company so thoroughly.

He smiled at me over the rim of his cup. "What are you thinking about so hard, O'Malley?"

I didn't get to answer because my phone began ringing. It was the same ring tone I'd heard a few minutes ago. But when I glanced at the screen, the caller was Australian. "It's your mother," I blurted.

My goodness, she was quick off the mark. But why pay me for another second when my services were now superfluous? I answered the call, because putting off bad news wouldn't make it go away. "Hello, this is Grace Kerrington."

"Miss Kerrington, are you alone?"

I flicked a look at Callan, who nodded.

"Um. Yes." I took a few steps away from Callan to make it less of a lie. "How can I help you?" I asked, basically inviting the woman to fire me.

"A complication has come up."

That was an understatement. But correcting her was really none of my business. "I'm sorry to hear that."

"My son is making trouble for me. I fear his grief has got the best of him and he's meddling in my brother's estate. I need you to keep an eye on him."

"W-what?" I was so startled she hadn't fired me yet that it

took me a long moment to figure out she was asking me to spy on Callan instead.

Callan, on the other hand, had both heard her and understood the request. He'd moved to stand right over my shoulder, probably so he could hear every word said. And now he was nodding his head vigorously. *Say yes,* he mouthed.

"You want me to..." Was there even a polite way to put it?

"Pay attention to his actions," his mother said firmly. "I want to know who he's talking to, who he's meeting with. Anything you can tell me, so I can attempt damage control."

"Okay...?" Callan was still nodding like a bobble-head doll.

"Thank you. I'll call you tomorrow. In the meantime, if you have anything in particular to report, please use my email address."

There was a click. She disconnected the call.

"Callan, what the hell?"

He looked grim. "My loving mother. Unafraid to show her true colors. Un-fucking-believable."

"I can't believe I just put myself right in the middle of the Walker family shitstorm."

He winced. "But only temporarily. Now you're fighting on the side of good rather than evil, even if evil pays your wages for a few more days."

"No, it doesn't. I'm calling the temp agency and telling them this job is done, and that they can add me to the list of workers who need an assignment."

He frowned. "You don't need another assignment—I need you here. I'll transfer the job to my own tab if it bothers you that much. Finding the will doesn't mean you're out on your ear."

"I can't work for you," I said.

"Why not?"

"Because we just did it on the floor in your uncle's bedroom!"

"And?"

"And I'm not sleeping with my boss. It was bad enough when I was working for your mother's company, but this takes it into *Pretty Woman* territory."

"Whoa. Are you kidding me?" he asked. He looked genuinely perplexed.

"I wish I was. And don't bother telling me you won't sleep with me during office hours because we both know I have no willpower where you're concerned, today being a perfect example of that. You wound up with your face in my panties at nine thirty this morning."

He made a rude noise. "Neither of us was really committed to that deal."

I widened my eyes and made an outraged noise. "Excuse me?"

"Okay, maybe you were committed to it, but I wasn't. But I promise I will be this time. No flirting, no touching, no eye-fucking, no dirty-talk between nine and five. And that includes lunch."

He stuck his hand out, waiting for me to agree. I stared at his clever, long-fingered hand and knew we'd both be fooling ourselves if I shook it.

"Be honest—if I took my shirt off right now you'd do me right here on the butcher's block."

He closed his eyes briefly, looking pained. "Grace, come on. Fight fair."

"I rest my case."

"We can do this," he said. "We'll fuck each other ragged at night, and by day we'll be consummate professionals. We can make this work, Grace. I'm not letting you go. I promised that you wouldn't be worse off if I found the will and I meant it."

"I'm not your responsibility. And there are other jobs out there," I said, hoping I was telling the truth. But the sooner I started looking, the better.

"But there aren't other temps out there who know the contents of this apartment inside out. There's no one who has spent as many hours as you have cataloguing Jack's estate. I need you, Grace. If you run out of here right now, all the inventory work you've done will be wasted. I'll have to start over. That's not helpful to the Robinson Center, is it?"

Oh, the man fought dirty. "Well..."

"Help me," he pleaded, a pitiable expression on his handsome face. "For a little while. Then, if you still decide you're uncomfortable, we'll revisit the problem."

"Okay," I said quietly. "But this business with Vicky makes me uncomfortable. I'm not going to pretend to spy on you."

He put a hand on my back and rubbed. "I don't like making you uncomfortable. I like making you moan my name."

"Callan!"

"Teasing, O'Malley. The moment you decide that you can't deal with Vicky any longer, I'll be fine with it. All right? I was just hoping to get a lead on her strategy, before she loses my phone number." *Numbah*.

This man would be the death of me.

———

I spent the rest of the day with Jack Walker's clothing, folding the shirts and casualwear into boxes. This was my gift to Callan. Taking the clothes out of the drawers of someone who wouldn't ever need them again was sad work, and I didn't want him to have to do it.

Callan spent the day at the lawyer's office and with Gavin from the Robinson Center. And if Vicky called to ask me about him, that's exactly what I planned to say.

At lunchtime I walked Lady in the park and bought myself some soup from a deli. Big splurge. But I was feeling somber, and it was cold, and I couldn't face another peanut butter sandwich.

Callan came through the door at five thirty, in high spirits. The first thing he did was kiss me. The second thing he did was invite me to dinner. "We need to celebrate. And you'll be off the clock, O'Malley. I can't think of a reason you could object."

"Olivia," I said, giving him my one-word reason.

"Oh, please." He made a comical face of dismissal. "She's obviously invited. We're dining at Le Petit Cochon in an hour. Get her on the horn and tell her to meet us there."

I wavered for about ten seconds. Olivia would be thrilled to eat dinner with Callan in a fancy restaurant. And, as he pointed out, I was off the clock. Even as the hourglass of our time together ran out forever.

Easy decision, then.

An hour later, I was seated by a maître d' with movie star looks in a chair more comfortable than any I owned. Olivia beamed at me from across the table, where she'd snagged the seat beside Callan's. The restaurant managed to appear both luxurious and spare at the same time, with leather chairs and sleek maple dining tables.

The waitstaff were dressed head-to-toe in black. And the kitchen crew toiled at the far end of the room, visible through an arched opening. It was meant to show off the enormous wood-fired grill, where orange flames licked away any ill feelings the patrons might have brought through the door.

This was what New York money looked like these days. Not ornate, but each dish on the menu had sixteen ingredients and a double-digit price tag. The first appetizer listed was a carrot and ginger soup. The carrots were from a small farm on the banks of the Hudson River, and the ginger was from the restaurant's own hydroponic farm on the roof.

It was nineteen dollars.

I made an effort to shrug off my low mood as Callan's feet found mine beneath the table. This was a celebration, after all. I slipped off my shoe and rubbed the arch of my foot over his ankle. His lips twitched conspiratorially. He knew I didn't want Olivia to catch a whiff of our affair. "Don't make me have any awkward conversations with her," I'd requested in the cab on our way downtown. It sounded better than, *"Don't disappoint us both when you leave.*

A waiter arrived.

"We would like one of everything, please" Callan said immediately. "Just kidding, mate. But could you bring us a bottle of champagne while we peruse the offerings?"

"Certainly. We offer the Mumm Blanc de Blancs, among some others." He flipped open the wine menu and offered it to Callan.

But Callan didn't take it. "Could you ask Jules to swing by the table? I have a question for him."

"Of course."

"Who is Jules?" I asked when the waiter retreated.

"The sommelier," Callan said, offering Olivia the bread basket. "I have a little proposition for him."

When Jules appeared, Callan turned his charms on the older man. "Callan Walker," he said, extending his hand. "I'm Jack's nephew."

Jule's face drooped. "So sorry for your loss," he said. "I enjoyed doing business with him. He was a lovely gentleman."

Callan's smile dimmed a little. "He was. One of the good ones. And now I have a warehouse full of his treasures to dispose of. If you'd like to make a final order that's, say, fifty percent larger than usual, I'll give you a break on the price. And the proceeds will all go to LGBT charities."

"Oh, interesting." Jules stroked his chin. "I'll need to have a look in our cellars, to see if I have the space. But that could work out."

"You can reach me on this number." Callan pulled a card from his shirt pocket. "In the meantime, we'd love a bottle of champagne. Surprise me."

"Will do." Jules squeezed Callan's shoulder. "Enjoy your dinner."

And we did. Jack ordered the saddle of rabbit, and Olivia gave him a hard time about it.

"You eat meat," he said. "We had sausage on our pizza."

"I don't eat any animal that's cute," my sister said, as if that made any sense at all. "No Bambi. No Thumper."

"Hmm." He took a sip of red wine and glanced at her steak. "Cows are cute, especially when they're little."

"I don't eat veal," she said with a shrug. Problem solved, apparently.

My phone lit up with an incoming text. Since I'd set it on the table in case Queen Vic called me, we all noticed. But I was buttering a slice of bread and didn't react quickly enough. Callan grabbed it first.

"Let's see which photo of mine they've got today," he said gleefully.

"Wait, you noticed those?" Olivia said, her eyes widening. "That's mortifying."

"Now she gets it," I grumbled. "I told him you did it. Threw you right under that bus."

"Um," Callan said, his smile vanishing. "This isn't me."

"Really?" Olivia grabbed the phone. "Oh. You're right." She turned her hand so I could see. My ex, Marcus, had sent me a selfie in front of a Welcome to New York sign—the kind they have at the airport. In the photo he was holding two gifts wrapped in green paper with red bows.

I took the phone from my sister and read the text. *Home for the holidays! I have gifts for you and Olivia. Can't wait to see you both.*

The fabulous sesame-encrusted salmon I'd been enjoying grew heavy in my stomach.

"Who's the bloke?" Callan asked, forking up a bite of meat.

"Her ex!" Olivia said gleefully. "We were going to move in with him, but then he got a job in Paris and bailed on us at the last minute."

"Right," Callan said, and I knew he was remembering the conversation we'd had about Marcus.

"He was a good guy," Olivia said. "Right up until the minute he left. But everyone does that to us. Grace and I repel men. Fathers. Boyfriends. We're like Kryptonite."

"Olivia," I said quietly, embarrassed. I could feel my face heating up.

Under the table, Callan's ankles hugged one of mine. But I didn't meet his gaze. I set the phone face down on the table and picked up my wine glass.

"Are you going to see him?" Olivia asked.

"Um..." *Fuck.* "Probably not." My sister's face fell. "I mean, if he has something he wants to give you, we could meet him for coffee or something quick."

She smiled again.

For dessert, Olivia and Callan split a raspberry-chocolate mousse. It was decadent, but I couldn't stomach more than a mouthful. Maybe I'd already had my share of decadence.

NINETEEN

Private Equity

Callan

I KNEW something was wrong the moment Grace came to work the following Monday. She was wearing her gorgeous red suit, but her face was grim.

"What is it?" I asked immediately, even though I wanted to pull her into my arms and kiss her. We'd texted over the weekend, and had one steamy phone call, but she'd been busy with her sister, and I'd caught up with an Aussie friend who was in town for a few days.

I'd thought about her all the time, though. Grace was officially under my skin.

"Vicky called just as I was leaving the apartment." She sighed. "She asked for a report on your activities. I told her you spent Friday at the lawyer's and at a non-profit where Jack had been funding an expansion."

"All right?" That all sounded dull enough to me. "What did she say to upset you?"

"Hello? I'm upset because I'm in the middle. She asked me another question, and I'm going to tell you what it was. But then

I'm not doing this anymore. I should never have agreed to be her spy in the first place. You won already. You're going to be fine. But I need to move on."

I just blinked at her for a moment. That was a lot to take in at once. "What was the question she asked?"

From her expression I realized I'd asked exactly the wrong question first.

"Vicky wanted me to let her know if you'd been in touch with any investment bankers. Specifically private equity."

"I wonder why she wants to know that?"

"No clue," she said, her voice flat. "I only did a single finance course. But whatever Vicky is after, I don't want to be her puppet. I'm quitting today. Then I'm going to call the temp agency and put myself on the list."

Fuck. We were back to this again.

I glanced toward Jack's front hall, picturing Grace walking out of it for the last time. Something went a little wrong in my gut. "I thought you were going to give me some time to get up to speed on the estate."

She crossed her arms. "I'll give you until Friday. But I'm telling the temp agency I'm available from next Monday."

"That doesn't sound like enough time," I said quickly. "Even after I petition for probate, there will be a lot of work to do here. I need help with the auctions and selling off Jack's inventory of wine. After seeing Jules's reaction the other night, I'm going to approach his customers instead of letting a wholesaler take it all. More money for the kids at the Robinson Center."

She smiled, but it was watery. "You're going to do a great job for them. But then you're going to catch a jet home to Australia, aren't you?"

I paused, thrown by her words. Yes, my permanent base— such as it was—was in Sydney. But just last week I'd become the head of a multi-million-dollar charitable foundation serving both Australia and New York. I had no idea what that might entail, what demands the new role might make on me. Right now, I was working hard just to keep my head above water and make sure I wasn't screwing things up for Jack.

"I honestly don't know," I said.

Her expression shuttered. "I need to plan for the future," she said quietly. "I need a permanent job in my field. I need letters of recommendation from people I'm *not sleeping with*. I can't live like you, Callan. I can't afford to."

Ouch.

"Believe me, it would be fun to say yes to you. I like it here. I like *you*." That last bit came out sounding like it cost her. "But I have to look out for myself and Olivia. I'm sure you can understand."

"But you'll still give me at least a week," I said. It was the first thing that came to mind, and I sounded needy to my own ears. "And longer if you can't find something better."

"The rest of the week," she repeated stiffly.

It was tempting to push, but my gut told me that if I did, she might just walk, here and now. I wouldn't let it end like this. Not on a bad note. Better to concede some ground now and try to talk her around another day.

The thought gave me heart. I'd talked Grace around before. I was sure I could do it again.

"Let's have a breakfast meeting," I said. "Your new temporary boss would like to take you out for waffles to learn what the art dealers told you."

"All right," she said, giving me a sad smile. "I can do that."

I hated knowing I'd been part of making Grace unhappy. I made a promise to myself that when all this crap was sorted with Vicky and the will, I'd take her and Olivia somewhere sunny and fun and dedicate myself to making them both laugh. For now, though, I'd settle for putting a smile back on her face.

"I should call your mother in the afternoon, right?" Grace asked. "If I call at six, do you think she'll be available?"

"Probably," I agreed, moving to open the door for her. "If she's not feeding on the blood of her competitors just then."

"Ew. So I won't make it a video call."

———

We worked hard the next couple of days. Digging into the facts of Jack's estate, I had a decent working theory for why Vicky was asking about investment bankers. But that was a problem for a different day.

My more immediate issue was with Grace. I was doing my best to convince her to stay on. As she took me through the things she'd learned about Jack's art collection, and helped me estimate the proceeds, I only became more certain she was the right person to help me.

That wasn't the only reason I wanted her to stick around, not by a long shot. I planned on telling her so the moment we had some clear air. I'd been thinking about the questions she'd asked —both spoken and unspoken—the day she'd tried to quit, and I had some answers for her.

"So that's how the auction houses do it," she said, sitting back from an old Sotheby's catalogue we'd been perusing together. "They keep a fat margin, but unless you know some terrific dealers and are willing to wait a couple of years to place everything, there's no better way."

"Thank you for educating me," I said. I wanted to touch her—needed to—but I'd been keeping my hands to myself during work hours, knowing how she felt about being on Vicky's, and now my, payroll. It wasn't easy, though. The pull I felt whenever she was nearby was as strong as it had ever been.

"Listen," she said, putting a hand on my knee.

"Mmh?" I said, distracted by my intense awareness of the weight and heat of her hand. Just because I couldn't touch her didn't mean I couldn't enjoy it when she touched me.

"I still haven't been able to get Vicky on the phone. When I called again last night, your sister said she was traveling."

"The cattle operation is spread all over the country."

"Right. It's just weird that she hasn't returned my calls. She's never done that before."

"I have an idea about the investment-banker thing."

"You do?"

"When my grandfather died, Jack and my mother each got a thirty percent stake in Walker Holdings. Claire and I each got twenty."

"You own *twenty* percent of Walker Holdings?" Her voice squeaked.

"I do." I cocked my head as I studied her. "You could have probably learned that from Google." Another woman would have already done a little sniffing around to try to calculate my net worth.

She shrugged. "I haven't Googled you. And Olivia was only after the pictures."

I put an arm around her then because I couldn't help myself. *Thank you for not treating me like a lottery ticket.*

The irony was not lost on me. The best, most real and admirable person I'd met in years wanted to get away from me so that she could go make minimum wage somewhere else.

"Anyway." I cleared my throat. "I hung onto my twenty percent for the sole reason that Vicky wanted me to sell to her. Right before we found the will I was almost ready to crack. Those shares are just tied up, right? The Robinson Center needed them more than I did."

"Wait..." Grace's eyes lit up as she got it. "If you're Jack's executor, you now control half the company."

"Exactly. I can distribute Jack's assets any way I wish. I could sell half Vicky's company to the highest bidder."

"Or take a seat on the board!" Grace was nothing if not sharp.

"Right. And I'm sorely tempted. I want to see the look on her face when she has to answer all my questions at board meetings."

Grace whistled. "Honestly, Vicky makes more sense to me now. I didn't understand her greed. She has a pile already, right? But if you could control her company, that's big. She might fight to the death for that."

"That business is her life. She loves it more than she's ever loved any living thing, including her husband and children." I ran a hand down Grace's hair. "If I had a seat on the board, there are things I could fix. Vicky's environmental record is poor. I could change that."

She gave me a more tender smile than I'd seen all day. "The party boy who saved the world."

I couldn't help it then. I had to kiss her. It was five o'clock somewhere, right? My lips grazed her smoother ones, and I heard the soft intake of her breath. "I miss you," I whispered against the corner of her mouth. "So badly."

Grace didn't say anything. But her arms came around my neck, and her hands gripped my back the way you'd cling to a life preserver. An urgent noise escaped my throat, and I pushed her down on the sofa, kissing her properly. Her mouth softened under mine. When I touched her lip with my tongue, she opened for me.

Fuck.

I got lost in her sweet taste and the feel of her curves under my body. But I took it slowly. Grace had let me know that our time together was fleeting, and even though I planned to change her mind, I knew how independent she could be. This might be it for us, and I had no idea how to handle that. So I kissed her as thoroughly as I knew how, my fingers stroking her skin through the silk of her blouse. I kissed my way down her neck, and when that wasn't quite enough, I unbuttoned her blouse in order to worship the curves of her breasts over her bra.

Grace kept me locked in her embrace, her fingers in my hair. I never wanted her to let me go. That should have been an uncomfortable feeling for someone who lived the way I did. But today it just...wasn't.

Now my discomfort came from the prospect of Grace leaving, of not being able to hold her and touch her like this again.

I smoothed a hand down her hip to the hem of her skirt. Her thigh was warm and soft as I headed higher. Her grip on me tightened as she anticipated my next move.

The distant awareness of Lady barking and tip-tapping her way through the apartment penetrated my lust-fogged brain, but by then I was palming the warm fullness of Grace's mound in my hand and the world had narrowed to just her body and mine, the couch we occupied, and the air we breathed.

Nothing else mattered.

"So *this* is what 'respecting Jack' looks like." The cut-glass of my mother's voice was like a bucket of icy water. My head snapped up.

There was Vicky, standing in the doorway like a bad dream. She wore an expression of icy disdain on her face. She was stouter than when I'd last seen her, her sturdy frame wrapped in a bland two piece suit that made her look like a Lego block wrapped in tweed. Beneath me, Grace stiffened. Then her hands were on my chest, shoving me away with almost superhuman strength.

"What are you doing here?" I asked stupidly.

My mother's heels clunked heavily on the parquet floor as she moved farther into the room. I was more worried about Grace, who was deathly pale as she scrambled to re-button her shirt.

"It's okay," I told her quietly.

Except it wasn't. Grace looked like a frightened deer, paralysed by the glare of car headlights. My mother stopped beside the couch, taking in every detail with a scathing glance.

"Grace Kerrington. I thought it was you. I suppose I shouldn't be surprised. My son never could resist a pretty face. I hope he was worth it."

Still trying to get past my shock, I stood, shielding Grace with my body. "Not another word to her."

"Do you know how much of a ridiculous cliché you are?" my mother asked, her focus on me now, which was what I wanted. "The finest education money can buy, opportunities other men would die for—and sleeping with the secretaries is the best you can do."

"Unfortunately for you, Vicky, I ceased giving a shit what you think a long time ago. Now, would you like to do me the favor of getting the hell off Jack's property?"

I was aware of Grace standing behind me and reached back blindly, offering my hand in silent support. She didn't take it.

"Until the will you found has been considered by the courts, I have as much right to be here as you do. More so, according to my legal team."

"Ms. Walker..." Grace stepped out from behind me, shoulders squared bravely. "I owe you an apology, and I want you to know that—"

"Don't waste my time. There's no excuse for what I just interrupted. Stephen told me you were hoping to become a permanent member of my staff. Should I assume you've been servicing him, also?"

Grace gasped, and two spots of hot color appeared on her cheeks. "*No*. Of course not."

I could see my mother winding up for another spray and shook my head. "Leave Grace out of this."

"You're the one who dragged her into it. Or maybe she leapt, legs akimbo, like so many stupid young women before her." She eyed Grace. "So, which is it, Grace? Are you a stupid slut or a naive slut?"

Grace made a choking sound, and I took a step forward. It was all I could do not to punch her in the throat. "If you don't shut your mouth I'm going to physically kick you out," I warned her.

She didn't bat an eyelid, her focus still on Grace.

"Neither," Grace said in response to my mother's insulting question. "I'm... I..." Her eyes got red.

"You just sent me an email last week telling me how *thorough* you've been." My mother skewered me with eyes as cold as steel. "Has she been thorough, Callan? Have you been getting good value for my money?"

Again Grace flinched, and this time her eyes welled with tears. I slid my arm around her shoulders and found she was trembling, her body vibrating with shock at my mother's verbal assault.

I'd done this to her—put her in the firing line, exposing her to this ugliness.

"Let's go," I said, ashamed to my core that this monster was my mother.

I'd barely taken a step before Grace shrugged me off. "No." She stepped away from me.

"Grace—"

"I'm done. Obviously." She took off like a shot, grabbing her coat off the coat tree before I began to react.

"Wait!" I called, finally moving to follow her.

But Grace had a head start on me. She'd summoned the elevator by the time I made it out the front door and I watched the doors slide closed on her furious face as I skidded into the foyer.

TWENTY

I Brought Tequila

Grace

"HERE," Jasmine said, passing me another tissue. "I brought tequila. But you have to stop crying before I can make you a margarita."

"Okay," I hiccupped. "I never cry!"

"I know, baby," Jasmine crooned. She got up to get me a drink of ice water.

"B-but I don't usually have days this bad!"

"Most people don't," she said when she came back. "I hate to have to remind you, but Olivia will be home soon, right?"

Shit. I didn't want Liv to see me like this. I took a deep breath and did my best to stop crying. "What am I going to tell her? She's going to notice when I don't get dressed for work tomorrow." My eyes filled again. Fuck! I'd never been so embarrassed in my life. Not to mention angry and hurt.

"The truth shall set you free. Tell her your boss is a psycho bitch from hell."

She was. But I'd made it easier for her by being stupid, stupid, stupid.

"Can I ask you something? Why didn't you tell your best friend your one-night stand had turned into something else?"

I let out a heavy sigh. It was a good question, and I wasn't proud of the answer. "I should have followed that old saw—never do anything you don't want reported in *The New York Times*. I didn't tell you because I knew fooling around with him was dumb."

"Hmm." She considered me. "There's a lot of ways to be dumb, though. Were you afraid you'd lose your job? Or were you really afraid you'd get attached to him?"

"Both. But mostly Option B. I don't want to be left behind again."

Her gaze sharpened. "Sounds like maybe it's already too late on that front. You really like this guy, don't you?"

"Jasmine, I love you. But get out of my brain." I felt another wave of anger rising up as I remembered the way Victoria Walker had looked at me. As though I was dirt on her shoe, or worse. I stood suddenly. "I'm going to splash my face with cold water."

"Great idea."

I'd just gotten myself under control when I heard Olivia's key in the door. Bracing myself, I came out of the bathroom.

"Omigod, what's wrong?" my sister demanded immediately. "Is it Mom?

"No," I croaked. Then I tried to smile. "This time I'm the fuck-up."

"Hey!" Jasmine said from the kitchen counter. "That is not true."

Olivia looked from me to Jasmine and back again. "What happened?

"Well..." I smiled nervously. God, why was I smiling? "I got fired from a job I should have quit anyway. That's the short version."

"What's the long version?"

I took a deep breath through my nose. "I told you that Callan's mother is the boss lady."

"In Sydney," my sister added helpfully.

"Right. Except she wasn't in Sydney today. She walked into the apartment, and Callan and I were, um... We were..." I couldn't say it. Not to my sister. It suddenly sounded so...tawdry.

Olivia's eyes grew huge. "You banged Callan Walker?" Her book bag fell to the floor with a loud thunk.

"No!" I said at the same time that Jasmine said the opposite. "I mean... He *kissed* me today on the sofa." I felt my face reddening again. "His mother was not happy with me. So...I'm out of a job."

The worst part of all of this was that I'd always known getting involved with Callan was a bad idea. I'd known it every single minute I was in his arms, and I'd done it anyway. Some of the awful things Victoria Walker had said hit close to home.

"Callan will fix this," Olivia said. "He has to."

Slowly, I shook my head. "It's more complicated than that. I can't go back there."

My sister cringed, and she suddenly looked younger than her fifteen years. "What are we going to do?"

"We are going to have Thai food and watch bad TV," Jasmine said quickly. "And tomorrow your sister will take a deep breath and figure out her next move."

To me, Jasmine mouthed, *my treat*.

Just this once I wasn't going to argue.

The next morning I made French toast before seeing Olivia off to school. I was trying to project an attitude of normalcy.

I was also trying very hard to ignore repeated texts from Callan. *Are you okay?* He wrote. *Can I call? I want to make sure you're okay.*

I was too furious to talk to him right now. That bullshit where Vicky asked me to spy on him and he'd encouraged me to play along... I'd *known* it was wrong, but I hadn't listened to my gut. I let him talk me into it because I'd wanted to please him. To help him.

I was such a fucking idiot.

And—holy hell—what kind of example had I set for Olivia?

Dismissing Callan's messages, I opened my email. And then my heart nearly stopped. There was a message from the temp agency with the subject line: *Please call in right away*.

Oh God. I had been just about to do that, in the hope that they'd have work for me. But somehow Vicky had reached them first. I opened the message to find it was even worse than I'd thought.

Grace—you need to call us immediately. Victoria Walker is very angry. She's ordered you off the job. And she says you stole a laptop computer belonging to her company. We've had to suspend you from our payroll while we investigate. But please call so you can tell us what you believe happened.

My hands began shaking and they didn't stop as I dialed the agency.

"This is Angela Jones," my supervisor said when she answered.

"Hi," I said, sounding nervous to my own ears. "It's Grace Kerrington. I just got your message."

"Grace! Victoria Walker has been a client for several years. Where is that woman's laptop?"

"It's right here!" I gasped. "She was yelling at me and I ran out of there. I didn't even realize I still had the computer until I read your message."

There was a long silence on the line. "Why was she yelling?" Angie asked.

And that question right there was why I knew I at least partially deserved the shitstorm I was facing. "I..." I cleared my throat. "She walked in when I was kissing her son."

The deep silence returned. "That was unwise," the supervisor said eventually.

You think? "I know that. It was incredibly stupid to let him get to me like that. It is not, however, a criminal act." I might have been ashamed of what had happened, but I wasn't going to let someone else shame me.

Angie sighed. "Bring the laptop to me by noon, okay? But I can't reassign you."

"But I need to work. Put me on anything. Even data entry. Please."

Angela knew my situation, and I'd been a loyal worker for the agency.

"No," she said, and my stomach fell. "She wants blood. And our policy is a thorough investigation. I can't ignore the complaints of a long-time client just because she's unpleasant. Victoria Walker is threatening to stiff the firm on your entire contract. If you want the chance to be reassigned, you'll get a meeting here with the supervisory staff where you can plead your case."

I swallowed, but my mouth was dry. "Okay," I croaked. "When can we do that?"

"I'll try to set something up for next week."

Next week. I couldn't go that many days without pay. "Okay," I said stiffly, wondering who needed a bartender on short notice. I realized I was about to spend my afternoon wandering into restaurants all over lower Manhattan. Right after I returned the fucking laptop.

After I hung up with Angela, I changed out of my suit and into a tight T-shirt and jeans. Underneath I wore a bra that hiked my boobs practically to my chin.

This was where I'd been headed the whole time, I supposed, from the first moment I'd set eyes on Callan Walker.

I told myself it wasn't so bad. Bartending was lucrative enough, even if it meant I'd barely cross paths with Olivia. The rationalization didn't make me feel any better as I pulled on my jacket.

Outside on the street, it was overcast, everything cast in monochrome thanks to the low cloud cover. The shop windows glowed with Christmas lights as I walked past.

The approaching holidays made me feel even worse. Jasmine would fly off to Aspen to have a white Christmas with her family. Meanwhile, I'd do a little baking and watch cheesy Christmas films with Olivia. But we'd probably both fight off the memories of better holidays. Before our mother's hopeless spiral, she used to love Christmas. We'd always get a real tree, no matter how much of our small living room it took up.

I remembered decorating the tree with a kindergarten-aged Olivia. She put all the ornaments on the lowest branches, where she could reach them. Mom and I would sneak some of them up onto higher branches after she went to bed.

In New York City, Christmas trees were sold on street corners. But even a tiny one was fifty dollars. Olivia and I wouldn't be getting a tree. I was too worried about keeping the lights on to shell out that kind of money.

I felt sick as I walked into the temp agency to return the laptop. I half expected Angela to come out and admonish me some more, just to pile on the humiliation, but I managed to hand the computer over and request a signed receipt without running into anyone I recognized.

Thank heaven for small mercies. Then it was onto the street to start trawling for work.

The first dozen restaurants turned me down, the restaurant managers shaking their heads at me. "We already did our holiday hiring," they said.

It was only after I'd decided to give up and walk home that I spotted an Irish pub called—of all things—O'Malley's. I'd never even noticed it before, and it wasn't very appealing from the sidewalk. But the name tugged at me, so I pushed open the door to find an elderly lady behind the bar.

"Hi," I said brightly, even though I was certain I was about to be shot down once again. "I'm looking for bartending work. My temp job fell through, and I'd be happy to take any hours you could give me."

"Huh." The old woman behind the bar glanced at her two afternoon customers. "The place picks up around happy hour."

"I'm sure it does," I said quickly. At least I'd hope so.

"How do you make an Alabama Slammer?" she asked me.

"Equal parts Sloe gin, SoCo and amaretto," I rattled off. "Splash of orange juice. Or more if it's for a pack of sorority girls."

She grinned widely, and I saw that even her wrinkles had wrinkles. "Well done. But nobody has ordered one of those in a good long time. You'll just be pouring beers."

"Will I?" I asked, my heart lifting.

"Not tonight or tomorrow," she said, and my heart sank again. "But the next night my shows are on, and I'll give you the whole shift."

"Thank you," I said, though I was still panicking inside. Two days without work was two too many. "Do you want me to fill anything out?"

She shook her head. "Just come back here in forty-eight hours and I'll show you around. The name is Martha O'Malley."

"Grace Kerrington. It's great to meet you." I reached across the bar to shake her hand.

I left feeling just the tiniest bit optimistic. But New York wasn't done testing me. Olivia came through the door at four o'clock, her eyes red-rimmed, her face puffy.

"What's the matter?" I said, hearing an echo of yesterday's conversation.

"I broke a tooth." It came out oddly, like she didn't want to open her mouth. "We need a dentist. Like right now."

"How bad is it?" There was a dental clinic charging a sliding scale rate that I'd taken Olivia to over the summer. But the wait for an appointment had been three months.

"Really bad." Her eyes teared up.

"Show me."

She opened her mouth but closed her eyes. "Oh, Liv!" My sharp intake of breath made her flinch. Indeed, one of her front teeth had a nasty chunk out of it. "How did that happen?"

"I tripped," she sobbed. "It was *so* embarrassing! Everyone saw. I missed a step on the stairs and went down. The nurse gave me ice but..." The tears rolled down her face. "It's really bad, isn't it?" She moved her tongue across her teeth. "It feels like a crater. And it's so sharp. I cut my tongue on it."

"Holy god." I sighed, reaching for my phone. "Let me see what I can find out."

I found Olivia an appointment for the next morning. "You'll have to miss the first two periods, maybe three."

"Okay," she mumbled, holding her mouth closed. "How much did they say it was going to cost?"

That was the truly terrifying part. "Until they get in there they won't know for sure. Something like three hundred dollars, though." *Right before Christmas.* I didn't say it aloud. But the way Olivia's eyes locked on mine, I felt like she'd heard me think it.

"Take them back," she whispered.

"What?"

She closed her eyes and then opened them. "The jeans you bought me. We live in a four-hundred-square-foot apartment, Grace. I found them weeks ago."

"Oh." Damn it. "Maybe we won't have to take them back."

"Yeah, we will." She blinked back tears. "I'd rather have my tooth fixed, okay? I know it's horrible timing."

"I'm going to pick up some shifts tending bar," I said. "Until something better comes along. So we're going to be okay, I promise."

"Where?"

"A place called O'Malley's."

She grinned, giving me a sudden view of the disturbingly broken tooth. "That's what Callan calls you. O'Malley. Why is that?"

I shook my head. "Just a dumb nickname. Apparently Australians nickname everything. It's pathological."

"Are you going to see him again?"

"No. That was never going to work out."

She looked uncertain. "I liked him. A lot."

So did I. "He doesn't really live in New York, though. And his life isn't like ours, Liv. So it doesn't matter how much we like him or not."

"I suppose not," my sister said. But she didn't look convinced. "Take the jeans back, Grace. I'm serious. It's okay."

It wasn't. But I'd probably have to do it anyway.

TWENTY-ONE

I Miss You (Both)

Callan

"HELLO, GRACE," I said into my phone. I was standing in Jack's apartment, looking out at the frigid winter landscape. It had snowed, and Central Park was covered by a blanket of white. "The park is very beautiful today," I told her. "Lady had a good frolic in the snow on our walk."

There was silence on the line. This was not unexpected, seeing as I was speaking to Grace's voicemail. I'd tried texting and email. Today I was desperate enough to switch to an audio assault.

Not that I expected it to work.

"Listen. I've had ten days and nights since you walked out. That's a lot of time to count all the ways I've *spectacularly* fucked things up with you." I paused for a breath. "Looking back over our time together, I realize I bulldozed you at every turn. When you tried to remain professional, I turned on the charm. I over-rode your objections, because I was the selfish prick who wanted what he wanted."

I paused a moment to think that through. I'd even used her pleasure-loving soul against her. There'd been nothing at stake for me. My big fat trust fund insulated me from the slings and arrows of outrageous fortune.

Not so Grace. She felt every sling, every arrow—all while also protecting her sister as best she could.

Jesus.

"I understand why you don't want to speak to me. My job offer still stands, but with Vicky circling, I can't imagine you're interested in hanging around this place..."

Beep. Grace's voicemail cut me off before I was ready. "God damn it!" I shouted at the windowpanes.

How appropriate, though, since my apology was shit anyway.

I'd made too many mistakes to count. As if seducing Grace into betraying her own rules wasn't enough, I'd then asked her to be the meat in the sandwich between me and my mother. She'd done it—against her wishes—out of loyalty to me.

And then she'd paid the price. She'd had to stand there and endure Vicky's acidic take-down.

It didn't matter that I'd been motivated by grief for Jack and outrage on his behalf. That was no excuse for the way I'd moved Grace around like a chess piece. What a perfect chip off the old block I'd become. What a truly fucking great scion of the house of Walker.

I'd spent much of the past ten days working with my legal team and talking to Gavin at the Robinson Center. I was trying to arrange a construction loan backed by my own assets, so that construction could continue before the probate court allowed me to liquidate.

I'd spent all my extra hours missing Grace.

The pain I felt in my chest every time I thought of her seemed fitting punishment for dragging her into my family mess and then failing to protect her. I deserved to never hear her laugh again, to never hold her in my arms or tease her till she gave me one of her patented raised-eyebrow looks.

The expression in her eyes the last time I'd seen her had been completely devastated. She'd been *ashamed*. She'd believed the shit my mother had served up. In those minutes, she'd felt like the quick lay my mother had accused her of being. She'd felt wrong and stupid and dirty.

It was so far from the truth, every time I thought about that episode my blood pressure spiked. After Grace had made her escape, I'd shouted at my mother until Lady got so agitated she began to growl.

Weirdly, that's what made my mother leave. Chased off by a grumpy poodle. It would have been funny if I hadn't been so livid. I'd changed the deadbolt locks that very night. Ten days later I was still expecting more trouble. It was unlike Vicky to give up so easily.

Whatever. I'd thought I was spoiling for a fight. But I was so worried about Grace that my guaranteed legal victory over Vicky didn't excite me the way it should.

I just wanted Grace back.

She was... Grace was fucking astonishing. A miracle. She'd offered me comfort and assistance, even though the price had been high. I'd made love to her over and over, and not once said the words she deserved to hear—that she was special, that this meant something, that I wasn't just amusing myself while I was in town for a few weeks. She'd asked me for reassurance, and I'd given her...silence.

For years I'd played the role of the careless, pointless family fuck up, a consummate piece of performance art designed to thwart my mother. When had the role become so second-nature?

My pacing took me past Jack's photo gallery in the hallway and I paused in front of a portrait of him and looked into eyes the same blue as my own.

"Jesus, I miss you," I told him.

Jack had always been there to talk sense to me. He'd been the most rational, human, *interested* sounding-board a man could find, never failing to call me on my bullshit or push me to be better.

"How do I fix this?" I asked him.

My answer was the snick of Lady's claws on the floor as she came to find me. I looked down into her questioning brown eyes when she nudged my thigh with her snout, reaching out to scratch her happy place behind her ear.

If I could turn back time, I'd do everything differently, from the moment Grace walked into the apartment talking about orgasms. But I couldn't. I couldn't even look into her eyes and let her know how sorry I was.

It was intolerable, literally. I felt as though my brain was going to explode, there were so many unsaid things in there that I needed to tell her. Lowering my head, I kneaded the space between my eyebrows.

"Fuuuuuck."

I lifted my head and started walking, Lady trotting at my side. Together we swept through the living room and into the study. Having spent so many hours ransacking this room for the will, I knew the contents of every drawer in Jack's desk by heart. I yanked the third drawer on the right open and pulled out a stack of his writing paper. Then I sat at the desk, picked up a pen, and started writing.

At first it was an incoherent mind-dump, a messy, disordered confusion of all the things I needed to explain and wanted to say. But after a while, I slowed and started thinking. I stopped writing and read what I'd written. Then I set it aside and started on a clean sheet of parchment.

Dear Grace, I wrote.

Because if she wouldn't talk to me, or answer her phone, I could still write to her. I could still make the effort. This was the single avenue I was left with, and I was grabbing it with both hands.

I had genuine sweaty palms as I drove over to Grace's apartment that evening. My letter sat on the passenger seat in a cream parchment envelope, thick with angst and honesty. Did I feel vulnerable? Fuck, yes. Had I spilled my guts like a lovelorn fifteen-year-old? All over the place, in Technicolor. But I'd finally put my heart on the page. I was giving this letter to Grace, even if she threw it back in my face.

Downtown, I got lucky and scored a park three buildings up from Grace's place. I took a moment to wipe my damp palms before grabbing the envelope and crossing the road.

I paused in front of the security intercom and took a deep breath. Then I pressed the buzzer for Grace's apartment. If she was home, there was a strong chance she'd ignore me once she learned who was on the other end of the buzzer. If that happened, I was prepared to wait until someone entered or exited in order to gain access to the foyer where her letterbox was located.

But I'd prefer to hand-deliver my heart if I could.

The seconds ticked by as I waited for a response.

"Hello?" a voice called. But it wasn't Grace's.

"Is that Olivia?" I asked. "It's Callan Walker."

"I know," said the voice. "Nobody else says Olivia like that."

"How do I say it?" I asked the intercom box.

"Like you're thinking there should be an R on the end, but you haven't decided."

"Is Grace home? And if I say her name funny, don't tell me."

"No." Olivia giggled.

"Can I come upstairs and give her something?"

"She's not here."

I could almost picture Grace standing silently beside her sister, shaking her head. Maybe I could negotiate a handoff at the door to the apartment. "Can I come up and give it to you, then?"

"Sure. Unless it's edible. Then I'm keeping it."

A smarter man would have also brought chocolates.

There came a mechanical hum, followed by a click. I tried the door and it opened in my hand. Once I stepped into the little foyer, another click admitted me to the stairwell. The seedy stairwell. The center for homeless youth I was helping to construct would be nicer than this apartment building. What I wouldn't do to get Grace and Olivia out of here...

On the landing above, one of the doors had *Kerrington* written on a piece of tape stuck beneath the peephole. I tapped on the door. "Open up, ladies. I just want to hand this off."

The door opened and Olivia's face appeared. I could hear the TV in the background. "She's not here. I said that already."

"Then why did you open the door if you're home alone at night?"

"Because you asked me to!" She rolled her eyes. "I'm not afraid of you, Callan Walker. Now get in here. I'm missing the final round of Cheftastic."

I followed Olivia over to a futon sofa, where she sat down. She took a handful of popcorn from a bowl and then passed it to me. "They're doing sushi. But it has to have a Christmas theme. Which is bullshit, since Christmas isn't exactly huge in Japan. But whatevs."

"Whatevs," I agreed, too busy taking in my surrounds, hungry for more clues about the woman I was crazy about.

Grace's apartment was small but cozy. There was a rack of suits and dresses standing against an exposed brick wall, and it looked like something from a fashion designer's studio. Indeed, a fitting mannequin stood just beside it, a tape measure around its neck. Beside that stood Grace's sewing machine.

Remembering the red suit she'd reimagined, I wondered what she might create if she had the time to do it.

"Omigod," Olivia scoffed. "He's laying out the salmon in the shape of a tree? That's weak."

It really was. "O, Salmon Tree, O Salmon Tree!" I sang, and she giggled. "Do you like sushi?" I never watched shows like this because they always made me hungry.

"Yeah. It's been a while, though. Kind of a splurge. Ten bucks says he uses the rice to make a snowy base at the bottom."

"I'll take that bet," I said, helping myself to some popcorn before passing it to her.

The dope used rice for snow, of course. I got out my wallet and passed Olivia a ten.

She looked surprised. "I was just teasing."

"Fair and square," I said, laying the bill on the coffee table. Then I put my envelope down beside it. "That's for your sister, okay? Make sure she gets it."

Olivia peered down at the envelope. "A paycheck?"

"No. A letter."

"Yeah?" She looked amused. "Did you write her a love letter?"

"Don't be a sticky-beak, missy." But had I? In many ways I had. It's just that the word *love* didn't appear anywhere. Walker family love would be a burden. I'd already proven it was a toxic substance.

"I'll make sure she reads it. And I won't read it first. Although it's really tempting." She grinned evilly at me.

"Happy Christmas, Olivia," I said, rising. "I should go. How long until Grace is home?"

She shrugged. "Her shift ends at midnight, but she was later than that the other night."

"Her shift? Where?"

"This bar on Avenue B."

"She's...a waitress?"

"Bartender," Olivia said, her eyes on the screen. "It's kind of a dive but the owner is giving her a lot of shifts."

"Which place?" I asked.

"It's called..." She turned, narrowing her eyes at me. "I don't know if I should tell you. Grace has been a big grump for a week and I think it's mostly your fault."

It was hard to argue that point. "What if I told you I was going over there to grovel shamelessly?"

"Hmm." She considered this, tenting her fingers in her lap. "Maybe I should see a demonstration before you try it on Grace."

I let out a bark of a laugh. "A demonstration?"

"Yup!" There was glee on her face. "Let's see you grovel."

Fuck.

I put the toe of one shoe on the corner of the coffee table, leaning down toward Olivia. "The Kerrington women are amazing people. I'm lucky just to meet you both. I don't deserve the honor of your company..." This was all true, of course. "I just hope I'm allowed to play a role in your life again. Even a bit part. Like Villager Number 7. Or even a shrubbery."

Olivia cackled. "Once Grace was the toothbrush in a school play about dental hygiene. There are photos. Keep going."

I put both hands over my heart. "If you would only answer my emails and text messages again, I swear to be a better man, and make you both lattes again. And let you choose all the toppings on the pizza."

Her face softened. "Not bad, Callan Walker. The bar where Grace works is called O'Malley's."

It couldn't be. "You're joking."

"Nope!" She kicked a foot onto the coffee table. "That's the place. It isn't much to look at."

"Thank you, Olivia." I put a nice fat R sound on the end, just for her.

She grinned up at me. "You're welcome, Callan Walker. Now go grovel. Make it good. You made my sister cry." She waved a hand, shooing me toward the door.

TWENTY-TWO

O'Malley's

Grace

TENDING bar at O'Malley's was not the hardest job I'd ever had. Neither was it the most fulfilling.

I scanned the room as I wiped down the bar with a clean cloth. There was a big table of eight college-aged guys near the window. I'd decided they were high school friends having some kind of Christmas vacation mini-reunion. At the bar, and watching a basketball game on TV, sat a couple of guys wearing shirts that read "Downtown Cooling and Heating."

The good news was that the place usually wasn't as dead as on my first visit. The crowd wasn't fashionable, though. The cheap beer and lack of decor brought in the sort of clientele who couldn't afford the more upscale bars in Soho.

This, I'd learned, was a typical weeknight crowd at O'Malleys. Pints and pitchers, mostly. Or Johnny on the rocks. The weekend had been busier, thankfully. I'd taken in enough tips to pay for a chunk of Olivia's shiny new front tooth.

I was feeling too heartsick to start sending out resumes again, and mid-December wasn't the best time to do it, anyway. So I planned to spend the holidays behind this bar, pouring tap beer. Though every so often some joker would ask for a frozen drink, and I'd have to deafen everyone on the premises with the chainsaw sound of Martha's aging blender.

As for Martha, she hung about while I worked, chatting with the regulars and disappearing at intervals into a tiny office in back where she watched *Judge Judy* and *Law and Order* reruns.

On this—my fifth night at O'Malley's—I wasn't feeling very relaxed, though. I was watching the door for a certain someone who had messaged to let me know he was dropping by. He'd said he needed a word with me, and I'd grudgingly agreed.

He appeared at nine p.m. I saw him at the door out of the corner of my eye, and braced myself for a first look at him in a long time.

Marcus. My ex.

He smiled immediately. And even as he made the short journey to the bar, I began to catalogue all the things that were familiar or different. His dark hair had recently been cut quite short. It worked on him, although it made him seem older. (Not that I'd ever advocate for a repeat of the horrible ponytail experiment of 2013.)

His smile had the same nervous quality that I'd seen on his face when he'd stumbled through his invitation to the winter formal my first year in the business program at NYU.

That was five years ago. We'd spent a lot of time together for most of those years, until his sudden departure in May. And now I stood here across the bar from this man I'd once thought I might spend the rest of my life with, and I felt...

Not much.

Funny how having her life implode can help a girl over her heartache.

"Hi there, beautiful." He set two gifts down on the bar and I mentally kicked myself. Those had been in the picture he'd sent, and I'd forgotten about it. I didn't get him anything. Not that it was customary to buy your ex a Christmas present. Fuck.

And now I'd made an awkward silence.

"Hi," I returned a beat too late. Then I leaned awkwardly across the bar so he could kiss me on the cheek. "You look good," I said, trying to break through my discomfort.

"You look *amazing*," he said, upping the ante. But if one of us here was supposed to be extra nice, it was him. And it was quite possible I *did* look amazing. I'd dug out some of my best bartending shirts, so I was showing a lot of cleavage, and I'd doubled down on the eye makeup.

He sat opposite me on a stool. "What can I pour you? I just opened a bottle of the pinot noir for someone else, and it smells terrific."

"Just a Bud Light?"

Hmm. I guess Paris hadn't changed him. I grabbed a glass and filled it for him. Then I dug a five out of my jeans and put it into the till.

"You don't have to buy," he said with a frown.

"It's my shout," I said. "Since I made you come in here to see me."

"Your...what?"

"Uh..." *Whoops.* "That's Australian for *my treat*. Sorry."

Damn you, Callan Walker. Get out of my brain.

Marcus sighed. "I came here to apologize, you know."

"It's okay," I said quickly. "I mean *I'm* okay." It was, of course, a total lie. There was no way I was going to admit to him how badly things were going for me.

He chewed his lip. "I brought you a present. And Olivia. Hers is the bigger box. It's a scarf that I thought looked like her. There are sequins."

"Aw. She'll love it. But you really didn't have to do that." *I didn't get you a thing.*

He pushed the smaller one toward me. It was the size of, say, a pint of strawberries. "Would you open it for me?"

"Right now?" I looked up to see the college kids waving to me. "One second."

I ran over to their table and took an order for two more pitchers.

Marcus nursed his beer and watched me work. If I were a nicer person I would have let him take me out to dinner. That had been his first idea. But it hadn't felt right. I didn't want to sit across a table from him like old friends. Not when I was still feeling touchy about his departure in the spring. And why should I dine somewhere nice while Olivia sat home eating leftovers?

Not to mention the fact that I was taking as many shifts as I could from Martha. Squandering a night's worth of tips to make Marcus happy wasn't a great strategy for me.

So here we were. O'Malley's was a dive bar, and not exactly the kind of place which announced to my ex, "See! I'm doing great without you." But you can't have everything.

When everyone in the bar had been checked on, I returned to the spot in front of Marcus. He gave me a nervous look and then pushed the box toward me.

I gave him a chipper smile and slit the wrapping paper with my thumb. If this gift was something that Olivia might like, I would shamelessly regift it to her on Christmas morning. Maybe it was French perfume or something.

Inside I found a wooden box. Like a tiny little chest, with ornate inlays. "It's beautiful!" I said in spite of myself. My finger traced a design on the top. "An antique?"

He nodded, smiling. "I spotted it at a Parisian flea market. It just caught my eye."

"It's pretty," I agreed. "Thank you."

"Open it," he said.

I carefully lifted the top. And what I saw inside confused me. A small velvet box.

Very small.

Robin's egg blue.

With Tiffany scripted on it.

No freaking way.

I picked up the box and opened it, stunned. A beautiful diamond solitaire winked up at me from inside. I lifted the ring from the box, feeling as though I was dreaming, maybe. My mouth was probably hanging open.

Across from me, Marcus put his chin in his hand. "When I said I missed you, I really wasn't joking."

———

Callan

Lucky I'm a nosy bastard. If I hadn't grabbed Grace's phone the night we celebrated the finding of Jack's will, I wouldn't have recognised the guy sitting opposite her at the bar when I entered O'Malley's. I would have just taken a seat and waited for Grace to notice me, never knowing that her ex was a few seats away.

But I did recognise Grace's ex, so I retreated through the front entrance. Standing in the cold, dark street, I contemplated my next move.

It hadn't escaped my attention that he'd brought gifts, the fucker. Two of them, if I wasn't mistaken. One for Olivia, one for Grace. Trying to buy his way out of his guilt, no doubt.

Sorry for abandoning you, but I bought you an Eiffel Tower snow dome and an I Love Paris T-shirt. Am I forgiven?

I really fucking hoped his gifts were that lame, because I was not enjoying the acid burn of jealousy eating a hole in my gut right now.

I glanced up the street to where I'd parked the Austin. The smart thing to do would be to wait in the car until Martin or whatever-his-name-was left. Then I could be the second man to accost Grace in her place of work this evening. Fan-bloody-tastic.

My hands were starting to burn with the cold, and I stuffed them into my coat pockets. Jack's coat pockets, technically, since I was wearing his jacket again.

Even though it made me feel like a creep, I stepped closer to the front window of the pub and peered through. Grace was opening her present, her expression unreadable. I couldn't tell if she was happy to see her ex or pissed off. I couldn't tell if she was excited by his gift or underwhelmed. All I knew was that he was in there with her, and I was out here.

They were talking. He leaned forward a little. He looked tense. Expectant. Grace lifted something small and square and blue from the wrapping paper in front of her. She looked shocked now. Uncertain.

Fuck, no. Surely he hadn't...

She opened the box, and even though I was twenty feet away, I saw the distinctive sparkle of light refracting off a well-cut diamond.

He'd given her a ring. A diamond ring.

An engagement ring.

I closed my eyes. Then I opened them again and made myself watch as he reached across the bar and took both Grace's hands in his. He talked earnestly, never taking his eyes from hers.

And she listened.

I turned away. It was like watching a bus crash. I couldn't do it.

I started walking, telling myself I should be happy for her. She'd all but told me he'd broken her heart when he went to Paris. He'd obviously had a few months to realise he'd made the biggest goddamn mistake of his life and had come back to try to redeem himself.

The Austin's leather upholstery was cold beneath my ass as I slid into the car. I stared out the windshield, trying not to imagine what was going on in O'Malley's right now.

Had she said yes? Did she still love him?

I wanted the answer to be no. I wanted to believe Grace wouldn't have responded to me the way she had if she'd still been in love with someone else. When we'd been together, we'd been the only people in the room, no ghosts hanging around to cast a shadow. That's what my gut told me, anyway. Or maybe it was my ego talking.

If only I'd got here first. If only she'd taken one of my calls during the week. If only I hadn't fucked things up so badly she was stuck serving beers in a shitty pub.

My thoughts went to the envelope I'd just left with Olivia. I'd said things in that letter that were going to be pretty fucking unwelcome if Grace had just accepted her ex's proposal. Hell, for all I knew, they'd be unwelcome either way.

I reached for the ignition key, ready to go take my letter back. I'd write Grace another one, this time strictly an apology. A safe letter, one that didn't leave me feeling as exposed and helpless as a landed fish.

I gripped the key but didn't turn it. I'd given Grace the truth in that letter. My truth. I didn't want to take that back, even if it made me look like a fool. Even if there was no hope of winning myself another chance with her.

Decision made, I started the engine, planning to head home. The shrill ring of my phone cut through the heavy silence. I pulled it from my pocket and glanced at the screen.

It was Vicky. Great. She was just in time to be the shit-cherry on top of the turd-sundae that was my evening.

"What do you want?" I asked. Her treatment of Grace had killed the last traces of civility between us.

"I'd like to make a time to talk to you" my mother said coolly. "As soon as possible, preferably."

"I've got nothing to say to you. And anything you want to say to me can come through my lawyer."

I was about to end the call when she spoke again. "I want to make you an offer for Jack's shares. Yours, too, if you're willing to sell them."

My thumb hovered over the phone icon, ready to hang up. "I have no interest in giving you that kind of power."

"I'm prepared to offer you ten percent above current capital value. Jack's foundation would be funded for decades to come."

"Look at you, always thinking of others."

"Callan. I strongly advise you to take my offer."

There was something in her tone that made the hairs on the back of my neck stand on end.

"Or what?"

"Or I'll be forced to pursue other strategies to secure the company's future. You have no interest in the business. Why not cash out?"

"What strategies?" I asked.

"I'll have no choice but to force your hand."

"Good luck with that," I said, suddenly tired to the bone. I didn't want to be sitting here in the dark, playing games with Vicky while Grace was maybe getting engaged half a block away. Whatever lever Vicky thought she could pull, she was welcome to have at it. I was going to go home and crack open one of Jack's bottles of expensive Scotch.

"It's a shame about your little friend," Vicky said before I could hang up.

I frowned. "Who are we talking about?" I asked. But I knew. Dread landed in my belly like a rock.

"Grace Kerrington. It's a shame about her situation. I ordered a background check when she took off with the company computer. It must be hard for her, looking after her sister on her own. Olivia. Is that her name? Were you aware Grace doesn't have legal guardianship of her?"

For a moment my mind went blank. Then her words hit home and I gripped the phone so hard it hurt my hand.

"*Don't*. Don't even think of going there," I said.

"Then don't make me go there."

Disbelief and anger flooded me in a hot rush. I wanted to smash something. I wanted to scream down the line, calling out her cold inhumanity. Because only a robot would use Grace and Olivia's vulnerability like this.

"Let me be crystal clear," I said. "If you jeopardise Grace's happiness, if you fuck with her sister's wellbeing, I will *bury* you."

"The offer for your shares will be delivered to the apartment first thing tomorrow," she said. "Do the smart thing for a change, Callan."

And then I was listening to silence as she ended the call.

"You fucking evil *cunt*." I stabbed at the screen to call her back and scream the words at her, but the broken screen refused to respond for a few seconds.

Just long enough for my brain to come back online. Vicky wouldn't be affected by insults. She'd heard worse in her time. She had enemies left, right, and center. She lived and breathed conflict.

Screaming at her might be satisfying, but it wouldn't change a thing. And it certainly wouldn't protect Grace and Olivia.

They were the only two people who counted in this situation.

My heart was pounding from an overload of adrenaline and rage. I took a steadying breath. Then I called up my contact list.

I'd been dealing with Jack's lawyers all week on probate issues. I didn't give a flying fuck that it was nearly ten. I dialed the senior partner and sat tensely as I waited for him to pick up.

"Callan Walker? How can I help you?" A certain reserve in Gerald's tone signaled he wasn't happy about the late hour.

"I need the number of the best family lawyer in New York. Someone who takes no prisoners and is used to dealing with custody disputes. And I need to talk to him or her right now."

———

So it was true—New York really *was* the city that never sleeps.

The bill was going to be steep, of course. I couldn't even guess the hourly rate for their counsel at this hour.

But it didn't matter. Nothing mattered except preventing Vicky from using Grace as a pawn in her dangerous games.

Back home, I sat at Jack's desk, I scribbled pages of furious notes as my newest lawyer described the process for granting legal custody of Olivia to Grace.

"Her case is strong," the lawyer said. "As long as you can prove Grace has adequate means and housing for Olivia—and adequate does not mean luxurious—there will be no likely objection. My investigator will hopefully turn up an arrest record for the mother. But even without that, your friend has already demonstrated willingness and capacity."

"All right. I'll get the information you need, and we'll speak in the morning."

"Hang in there, Callan. This will work out fine."

I hung up with him, and then sat a little longer in the study, considering my next move. I had to let Grace know about everything I'd just learned. It wouldn't be easy. If she was mad at me before, this would make her livid.

But there was no helping it.

My phone rang in my hand. And in spite the complete impossibility that Grace would finally be calling me back, it's the first thing I thought of at the sound of the ring tone. *Please.*

No dice. The caller was my sister Claire.

"I'm worried," she said immediately when I answered.

"About me?" And then I almost made a joke. *Aw, shucks. You shouldn't have.* But things were still fragile between my sister and I. We'd talked more during the last week then we had during the previous year. But it all still felt quite tentative.

"Don't sound so shocked," my sister said with a sigh. "But I just thought you should know that Mum blew off her fourth-quarter wrap-up meeting. She's never done that before. And she won't tell me what she's working on, which is also quite strange. But I just paid the bill for a private investigator in New York. In the last two weeks she's given him a lot of hours, Callan. I don't know what she's planning, but it won't be nice. For someone."

My chuckle was dry. "I appreciate the call, Claire. But unfortunately I already know her evil plan. I've been involved with someone, and Mother has just threatened to make my girl's life miserable unless I do her bidding."

"She wants Jack's shares."

"She must want them very badly. Because this is low, even for her. I can't imagine what Grace or I did to deserve this."

"It's what you *didn't* do. She runs the company, but now you'll control half of it."

"She draws a handsome salary for her efforts," I said with a snort. "And let's not forget, she bulldozed every effort I made to do anything innovative when I worked for Walker."

"Because you didn't do things her way. You're just a young punk with big ideas and no experience."

"Jesus, Claire." *Remind me why I never call you?*

"I'm not saying she's right! But that's how she looks at the world. She doesn't see herself as a Marvel villain, but as the matriarch of a pack of ungrateful beneficiaries."

"But if you put her in a vinyl bodysuit, Claire, in a lineup with Marvel villains, nobody could tell the difference."

My sister snickered. "Thank you for that image."

"You're so welcome." I found myself grinning into the phone. That was a new thing, I guess—laughing with Claire. But it begged a question. "How do you put up with it?"

"With what?"

"With her bullshit. It must blow back on you all the time."

"Oh. With wine, I suppose." She sighed. "There are days when

I feel like pulling a Callan, when I want to run off and take a four-year vacation."

I snorted. Because all good jokes were based in the truth.

"She's not easy, but I've learned a lot. She's very smart. She doesn't take any shit from anyone. I've learned more from her then I did at University."

"Well..." I cleared my throat. "If you feel a vacation coming on, you could join me in New York. Looks like I'm going to be here a few months."

"New York in January. The sandy beaches. The fine weather."

"Ten-thousand miles from Vicky."

"I'll consider it."

"Thanks for the call, Claire Bear." I hadn't called her that in a lifetime.

"I hope your girlfriend is all right."

I flinched, wondering if Grace was now someone's fiancé. "Thank you. I'm doing what I can to fix things." For Grace, anyway. "Have a good one."

After I hung up with my sister, I left the apartment and got back in the car. I jumped downtown once again. There was almost no traffic this time. The Broadway shows had all let out, and the streets were quiet. When I reached Avenue B, I easily found a parking spot. My watch said one a.m.

I waited outside the bar, wondering how Grace usually went home from her shift. I hoped she didn't walk anywhere alone at this hour.

She emerged ten minutes later, alone, bundled up in coat, gloves, and scarf. I saw her look around, as if for a car. But then she spotted mine. She shoved her hands in her pockets and stared.

I opened my door and got out. "Hi there, O'Malley. I see you've opened a bar." I indicated the sign above the door. "That's quick work."

She dropped her chin and looked at her shoes. "How did you find me?"

"Olivia."

"Little traitor," Grace mumbled.

"Can I drive you home? There's something I really need to tell you and unfortunately it's urgent."

She met my gaze then. "Does it have to be right now? It's been a really long night already."

Interesting. I tried not to wonder what that meant. My gaze dropped to her hands, but she was wearing gloves. Was she wearing what's-his-name's ring? Then I reminded myself it was none of my business and that she and I had a much bigger problem. "I'm afraid it can't wait. And here you are, needing a lift home anyway."

She scanned the street again. "I was going to use Uber, but I don't see the driver."

"Please?"

She made me wait for what seemed like an eternity before she pulled her phone out of her pocket, opened the app, and canceled the ride, I assumed. "All right. You have ten minutes. Make 'em count."

We got into my car, but I didn't start the engine. I just looked at her for a moment. She'd just worked I-don't-know-how-many-hours behind the bar. It was late and she ought to have looked exhausted. But she looked gorgeous to me. All I wanted to do was pull her into my arms and take her home.

"I thought you had something important to say," Grace prompted me.

Right.

I took a deep breath. "I've been on the phone with lawyers tonight, because I needed to take care of something for you. But I don't want you to panic."

She blinked. "You do know that 'don't panic' is a tough opener, right?"

Fuck, this was hard. "Vicky wants me to sell her Jack's stake in the company. So she went on a fishing expedition to figure out how to make me do that."

Grace's eyes widened. "And...she decided that I might have something to say about it?"

Slowly, I nodded. "Specifically, she's discovered that you don't have legal custody of your sister. And she's threatened to make trouble for you and Olivia."

Grace braced herself against the door of the car and stared at me. "You are fucking kidding me."

"I've already got you covered. I've hired the best family lawyer money can buy. And he thinks you can get a judge to give you custody almost immediately." It all sounded so freaking lame when weighed up against the potential of losing Olivia to the welfare system. "I'm sorry..."

"*Fuck* sorry! This is all your fault! What is her goddamn problem?"

I cranked the ignition. If Grace was going to bail on me and slam the door in my face, I wanted her to do it in front of her own apartment building.

As I pulled away from the curb, she fumed from the passenger seat. "I wish I'd never, *ever* gotten that temp assignment!"

What could I say to that? It depressed the hell out of me, but she was right—her life would be demonstrably better without me in it. I pointed the car toward her neighborhood. It was only a five-minute drive, even if I hit all the lights red. "The lawyer is on the case. I've made notes for you, and booked an appointment with him for ten thirty tomorrow. He needs Olivia's birth date and some other key data. Providing that you want custody."

"OF COURSE I WANT CUSTODY!"

"Sorry. That was a stupid thing to say." So much for my much-vaunted charm. "Just so it's clear, I'm paying for all of this. In case you were wondering."

She was silent. We were only a block from her apartment

building before I hit a red light and chanced a glance at her. She was hunched in her seat, a hand over her eyes, quietly crying.

My heart broke in two right there in the Austin-Healey.

I pulled the car over to the curb. "Come here." I reached for her. She resisted me for a second. But when I cupped her chin to wipe tears off her cheek, she let out a sob. I pulled her in, and she shook against my shoulder. I had to grit my teeth, I was so angry. At myself, and at Vicky.

"I s-swear to God," she gritted out. "After all this, if she ends up in some foster home I will—"

"Not going to happen," I said quickly. "The lawyers won't let it happen. I won't let it happen. And even if something went wrong, I'd show up there and boost her out of the window myself."

"You say that," she whispered. "But who knows where you'll be?"

Right here, my heart said. It was slowly dawning on me. I'd never said I was a quick man. But you'd think I would have realized by now how much Grace was coming to mean to me.

Watching her take that ring out of the jewelry box tonight had practically cut me down. It was just the sort of bludgeon I needed to get it through my thick head. Grace was worth sticking around for.

After a few more precious minutes, she pushed me away and moved back to her side of the car.

"I'm okay now," she lied.

I let it slide and finished the drive home, pulling into the same spot I'd been lucky to find earlier, when I visited Olivia. At least the parking gods were smiling on me tonight.

"You know, in the early days when Olivia first came to live with me, I was afraid of every person who knocked on our door, every teacher I spoke to, every neighbor who saw us going about our business." Grace stared out the windshield, her gaze bleak. "I was convinced the welfare people would find out she was living with me without the proper paperwork, that they'd take her away and I wouldn't have the knowhow or resources to get her back." She fell silent but I didn't say a word, because I knew there was more, and I felt privileged she still trusted me enough to share anything.

"I used to have nightmares where she was dragged away, and I couldn't get the phone to work. Then, when I did, I kept mixing up my words and I couldn't explain why they'd made a mistake and had to bring her back."

I shifted in my seat. The need to fix this for her, to shield her from the hurt I could see in her face and hear in her voice was a physical pain in my gut.

"Then I realized most people were too busy living their own lives to care about ours. That, or they had clued in to our situation and weren't about to rock the boat because I wasn't messing up too badly. I was doing better than when Mom had been on board, anyway. After a while, the dreams stopped."

She turned her head to look at me, and all I could say was, "I'm sorry. If there was any way to stop this from happening, to make it go away, please know that I would do it in a heartbeat."

She bit her lip, then glanced over my shoulder toward her building.

"I need to get up to Olivia. Who do I need to see tomorrow?"

Reaching into the back of the car, I grabbed the notes I'd made while talking to the lawyers. For the next ten minutes Grace and I talked custody and court hearings. I did everything I could to emphasise the strength of her case as conveyed to me by the lawyers, desperate to reassure her.

"He kept saying that the courts don't want to put kids in the system unless there's a good reason for it," I told her. "Taking her away from you would be the absolute last resort."

"But I have to demonstrate I can provide for her," Grace said. She was plucking at the wool of her gloves, tense and unsettled.

"I'm going to give you a letter of employment from the Jack Walker Foundation."

She made a low growl.

"That doesn't mean I'm going to pressure you to actually work with me. That will be completely up to you." I heard myself and wanted to choke on my own hypocrisy. " Okay—I acknowledge I have pressured you in the past to do things you maybe didn't want to do. I promise it would just be a cover until you found something on your own. Unless, of course, you decide to take the job for real."

I stopped talking before I dug a bigger hole for myself. I had so little credibility right now, why on earth would she believe me when I'd pushed her around so much in the short time we'd known each other?

"I don't want to work for you," she said bluntly. It was surprising how much the truth hurt. "But I'm not lying to the courts about a fake job, either. So I'll take the job and the letter, until I can fix things with my agency and find something else."

"Wait, what? Why do you need to fix things with your agency?"

She gave me a hard look, and I finally caught up: *Vicky*.

Of course. So Grace had had that to contend with, on top of everything else.

"Jesus, Grace. I'm so sorry." For a moment I was overwhelmed by the carnage my family had inflicted on her life. How could I possibly imagine that this woman might still have feelings for me when her world was in tatters, courtesy of my mother's sociopathic need for control?

"I have to go," she said, reaching for the door handle.

"Your appointment is at ten thirty tomorrow, okay? He's the biggest shark in New York so his advice is worth taking. Call me if you need anything—money, references, anything."

"Don't worry, I will do every little thing the lawyer says, no matter how demeaning."

I hated hearing the anger and resignation in her voice. She got out of the car and fumbled in her bag for her keys. I watched as she grew increasingly frustrated before yanking the glove off her left hand to improve her dexterity. I caught a flash of pale, bare fingers before they disappeared into the bag.

I scrambled out of the driver's seat, facing her across the roof of the car.

"You're not wearing the ring," I said.

"I didn't—" She frowned at me. "How do you know about the ring?"

"I came to talk to you at the bar, but Marvin was there."

"It's Marcus. His name is Marcus."

I didn't say anything, simply watched her, waiting for her to answer my question. After a short beat, she dropped her gaze to the keys in the palm of her hand.

"I'm not wearing the ring because you can't turn back the clock."

She lifted her gaze then, for the briefest of moments, and I understood that the message applied to me, as well as the hapless Marcus.

There'd been too many fuck-ups, too much ugliness. Deep inside I'd known that, but I'd still had a kernel of hope. Why would anyone want to voluntarily wade into the cesspit that was my family? Grace was wise to run a mile.

She walked across the road, and I watched her leave, waiting until she was safely inside the building before getting back into the car.

I started the engine, but I had nowhere to go.

Still, I couldn't stay here. Putting the car in gear, I pulled away from the curb.

TWENTY-THREE

Best Grovel Ever

Grace

I DIDN'T KNOW how to feel as I trudged up the stairs to my apartment. What Victoria Walker had threatened to do to my family...it made me want to Hulk-out and tear down half of Manhattan. It also terrified me, in a way I hadn't been scared for years. Those feelings were pretty clear—anger and fear. I was familiar with them.

But the way I'd felt when I saw Callan waiting for me outside the bar, and the way I'd felt when he'd pulled me into his arms, and the way I'd felt when he asked me why I wasn't wearing Marcus's ring? That was confusing as hell.

After everything that had happened, I should never want to see his face again. He'd been part of one of the most humiliating scenes of my life—and after dealing with my addict mother for years, there were some pretty serious contenders for that title. He should be filed under Huge, Catastrophic Mistake in my memory and banned for life.

But when I'd seen him tonight, my heart had given a little leap —almost the exact opposite of the way it had thumped steadily away when I'd seen Marcus. And when Callan had held me in his arms, all I'd wanted to do was stay there. He'd felt so familiar and smelled so good, I'd wanted to crawl into his lap and let him wrap me up in his strength until the world disappeared.

I paused before opening the apartment door, trying to work out what that said about me. Rationally, I knew Callan was bad news—and that was before his mother even came into the equation. He was too good-looking, too sexy, too charming, too rich, too sophisticated. He was not for me. He had never been for me —I'd just had him on a very short loan for a while.

Rent-a-fantasy.

Emotionally, though...emotionally, I was invested in Callan. There was no point kidding myself on that score. Even after everything I'd done to be smart and protect myself, I had let myself believe the way he made me feel was real. That when we held each other and kissed and fucked, it was more than two people creating pleasurable friction and exchanging pheromones. I had ignored the fact that we could not have two more wildly divergent lifestyles. I had ignored everything and let myself get swept away.

"Yeah. I think that's what they call a self-inflicted wound," I whispered to myself.

And now I was suffering the consequences. Lucky me.

I shoved the key into the lock and let myself into the apartment. The television was on with the sound muted, the flickering images casting a strange blue light over the room. Olivia lay sprawled on the futon, the remote control resting in her lax hand, her mouth slightly open as she dreamed the dreams of a fifteen-year-old girl.

I stood looking down at her, struck by how much younger she looked when she wasn't pushing attitude at me and testing every boundary I set for her. If these lawyers couldn't do what Callan had promised they would do... A shiver of visceral, primal fear ran through me, swiftly followed by a burst of welcome rage.

I wouldn't let them take her. I would set the world on fire before I let that happen.

Olivia's eyelids flickered and I sniffed back the tears that had flooded my eyes.

"Oh, hi," she said. "What time is it?" She yawned, giving me a ringside view of her new tooth.

"I love you," I said. "I know I don't say it enough. But I do—I love you more than anything."

"Um. Okay." Her face scrunched up in a confused frown. "Is everything all right?"

"Yes." I sat down beside her and took her hand.

"Just so you know, you're freaking me out here," Liv said. But she didn't pull her hand away.

"Relax and enjoy it. I'll be back to nagging you to clean your room tomorrow."

She peered at me out of the corners of her eyes. "Sure." Then: "I love you, too. For the record. If we're keeping one."

"We're not. Sisters don't need a record."

I squeezed her hand, marveling that it was as large as mine now.

"I thought maybe something might have happened at work. Because I told Callan where you were," she said hesitantly, guilt evident in the way she didn't quite look at me.

"Thanks for that, and for the heads up, by the way," I said.

She winced, because we both knew she hadn't tried to warn me.

"He said he was going to grovel. How'd it go?"

I shook my head. "No groveling. We just talked about a work thing."

There was no way I was letting Olivia know what was going on regarding her custody, not until I absolutely needed to.

"Really? Are you sure? Why did he leave you this, then?" Olivia pulled an expensive-looking cream-colored envelope from the throw blanket tangled around her legs. I recognized Callan's sloping scrawl immediately.

"Where did you get that?" I asked.

"He came over tonight. He left it for you. I felt sorry for him because he looked so whipped. So I told him about O'Malley's." She passed me the envelope. "Can you please open it right now, because I was *this* close to steaming it open before I fell asleep."

I stared at the textured paper, at my name in his bold handwriting. Then I flipped it over and tore it open with what was probably indecent haste. The letter was thick, at least three pages. I unfolded it and started to read, vaguely aware of Olivia scooting in close so she could read over my shoulder.

Dear Grace,

I'm sorry, for everything. You deserved so much more from me, and I let you down. I want you to know I will never forgive myself for that, or for the way Vicky spoke to you. What she said was unforgivable, and I fully understand your decision to have a lot less Walker in your life from now on. I promise to leave you alone once I've had my say—only because there are things between us that should be said, not because I am expecting anything from you.

When I first met you, I made the mistake of assuming I understood you. I thought you were ambitious and ruthless, but I soon discovered how wrong I was. Your honesty, your generosity, your integrity blew me away. You put yourself on the line to help me honor Jack's memory, even though it meant risking your livelihood. I'm sorry I put you in that position. I had my head too far up my own ass to recognise what I was doing to you.

I want you to know the nights we shared together were

important to me. You are important to me. (And not just because of that thing you do with your tongue).

You wouldn't know this, but it's been a long time since I said that to anyone. A few years ago I decided I would never share my life with anyone. Betrayal and fucked-up family dynamics had me convinced I'd never find someone to stand by me, someone who made it all worthwhile. I told myself I had all I needed—more money than I could spend in a lifetime, a few close friends, and enough interesting acquaintances to keep things amusing.

And then I met you, and the horizon shifted.

You made me want things I haven't wanted in a long time. You made me care about someone again. But I'm so out of practice, I didn't let you know that. If I had, this is what I would have told you the last time you were in my arms:

You are incredible. Your strength, your determination, stagger me. The way you look at the world, the way you handle yourself, the way you love and care for your sister...I admire you more than I can say. The many small kindnesses you showed toward my uncle, a man you will never meet, will stay with me forever. I'm humbled by your huge, beautiful heart, and I'm wild about your gorgeous body and clever, steel-trap mind.

Then there's the way you look at me. That's the most amazing part. You look at me like I matter. Like I'm good for more than picking up the dinner check and a one-night stand on a yacht.

(Not that we should rule out yacht sex. But I digress.)

Grace, you recently reminded me that I'd be leaving to return to Australia soon. I think I agreed with you,

*because, as I believe I've already established, I had my
head up my ass.*

*What I should have said was that I didn't need to go
anywhere that you weren't. But I didn't, and so I'll
wind this up with my final apology to you—I'm sorry
I wasn't brave enough and smart enough to
understand who you are and what you mean to me
when I had a chance to do something about it. It will
be the stand-out regret of my life, bar none.*

*I wish you every happiness, because you deserve it more
than anyone I know.*

Yours,

Callan Walker.

For a moment after I finished reading, there was nothing but the
sound of traffic outside and the low hush of my and Olivia's
breathing.

Then she stirred beside me. "Omigod. That's the best grovel I
ever read."

I stared down at his words and realized the page was trembling, because I was trembling.

"What are you doing to do?" Liv asked, her tone a little
awestruck.

I turned my head to stare at her. And then I was on my feet,
shoes slipping on the floor as I tried to get to the door as fast as I
could. I wrenched the door open, sending it slamming into the
kitchen cupboard. And then I was racing down the stairs, taking
two at a time, the balustrade burning beneath my hand, I was
moving so fast.

I exploded out the entrance and into the street, almost falling
over as I came to an abrupt halt on the sidewalk.

The Austin was gone. *He* was gone.

I don't know why I'd thought he'd still be there. He'd dropped me off more than five minutes ago. Why would he be still hanging around after I'd told him we couldn't turn back the clock?

Frustrated and disappointed, I turned to go back inside, a cocktail of urgency and hope bubbling inside me. I needed to find Callan, and tell him—

I froze mid-turn as I recognized the distinctive shape of a set of taillights halfway up the block. The car was double-parked, the glow of the brake-lights very red in the darkness.

I started to run. My coat flapped against my legs as I accelerated down the sidewalk. After a quick glance over my shoulder to ensure this wild night wouldn't end up with me causing a traffic accident, I ran across the street.

Then the traffic light changed, and I was sure the brake lights were about to wink off, and that the car would pull away. It didn't, though. For once in my life, the thing I wanted didn't slip through my fingertips like I expected it to.

Since the driver's seat was on the wrong side, I could see Callan even as I stumbled towards the car. His arms were crossed on the steering wheel, his head bowed.

I leaned in to tap on the window but he must have caught the movement in the corner of his eye, because he turned and then did an actual double take.

For a long moment we simply stared at each other. I could feel my heart pounding in my throat. His eyes were dark with uncertainty. He reached for the window controller, winding it down.

"Put me out of my misery, O'Malley, and tell me you're here because you left something in the car," he said.

"I read your letter," I said. I didn't know how to say what was in my heart, how to describe the hopeful, happy warmth spreading through my chest.

It had been so long since life had been generous to me.

"In case you're wondering, I meant every word," he said, his smoky blue eyes more serious than I'd ever seen them.

It was more than enough for me. I launched myself across the window frame, grabbing his shoulders and angling for his mouth. His lips were cool and firm, but his mouth was hot and needy when he opened to me. A wide palm caught my chin and stroked my cheek as we consumed each other.

This was what people who spoke of chemistry were trying to describe. If Marcus had never left me, I never would have known. I would never have met this man and felt the feelings he inspired. I would never have embarked on the crazy rollercoaster ride of falling for Callan Walker.

Callan broke off our kiss suddenly. "Tell me about Merwyn."

"Marcus?"

"Did you say, 'No, but I'll think about it'? Or did you say, 'No, and lose my number.'"

Numbah. I kissed him one more time, because that accent still did indecent things to me. "I can't marry him."

"Why not?"

"Because I'm hung up on this Aussie bloke. Maybe you know him? Smart mouth, with a poodle for a sidekick? Psycho family?"

"Sounds like a wanker," Callan said. "But there's no accounting for taste." He grabbed me again and we tried to swallow each other's mouths while I dangled half-in, half-out of the car. "Beautiful, amazing Grace," he said a moment later, breathing hard. "I know we've only known each other a short time. But I swear it isn't grief talking, or infatuation. I'm ready to make changes. I'm ready for *you*." He punctuated that with a kiss. "If you think you could love me someday, I'll do whatever—"

I cut him off with another kiss, overwhelmed that he'd poured his feelings onto the page and made himself so vulnerable when he was so uncertain of me. I slid my hand up to cup the side of his face, my thumb resting on the strong line of his jaw as I broke the kiss.

"Consider it done," I said.

He stared at me. His smile started as a lip twitch. Then a full-on grin. It warmed his eyes, the corners crinkling in the way that always made my belly flop over. He tipped his head and just considered me a moment. "Be with me, O'Malley. Not that it's easy."

"I'll try," she said shakily. "I want to. Is that good enough for now, do you think?"

His gaze softened as he scanned my face. "I think I'm the luckiest man alive."

The sudden blare of a car brought us both down to earth. Callan craned his head to check the rearview mirror.

"I 'spose that was always bound to happen," he grumbled.

"Park the car," I told him.

"Great idea."

I unthreaded myself from the car window and gave the car behind us an apologetic wave before moving to the sidewalk. My courtesy earned me a one-fingered salute as the driver pulled around the Austin. Ah, New York, city of romance.

I wrapped my arms around myself as I waited for Callan to park the car, dizzy with happiness and disbelief.

Could this really be my life? Could the handsome, irreverent, clever man walking toward me really be mine?

As if to answer my question, Callan swept me into his arms, locking my body against his as we kissed again. It had been nearly two weeks since I'd been naked with him, and the need to be skin-to-skin was like a fire in my blood.

"Upstairs," I managed to say in between kisses.

"Good idea."

We stopped every third step to kiss some more, Callan's warm hands sliding beneath my beer-stained T-shirt to palm my breasts. I pressed myself against him shamelessly, reveling in the small words of praise he whispered against my mouth, telling me how much he'd missed me, how he'd dreamed of kissing me again.

I didn't remember my sister until we reached the apartment, a testament to exactly how wild I was about Callan Walker.

"God. Olivia," I said as the thought hit me.

Callan went very still, his fingers digging into my hips. "Right. Liv. Of course."

It took us both a moment to release the monkey-grip we'd had on each other and step backward.

"I'm sorry," I said.

"Never apologize for Liv. She's awesome."

That didn't mean we weren't desperate to jump each other.

I took a moment to make sure my shirt was straight, then I tried the door handle and pasted on a smile.

"Look who I found hanging around downstairs," I said, as if I hadn't just torn a hole in the floorboards scrambling to get to the man following me into the apartment.

Silence greeted me.

"Liv?"

That was when I saw the note propped up on the kitchen counter.

Gone next door to stay the night with Tracey. It's no yacht, but you can thank me later.

Callan read the note over my shoulder. "She really didn't need to do that."

Then he grabbed me and threw me on the futon.

All I could say later, in our defense, is that we were both starved for it. A whole night alone, and we were raring to go. That's why we tore off each other's clothes within seconds of landing on my bed.

What followed was a frantic reenactment of the karma sutra. There were probably yoga classes that used fewer positions than we did. It was energetic and combustible and joyful. When we finally collapsed into a sweaty heap on the mattress, Callan's smile was bright enough to power all of Manhattan above 42nd Street.

"You'll be the death of me, O'Malley," he said.

"But what a way to go."

"God, yes. Come here and kill me again." He dragged me

across his body so that I wound up sprawled across him, his big body my mattress. He wove his fingers through my hair and smiled up into my eyes. "I missed you like crazy," he said. "That's another thing I never say."

"What else do you never say?" I teased.

"I'm wild about you. I adore you. I worship your mind. I lust after your body. I want to make you happy as often as possible."

"Just as soon as we fix the fine mess you've gotten me into."

His smile died. "Right. But I will fix it. You have my word." Somehow he managed to look both fierce and tender as he looked up at me. Not so long ago, we had been sailing our separate courses, unaware that our paths were soon to collide. Looking into Callan's beautiful face, I knew that my life would never be the same again, and that was a damned good thing.

———

Callan

We made sure we were dressed and decent by the time Olivia returned home the next morning. She opened the door cautiously, peering around the corner with comic wariness.

"Funny," Grace said dryly.

"I'm only fifteen," Liv said. "I don't want to be exposed to anything that might stunt my emotional growth."

"Morning, Livvie," I said.

"Good morning. I have to get ready for school now, so you should probably go."

"Guess who's getting etiquette lessons for Christmas?" Grace gave her sister a dark look.

"Hey," Olivia said. "I abandoned ship last night so you two could have a booty call. You should be thanking me for my etiquette."

I had the good sense to hide my smile behind my hand until I could get my mouth under control. One thing was sure, life would never be dull with Livvie around.

I turned to Grace. "I'm going to go back uptown to change. I'll pick you up at ten, okay?"

She nodded, the bob of her throat the only visible sign she was nervous about the appointment I'd set up for her today. I kissed her briefly and palmed the nape of her neck.

"Stop worrying," I said quietly, for her ears only. "We've got this."

She nodded, but I knew she'd never really relax until she was holding a court order that said she was Olivia's guardian. I couldn't offer more assurance without pinging Livvie's acute radar, so I simply gave her neck a final squeeze and headed for the door.

Four hours later, Grace and I emerged from a shiny Manhattan tower and stopped on the busy street to regroup.

"Feeling better?" I asked.

She let out a heavy sigh. "Much better. A thousand times better."

Later in the afternoon, Grace's lawyer would file a petition with the Family Court asking that Grace be made Olivia's guardian. There was paperwork to gather, and Olivia would have to be told since her wishes would be taken into account during the hearing that would follow, but the lawyer had been both reassuring and confident. The tightness I had felt ever since my mother's phone call last night had finally started to ease.

Speaking of my mother.

"There's something I need to do," I told Grace after I'd driven her home. "Can I take you and Olivia out for dinner tonight?"

"You don't need to do that," Grace said. She'd started to lose the scared look she'd worn for half the morning, thank God.

"I owe her for helping me last night. And it has to be sushi. That's what the chefs on our show were making last night when we watched together."

Grace got a look on her face I was beginning to recognise as her sentimental look. "Don't go soft on me, O'Malley. It's just dinner."

"Sushi sounds great," she said with a smile. "I love that you watched a cooking show with my sister, by the way."

"Yeah, yeah, I'm a saint. I'll pick you both up at seven."

I waited till she'd gone inside before hitting the accelerator. All the parking allocated to Walker Holdings was taken when I arrived at the garage beneath the building.

"Fuck it," I said, and double-parked behind the CEO's spot.

Heads came up as I entered the offices. I ignored the curious gazes and headed for the executive board room, where my mother always set up shop when she was in town. The door was closed, but I pushed it open and watched as the handful of people in the room gaped in surprise.

"Afternoon," I said. Then I met my mother's wary gaze. "This won't take long."

"If you could all give us a moment," Vicky said to the room.

She was in another of her tweed suits today, her hair pulled up in a chignon. She looked uptight and uncomfortable. She was about to get more so.

I waited until the last person had filed out and the door was closed before speaking.

"I'm here to tell you in person that there is nothing you can do to threaten Grace Kerrington and her sister. As of this afternoon, Grace will be Olivia's legal guardian."

My mother's expression was unreadable as she sat back in her chair. "You didn't come here to tell me that."

"You're right. I came here to let you know that if you ever so much as mention Grace's name again I will make sure that every questionable deal you've made, every regulation you've skirted, every corner you've cut becomes public property. I know where your bodies are buried, Vicky, and I will not hesitate to dig them up if I have to."

She stared at me for a long beat, then flicked a glance at her hands, which were resting palm down on the table in front of her.

"If you destroy my reputation, you destroy the company," she said. "You wouldn't kill the golden goose like that."

"I'd do it in a heartbeat. You think I give a fuck about the great Walker name?" I pulled a sheaf of papers from my back pocket and tossed them on the table. "Here's your share offer. I'm not interested—"

"Of course you're not. You'd rather cause trouble than do something constructive," she said, her chin jerking up aggressively.

She was so sanctimonious my temper slipped its leash for a second. "*Be quiet*," I said, my voice a whiplash. "I haven't finished. I'm not interested in your shitty offer. But I will sell you the lot for fifteen percent more than the current market value."

She glanced down at her hands again, and even though she had her best poker face on, I knew she was pleased. What a broken monster she was. She probably thought her gambit with Grace had paid off. The money would hurt her momentarily, of course, but she was finally getting what she wanted: absolute control.

I hoped she choked on it.

"I'll have to consider the numbers and see if that's possible," she said.

"This is not a negotiation, Vicky. Take it or leave it."

"Then I'll take it. I'll have the papers drawn up immediately."

"And then we're done. We never need to speak again. Ever. Are we clear?"

She blinked twice, the rapid movement the only giveaway I'd struck a nerve. "You always did have a flare for the dramatic."

"I'm not being dramatic. There's something wrong with you, and I'm done pretending it will ever change. You tried to fuck with someone I love. That will never happen again."

I left her then, not stopping until I was in the elevator, heading down. I yanked my tie loose, then undid my top button.

When the elevator got to the garage, I strode to the Austin and slid behind the wheel.

The thought of Grace, of her good and loving heart, made my chest ache as I started the engine. I needed some of that goodness right now, to counteract the poison of dealing with my mother. But I'd deliberately left Grace out of this, and I wasn't about to unload on her now. Later, I'd tell her what I'd done, but right now she didn't need to hear about more Walker bullshit.

The important thing was that it was done. I'd finally severed the last ties that bound me to my mother. I was free.

Free to have a real life, with Grace and Olivia. Free to finish my uncle's work.

It felt *good*. Better than good. It felt fucking amazing.

A slow smile curved my mouth as I accelerated up the exit ramp. By the time I reached daylight, I was grinning like a lunatic.

———

Grace

"Are you freaking kidding me? Nobu? You said we were having sushi," I hissed at Callan as the waiter showed us to our table that evening.

"They have great sushi here," Callan told me blandly, only the glint in his eye letting me know he was enjoying my reaction.

"This is so cool," Olivia said beside me. "It's so dark I can barely see my hand in front of my face."

I suppose I shouldn't have been surprised sushi came with Michelin stars for Callan. And he *had* said he wanted to reward Olivia.

Callan flipped through the wine list. "How do you feel about pinot gris?" he asked.

"I feel absolutely fine about it."

"It's a Jack Walker import." He snapped the menu shut.

"Wow, really?" Olivia asked. "Your uncle sold wine *here*, too? Fancy."

Callan grinned. "He had a good thing going. I've been thinking about it. If I kept Jack's import business up, I could produce a steady income for the foundation. There would be more money for charity."

"Sounds like a lot of work," I pointed out. And he was going to be very busy setting up and running the foundation.

"It does, doesn't it?" he asked, giving me a wink.

Olivia and I chose a couple of dishes, and then Callan added even more. Gorgeous delicacies began appearing at our table almost immediately.

"Omigod," Olivia said after tasting the yellowtail tartar. "That was amazing. But why is it not in the shape of baby Jesus?"

She and Callan howled at what was obviously a private joke. Honestly? It made me swoon that he seemed to enjoy her so much. And it really wasn't so hard to believe—when my sister was on her best behavior, she was nearly irresistible.

"Have some more," Callan urged, nudging a plate toward me.

Every morsel of sushi I'd tasted seemed to melt on my tongue like butter. And each one of them cost the GDP of a small country, I was fairly certain. I didn't even want to see the bill, let alone argue to pay our share.

Dessert was some kind of panna cotta with monk fruit. I didn't know what that was, but it was delicious.

"Well," Olivia said with a sigh. "That was amazing."

I waited until we were leaving the restaurant before slipping my hand into Callan's. "Thank you. That was really special."

"Yeah, it was," he said, squeezing my hand.

I'd caught him looking a little pensive a couple of times during the evening. I knew he still felt bad about what his mother had tried to do. But none of that had been on Callan. I'm sure if he'd been given the choice, he'd prefer to have a run-of-the-mill mom, the kind who made peanut butter sandwiches and drove him to soccer practice, just as I would have preferred a mom who loved us more than she loved being high.

The important thing was that we had both survived our fucked-up starts in the world, and somehow found each other. I didn't want to look back, and I'm pretty sure Callan didn't, either.

I love you. The words were right there on my tongue. But I didn't say them. It was too soon, and I'd been burned before. Still. He deserved to know that I cared.

"You make me happy," I said instead. "I don't know what happens next, but I'm looking forward to finding out."

"What happens next is that I try to get you alone as often as I can, and spoil you both as frequently as possible. And then beg you to help me with the foundation."

I still didn't know about that last thing, but most of it sounded good to me.

"Can I run something by you?" he asked.

"Sure. I'm too full to say no."

"Ah, perfect. Keeping the wine importing business going—I really like this idea. When I was younger, I tried to work in organic Australian beef, but my mother undermined me at every turn. She isn't mixed up in the wine business, though." His eyes were alight with excitement.

"That sounds like fun." It was good to see him so fired up about the prospect. It also sounded like a big commitment.

"I've got a mate who knows about wine. We can visit him in Australia and pick his brain about what's hot down there, who's worth watching..."

I frowned, even though my heart leapt at the idea of a trip to Australia. It would be so easy to slip into being Callan's tag-along girlfriend, but that's not why I'd gone to business school.

"The thing is..." He gave me a sideways glance. "The wine labels are a bit fusty. You said so yourself. I'm thinking the brand could do even better if some sharp person with a business degree and an eye for design helped me with it."

I hadn't seen that coming. The idea made me fall silent for a moment. "How would that work?"

"That bit isn't worked out yet. You could run the whole damn company, O'Malley. We'd have to dine out a lot and schmooze with restaurateurs. But the business could use your marketing brain."

So, not a tag-along girlfriend at all, but a real part of a real business, doing something I'd enjoy.

It couldn't be that easy.

We walked in silence while I thought about the scent of wine corks and bolder, brighter wine labels. "The patterned silks of the smoking jackets. They would make really interesting label designs." Brainstorming business ideas would be so much fun. I stopped walking. "You tempt me, Callan Walker. You really do."

He smiled. "Just think about it, okay?"

Olivia was a little ahead of us on the sidewalk, so I took the opportunity to stand on my tiptoes and press a kiss to my new boyfriend's mouth. "I will."

From up ahead came a critical voice. "You guys are like the worst Hallmark card ever. I should put this on Instagram and we can watch the world throw up."

Sure enough, she had her camera out. The flash momentarily blinded us. Then Callan was laughing and holding out his hand.

"Do not put that on Instagram, Trouble," he said.

"Trouble? Did you just call me Trouble?" Olivia yelped.

"It's the nickname thing," I told her. "Go with it. It's an incurable national affliction."

"If I'm Trouble, I'd better live up to my name, then." She started tapping at her phone, and Callan gave a growl.

"Give me that," he said.

He reached out, and Olivia took off, and before I knew it my boyfriend was chasing my screeching, laughing sister up the street.

I watched them cavort like children, my hands deep in my

coat pockets, and it hit me in a rush of certainty that we were going to be okay. All of us, together.

It wasn't going to be perfect or easy, but we had the best glue in the world to hold us together.

I savored the moment, tucking it away to share with Callan later. Then I lengthened my stride to catch up with them.

TWENTY-FOUR

Three Months Later

Grace

"THIS BOOK COLLECTION is going to take *days* to catalogue," Olivia said, looking up from where she was typing in the details of a first edition at Jack's desk. She was practically salivating, and I shook my head.

"I told you fifteen dollars an hour was too much," I said to Callan.

He looked up from reading a text on his phone, a distracted expression on his face. Then he tuned in to what I'd said and smiled. "But how else is Liv supposed to save for those boots she wants?"

"Exactly," Olivia said. "Stop trying to undermine the rights of the worker."

"Not much work going on that I can see."

She poked her tongue out at me and went back to typing, carefully noting down every detail of the book so we could get it appraised for the estate.

Callan had been officially appointed as his uncle's Personal

Representative last week, and given Letters of Testamentary that meant he could now act in Jack's stead in regard to all of his affairs. It had been frustrating waiting so long for the courts to probate Jack's will, but we hadn't been idle while we waited. Every item of value Jack owned had to be documented and appraised—an ongoing process—assets had had to be chased down, creditors paid.

And then there was the work required to get the Jack Walker Foundation off the ground. When Callan hadn't been working side by side with me, chasing down dealers and researching auction prices, he'd been in meetings with lawyers and accountants, slowly getting his head around the responsibilities he'd be taking on.

Meanwhile, I'd begun tinkering with new designs for Aussie wine labels. And Callan and I had been making a slow circuit of all the restaurants where Jack did business, introducing ourselves to Jack's contacts. This required candlelit dinners in lovely locations two or three nights a week, sitting across from the most handsome man I'd ever met.

Oh, the hardship.

Callan glanced up from texting and caught me looking at him, no doubt with my "tragic love-sick face" (Olivia's description) on full display. He smiled, and my stomach did a slow flip as I saw the dirty thoughts behind his eyes.

My own lips quirked into a smile, but I shook my head, silently admonishing him for looking at me like that with Livvie in the room. She was too absorbed in her work to notice us, however, and he jerked his chin toward the door, inviting me to step outside for a moment.

I unfolded myself from my cross-legged position on the floor, where I'd been sorting through some of Jack's smaller volumes. Callan led me into the living room, then through into the dining room. The better to have some privacy, I assumed.

On the table, though, sat a pretty box all wrapped up. "What's this?"

Callan grinned. "For you. Because it's the eleventh of March.."

March eleventh. That date meant nothing to me. "Um, my birthday isn't until June."

He rolled his eyes. "I know that, darling. But you've done it. You've survived."

"Survived what? I'm not following you at all."

His laugh was rich and sexy. He pulled out a dining chair, sat down, then tugged me onto his lap. "You." He punctuated the word with a kiss. "Have survived." Kiss. "One hundred days of Callan Walker."

The next kiss made my thoughts scatter. His mouth was firm and bossy, and he palmed my ass in a way that implied great things to come. I pulled back, laughing. "It's business hours."

"I know," he said against my mouth. "That was just a preview of coming attractions."

"So, one hundred days ago we…"

"Did it on the sofa for the first time."

"Ah. You're right—those pictures on my phone stopped, and I hadn't noticed."

Callan made a strangled noise. "You didn't *notice?*"

"Why would I? I have the real goods every day."

"Not *every* day," he pointed out, kissing me again. "By the way. I had an interesting conversation with a realtor this afternoon."

It took me a moment to change gears. "What about?"

"She said I'd be smarter to hold off on selling the apartment for another six months, since the market's going up, and that it might take a few months to move something at this price point. So I might be here for a while."

"Huh. I guess you'll have to suck it up and do it tough until then." We both knew it was no hardship to live in Jack's beautiful apartment.

"I don't know. It's a lot of space for one person."

"One person and one dog," I said. Right this moment Lady was lying in a patch of sunshine in the other room, beside Olivia. We'd all grown very attached to her in the past months, and even though no one had formally acknowledged it, it was clear that Lady wasn't going anywhere. She was ours, and we were hers.

"Still, I don't know how Jack did it. Rattling around all these rooms on his own." Callan was watching me carefully, and it took me a second to understand where this might be going.

"So... What are you thinking?" I asked, because I didn't want to get ahead of myself, even though it killed me to say goodbye to him most nights. I wasn't comfortable with Callan staying over at our tiny place, and while Olivia was a trouper, arranging sleep-overs at her friends' places whenever she could, my living arrangements had definitely cramped our style more than a few times.

"I was thinking that it's crazy, bordering on insane, for you and Livvie to be crammed into your matchbox when Lady and I are here with all of this." He kissed my neck, his mouth hot and hard. "Also, I can't have a girlfriend this beautiful and not get it on the regular. I want to wake up with you every morning."

"How do you know?" I pointed out. "You might get sick of seeing my pillow-face in the morning. And maybe I'd steal the duvet and leave the lid off the toothpaste. And then there's Livvie. In case you hadn't noticed, she can be a handful."

I was only partly teasing him. Us moving in with him would be a big deal, for all of us.

He pulled me further onto his lap. He was hard, a discovery that made me purr in the back of my throat.

"Say yes, Grace, and stop teasing me," he said, nibbling on the skin just beneath my ear. He drew my earlobe into his mouth and sucked. Every nerve in my body sat up and cheered. Exactly who was teasing who in this scenario? His hands began to wander my body. Would I ever get enough of this man?

"O'Malley," he whispered, stroking my skin. "Move in with me.

Save me from myself and make me the happiest man in the world. I love you."

My heart thumped loudly in my ears. It had been a long time since I echoed those words to anyone. But it was true. I loved Callan Walker, even though fear had held me back from saying so over the past three months. Today, though, I looked over that scary precipice and jumped.

"I love you, too," I whispered.

He kissed me quickly, his eyes telling me how much he'd needed to hear those three little words. "Then say yes."

"If we move in with you, your mother will accuse me of being the gold-digger she already thinks I am."

Callan snorted. "That's your big objection? Sweetheart, I invite you to decide what course of action will most enrage Vicky, and then *do that very thing*."

"That can't be my reasoning," I teased, ruffling his hair. "If I do this, it's definitely for the sex."

He kissed my neck. "Whatever. Just do it."

"Okay," I said. It was funny how easy it was to say yes. I ought to be terrified. But I trusted him. I knew now, without a doubt, that his heart was in the right place—I could feel it, pounding steadily against my own.

"When we sell this place, we can start looking for something of our own," he said, the words muffled as he kissed my neck.

"Okay," I said again.

He lifted his head to look at me. "You're very compliant this afternoon. Maybe I should try a few more tough questions on you. But you have to open your gift first." He reached for the ornate box and set it in my lap.

The fancy ribbon came loose with one tug. I lifted the top off the box and poked aside some tissue paper. "It's...?" Something in a heavy, silk fabric. I lifted the beautiful thing from the box. "A gorgeous... bathrobe?"

"Your own smoking jacket." Callan chuckled. "If you're going to live a hedonist's life, you'll need this. Standard issue."

"You crack yourself up."

"I do. Besides, I want to see you in this and nothing else..." He kissed me again.

"Alert, alert! Impressionable young adult coming your way," Olivia called from the living room. The sound of her deliberately loud foot-steps preceded her before she appeared in the doorway carrying a heavy-looking book. "Good, you're both decent. A minor miracle."

I rolled my eyes. *One* time she'd caught me with a couple of buttons undone and she'd been getting mileage out of it for weeks.

"You'd better have a good reason for interrupting me when I'm hard at work, Trouble," Callan said.

Liv smirked. "Work, right." She pulled a yellowed envelope from between the pages of the book she was carrying. "I found something in one of the old bibles," she said. "I didn't want to open it in case it was important. Plus, it says it's confidential."

I got off Callan's lap, and he took the envelope from Olivia. My sister and I watched curiously as he slid some papers free.

"There's an invoice." He read the closely printed type, a frown forming. "From a private investigator. And..." He flipped the page and read a few lines before glancing up. "A report. On someone with the initials P.M."

I moved so I could see over his shoulder, and together we read what I assumed was a background check on someone. *P.M. graduated from Harvard Business School... P.M. was then promoted to senior partner...* And on it went, all of it pretty innocuous. P.M. had no criminal record, a clean credit rating.

"Do you have any idea who P.M. might be?" I asked Callan.

"No idea. I can't even imagine Jack hiring someone to do something like this." He sounded uneasy.

When we'd both read to the end of the report, he flipped to

the last remaining page. It was a letter, hand-written in a sloping scrawl.

Jack,

Good to see you last night. As promised, I've enclosed my invoice for checking into Moore. Before we go any further, I'd encourage you to sort out your intentions. If your sister is unwilling to make contact with the biological father of her daughter, I'm not sure it's wise to continue. I've got the time, and I know you have the money to keep chasing this, but I question the wisdom of collecting evidence for a legal action V doesn't want to pursue. Facts are wonderful things, but they're only valuable if you have a purpose for them.

Yours, Harry McLean

"Holy fuck," Callan said, looking pale.

"What?" Olivia glanced from me to Callan and back again.

"Could this be accurate?" I asked. "I mean, do you think your mom could have...?"

"With Vicky, anything is possible."

I reached out to slide my hand into his. He looked so shocked. As though the world had shifted beneath his feet.

"Will someone please tell me what's going on?" Olivia demanded.

I glanced at Callan for permission and he gave a distracted nod. "There's a letter here that seems to be saying that maybe Claire and Callan have different fathers."

Olivia frowned as she joined the dots. "You mean...Vicky had an affair?"

"That seems to be the gist of it, based on what's here," Callan said.

"Bloody hell," Olivia said, using her favorite adopted Aussie phrase. "What are you going to tell your sister?"

Trust Olivia to cut straight to the heart of the matter.

"That's the million-dollar question, isn't it?" he asked.

We all stared at each other for a beat. Claire had been to New York on a visit since the thaw between brother and sister, and both Liv and I had decided we liked her—even if she did still work for the She-Devil. If the information in the letter was correct, this was going to change her world.

"Welp," Olivia said. "Now that I've dropped this bomb, it's time for my break. I think I'll take Lady out for a walk." The poodle had sharp hearing. She bounded into the room a second later, pink tongue hanging out in anticipation.

"You have to now," I pointed out as the dog's tail wagged frantically.

Olivia departed. Callan sat down heavily in the same dining chair we'd been cuddling in a few minutes earlier. He reached for me, and I sat down on his lap again. He put his chin on my shoulder and rubbed my back slowly.

His silence indicated he was deep in thought, but his touch was still affectionate, as it always was.

I loved him. I'd said it, finally, and it didn't even feel scary. "Tell me what you're thinking," I whispered.

"I have to call her. It might be bullshit, but either way, she has to know. It's..." He checked the time. "Seven o'clock there. She'll be up, and I want to catch her before she's in the office."

"Maybe she knows already," I pointed out. "If she and your mother are close, maybe this isn't a secret."

"I hope you're right," he said slowly. "But Vicky loves secrets and has very little respect for others' feelings. I have a bad feeling about this."

"I'm sorry your mother is a shrew." I wrapped my arms around him.

"She is." He sighed. "But I'm used to it. If she was cheating on my father, I won't be surprised. Might even explain why they got divorced." He lifted his head. "I'm going to call Claire and check in. If it's a calm moment, I'll try to bring it up."

I vacated his lap and gave his hand one more squeeze before he pulled his phone off the table and found his sister's number. He paced the room while the call connected.

"Hey, Claire Bear," I heard him say. "Do you have a moment? There's something a little confusing I found among Jack's papers. And..." He sighed. "I thought you might need to know..."

The End

Also By Bowen & Mayberry

More Australians:

Satisfaction by Sarah Mayberry

Anticipation by Sarah Mayberry

More Americans:

Bittersweet by Sarina Bowen

The Year We Fell Down by Sarina Bowen

Acknowledgments

I want to thank Sarina for her generosity, creativity, amazing sense of humour and work ethic. Working with you has been inspiring and challenging (in the best possible way!), and I am very proud of the book we have made together. Thanks - again! - for thinking this might be a cool idea. *-Sarah Mayberry*

Back atcha, babe! It was so much fun to learn your lingo! And thanks for the killer care package from Australia. A girl can't write about Iced Vovos until she's tasted them herself. *-Sarina Bowen*

And we'd both like to thank Mel Scott for her beta read! And Hang Le for her hard work on our cover. You missed your calling as a dress designer.

9 781942 444459